M000288495

THE HEIGHTS

PRAISE FOR THE HEIGHTS

"Chicago Heights, Illinois, was a hotbed of organized crime and an important center of Chicago Mob operations for decades. Ray Franze nicely blends fact and fiction in his debut novel, *The Heights*, which tells the fascinating story of the Boys in Chicago Heights. The author may not know exactly where the bodies are buried, but after careful historical research he knows who put them there. A great read!"

—JOHN J. BINDER, author of *Al Capone's Beer Wars* and *The Chicago Outfit*

"In *The Heights*, author Ray Franze takes the reader inside The Chicago Outfit, from Capone to Accardo. This is historical fiction that is more historical than fiction."

— GARY JENKINS, *Gangland Wire*

"Reads like the mobster himself is telling the story. It is so well-researched it is virtually impossible to tell the difference between the true story and fiction. If you liked the nonfiction book *Wiseguy* by Nicholas Pileggi, and the movie adaptation *Goodfellas*, then you'll love *The Heights*. I have read a lot of mobster stories, both true and fictional. *The Heights* will be right up there with the best of them."

— *THE YARD: CRIME BLOG*

THE HEIGHTS

A novel

RAY FRANZE

Blue Handle Publishing | Amarillo, Texas

Blue Handle Publishing, 2607 Wolflin #963, Amarillo, TX 79109
bluehandlepublishing.com

Cover & Interior Design: Blue Handle Publishing

Editing: Book Puma Author Services
BookPumaEdit.com
BookPumaLive.com

ISBN: 978-1-955058-08-7

For Nicole and our three daughters, Ellie, Lia, and Kira: Your dreams are mine.

PROLOGUE

A sturdy, balding man in his late sixties sits on his wraparound porch near Linden in California's Central Valley, just east of Stockton. It's a beautiful September afternoon in 1969. He is sipping Dewar's on the rocks, overlooking his horizon of tomato plants and watching workers load a wholesale pickup into an old A. Morici truck for the Chicago Macaroni Company. The man hopes his LOOK magazine arrives in today's mail. Call it his guilty pleasure.

As he eases into the outdoor sofa, the man smirks and shakes his head in disbelief. He knows his cousin, Dominic, is proud of him. And this man who still oozes power transports himself back to where it all began, back to Chicago Heights, Illinois—better known to the predominantly Italian locals as The Heights.

CHAPTER 1

Welcome To The Heights

I took just a couple steps inside our house and flopped my suitcase on the floor. It was the summer of 1913 and The Heights, which resides thirty miles south of Chicago's Loop, was booming. More than three thousand Italians made up twenty percent of the town's bustling population.

I was twelve years old when I moved to The Heights with my parents and two younger sisters. We left the poverty and terrible unemployment plaguing Sambiase—part of the city of Lamezia Terme, in Italy's southern region of Calabria—after hearing about opportunities in The Heights's growing steel and railroad industries. But my father, Luca, had his eyes set on opening grocery stores to service the growing population. He had worked in his family's stores and owned his own after getting married and starting our family in Sambiase.

After we settled in, I'd run through The Hill—my old neighborhood in The Heights—all day long. When I left each morning, my mom would call out, "Salvatore, torna a casa prima di cena!" Come home before dinner! Though it was called The Hill, we always referred to it as Hungry Hill for how hard the Italian immigrants residing there suffered and struggled at the turn of the century. Most of us settled close to those from the same region in Italy, predominantly on The Hill or the East Side because of their proximity to manufacturers. Nearly half the Italians in The Heights lived on the East Side, many along 16th Street. A lot of East Siders came from the seaside town of San Benedetto del Tronto in Marche, but those who settled along 16th Street and its immediate surroundings came from Campania and Sicily. Hungry Hill residents came from the areas around Rome, Naples, and Calabria. The Abruzzese, mostly from Sulmona, were some of the few who settled on the West Side.

Growing up in The Heights, you could be the nicest kid in the world but still have to fight, or have someone make it clear you were not to be touched. And there were always a handful who needed to be put in their place. Our neighbors a few doors down, the Fazio family—with five boys and three girls—had come from Stefanaconi, just twenty-five miles south of Sambiase. Those boys were always defending their sisters' honor. I was helping my mom in the kitchen one day when I heard a commotion coming from the middle of the street. The oldest Fazio brother, Dante, was walking toward his house with some lady hustling closely behind, yelling and cursing at him in Italian. Dante was stone-faced and bloody handed as he made his way back home. We found out that the second-oldest brother, Tony, had found one of his sisters crying inconsolably after school. Tony had a reputation. Not as a fighter, but as a goofy, fun-loving kid.

That ends when you need to protect your family.

The bully had said something so horrible the Fazio girl refused to repeat it. He was a few years older, but Tony had a point to prove and they mixed it up for a few minutes before Tony's friends stopped the melee. A week or so later, Tony told me he was fully aware that he'd end up on the short end in a fight, but he was so pissed off he had to exchange more than words. Tony was just happy to land a few good ones across the bully's face and ribs.

Dante got home soon after the fight, and since word always spread fast throughout The Hill, he ran out of their house seeing red. Dante, who was the same age as this strunz, picked up a loose brick as he ran toward the bully's house. He kicked in the front door and the bully flew down the stairs. The bully pulled a short skinning knife and slashed Dante across his forearm, but Dante landed a punch with the brick across the bully's jaw. That was it. From that day forward, the Fazio boys had a reputation for not only being nice and sweet, but they were also not to be messed with.

Stories like this played out every day in The Heights. I learned quickly that no one looks out for your family like family, and I admired those who did the protecting. I also learned that respect must be earned, as the Fazios had done in one afternoon. Little did I know how intertwined our two families would become.

Though I enjoyed playing with the neighbor kids, I was naturally a serious young man. I took pride in my work ethic, and my parents needed my help when they kept having kids. Actually, they kept having daughters. I worked in my dad's two grocery stores; mainly the one at 16th and Shields but occasionally at the one at 22nd and Wentworth. Dad's patrons would often tell him about their daily struggles and working conditions. Small things like breaks, breakrooms, or even employee restrooms were almost nonexistent. Many of my neighbors worked at Canedy-Otto Machine & Tools, Inland Steel Company, and the National Brick Company. Italian women and children often worked the onion fields owned by Dutch farmers in South Holland, five miles north of The Heights. Most would ride the Chicago and Eastern Illinois train back and forth, and their fellow commuters would gripe about having to share a train car with smelly dagos on their way home from work. After hearing and seeing such struggles, I knew I wasn't going to work in those conditions or deal with someone disrespecting me because I was Italian. My dad would say, "Son, when someone shows me kindness and respect, I'll show them more. When someone disrespects me or my family, I'll show them less." That always stuck with me, and I would eventually follow that motto daily, knowingly or not.

Just a few months after moving to Hungry Hill, we heard a barrage of knocking on our front door during dinner. I pushed my chair back from the table at the same time as my younger sisters, and we raced. I barely stepped in front of them, our parents right behind us, then swung open the door to reveal my cousin Dominic Scalea, arms wide open and grinning ear to ear. We all screamed and hugged and kissed each other, and Dominic wasted no time in congratulating my very pregnant mother.

"Dom! What in the world are you doing here?" I screamed and yanked him by the sleeve.

Dominic was my mom's nephew. Eyes wide from shock, she immediately made him a place at the dinner table, poured a glass of chianti, and scooped a plate of angel hair and meatballs. "It's so good to see you," she said, gently placing a folded napkin on his thigh.

"Yes," Dad said. "This is such a pleasant but shocking surprise. Are you okay?"

The families had gotten together only a month before we left Sambiase for America, and Dominic made no mention of joining us.

"Auntie, it's good to see you, too. My mom misses you so much. And yes, Uncle Luca, I'm okay. I just needed to get here. But let me tell ya, I almost didn't make it." Dominic twirled pasta around his fork, dipped his bread in gravy, and shook his head. "Madonna mia, Auntie, your homemade bread smells unbelievable!"

"What do you mean?" I asked. "Why did you almost not make it? What happened?" The story had to be good if Dom was involved. He was always fun and crazy. No fear.

"Almost drowned," Dominic said nonchalantly, stuffing the last bit of pasta into his mouth.

Half the forks hit their plates in unison.

Dominic looked between my parents seriously. "I crossed illegally, on foot through Canada, near International Falls."

"In Minnesota?" I asked, my pubescent voice cracking.

"Yeah, Minnesota. There were moments I didn't think I'd make it. I tried to find a really dark area to enter and exit, and I had to make sure my eyes had adjusted. Then, with only starlight to light my way, I waded into the freezing Rainy River. I figured it was a couple hundred yards across, but it could've been more. The darkness was my friend and foe at the same time. I thought if I was a few miles west of the border patrol, I would end up in a secluded area, even with the current trying to dump me off in front of the border agents. Unfortunately, the area had storms the last few days, and the river was nearly flooded."

He sat back and sipped some wine. "Nerves were setting in hard at this point. I realized that I'd underestimated the river's conditions, but I was fully committed to going. I rolled my wrist and glanced down at the time. It was 10:40. I stared across the choppy Rainy to the U.S. side, took a deep breath, thought about my family in Canada and back in Sambiase, and waded even farther into the rushing river. About a quarter of the way across, the current took me by surprise. I was barely able to keep my head above the chop and not swallow water with every breath. When I finally made it across, I laid on the shore, panting for what felt like an eternity. I tried to check the time, but my watch was flooded, stopped at 10:44. I almost skipped it into the river, but at the last second I decided to keep it so I would always remember the journey. I hitched rides toward Chicago over the next week and found myself here, knocking on your door."

As Dominic finished, we all sat there, silent, holding onto his last word with mouths agape.

My dad cleared his throat. "Well, we're sure happy you made

it, Dom. Welcome to The Heights."

I was glad to see my cousin, but something was ominous about his sudden appearance. I was young, yes. But I was not naive. I knew the stories of certain men from Sambiase, some of which included my cousin. I knew that while these men carried great respect and influence within the town, they were looked upon unfavorably by the authorities for their unsavory activities. Many had records that would have prevented lawful entry into the country. At the same time, these characters could be beneficial to some of their amici in the United States. Things were coming to a head in The Heights between different Italian factions.

No, Dominic's appearance was not unplanned. His illegal crossing was quite deliberate. I just wasn't sure how he would fit in.

Over the next week or so, Dominic worked in my dad's stores. Once in a while, I would see them talking quietly in the corner. Dominic seemed to be asking a lot of questions. One day, my dad told Dominic, "I have someone I want you to meet. Jon Allen."

Jon Allen was born Giovanni Avellino. He got married in the Calabrian town of Cosenza in early 1912. He and his new bride left for America a few days later. They boarded the SS Hamburg in Naples and arrived in New York by mid-February, settling in Chicago Heights a week or so later. The young couple was exhausted but excited to start their new life together in the land of opportunity. After seeing the factories' horrible working conditions, Giovanni wanted to open his own business. He believed that having an American-sounding name would help him better assimilate, so he started going by Jon Allen.

Jon would tell my dad stories about how he tried going to local banks for a loan so he could open a lounge. Every single bank gave him bullshit excuses for why he didn't qualify for the loan. Jon's wedding dowry would have been enough collateral if he'd been

German or Dutch. Lack of access to legitimate loans often sent law-abiding businessmen to illegitimate sources, a common occurrence for Italian immigrants. "You never want to borrow money from gangsters," my dad always told me. "If anything, you want to do the lending." He was unknowingly planting the seeds in my head. Jon would eventually ingratiate himself with some of the local Italian—mostly Sicilian—politicians, as this would be the only way to start his business.

By 1915, Italians were becoming more influential in local politics. Jon had made enough connections to hustle his way into their circle and started making money from the little bit of gambling they allowed him to run. A few months later, he parlayed his earnings and marriage dowry into the purchase of the Lucky Lounge—a large, white, rectangular two-story farmhouse with black shutters.

You always knew when someone was walking around the Lucky because its floors were slightly uneven and squeaked. The ornate wooden bar, with large mirrors laid in the woodwork behind it, ran nearly the length of the room opposite the windows. It was fairly musty when you walked in because there was never enough cross breeze to clear out the cigar and cigarette smoke, even with the large windows. The bare wooden tables were scattered in the room with four wooden chairs around each one.

There were also a few large rooms down the back hall. Jon's office was halfway down on the left. Shortly after he took over the Lucky, Jon began running his gambling operation in back rooms on the first floor and running girls on the second. The steep narrow staircase to the second floor was somewhat hidden by split-panel red velvet curtains acting as a door. The four small rooms the girls worked in had white linen curtains, a small vanity with a mirror where they could fix themselves, and a small bed along one of the walls. The rooms usually smelled of cheap perfume to help cover the smelly factory and railway workers who frequented them. Farther down the hall on the second floor was a small efficiency apartment. Jon's building also housed a gym in the cellar for the boxers he promoted and trained.

The Lucky Lounge quickly became known as a one-stop shop where workers could gamble their checks away and have some fun with an easy gal. As Jon's activities expanded, he needed help to manage the business and negotiate with the Sicilians. Dominic was all in, and he encouraged me to join and make some extra money to "take the girls out or help out at home." I almost felt guilty if I didn't go. And I did like the money.

Around this time, alderman Lorenzo Sanfilippo emerged as the first crime boss in Chicago Heights. Rocco Lambretta and Matteo Pacenti, both Sicilian, were his lieutenants. Lambretta and Pacenti became entrenched in the Unione Siciliana, which solidified their political reach. At this point, Chicago Heights was not part of the Chicago Outfit. Sanfilippo was The Boss of The Heights and had his own territory, completely independent from Big Jim Colosimo and Johnny Torrio's thing up north. Jon Allen realized Sanfilippo needed help and enlisted his new best friend, Dominic, who leapt at the chance to be part of a Calabrian-based gang.

By mid-1917, Dominic was living in the apartment above the Lucky. I was nearly sixteen by then and spending more time helping out, mostly dropping off envelopes without asking questions. I still worked at the family grocery stores, but I wasn't interested in being a shopkeeper. I was also spending a lot of time away from my five younger sisters, who constantly turned the house upside down. My parents enjoyed the chaos. Not me, though I loved my family unconditionally. Jon was always asking my dad if he knew where I was because he could see the path I was heading down. Yes, I was working at the Lucky Lounge and occasionally running errands for or with them, but I didn't see it as my career. I saw it as extra work.

I figured I would take over my dad's stores when he was ready to retire because it seemed like the easy and logical choice. I could be my own boss and it sure as hell was better than working in some shit factory.

BY 1918, GANGSTERS from Chicago started pushing south and opening joints around The Heights. Johnny Torrio, acting in the interest of the Chicago Outfit for Big Jim Colosimo, opened the Shadow Inn in Stickney, the Roamer Inn in Posen, the Burr Oak Hotel in Blue Island, and the Coney Island Café and the Barn in Burnham. This wasn't so appreciated by the Chicago Heights guys, who didn't like Torrio moving so close, though those areas were technically anyone's game. Jon and Dominic were bringing in pretty good cash, but the Sicilians didn't give them the respect they deserved. They were one of the best-earning crews, yet they got brushed over as unimportant in meetings because they were Calabrese. This enraged Dominic, but Jon was cool. "Patience, paisan. Patience," he would tell Dom. "We will have our day." Dominic believed every word because Jon always followed through with fervor and unwavering determination.

This was also when I really started really working for Dom and Jon.

I was barely helping out at the family store and spending all my time with Marie—the girl who stole my heart—or at the Lucky. Dominic and Jon were no longer giving me that look to leave the room so they could talk in private, though. I never spoke unless spoken to, let alone offered an unsolicited opinion. But once in a while, if they couldn't make a decision, they would ask me. I always explained my rationale. They'd smile and say, "This kid has a future." I found comments like this a sign of their growing respect for me. To be honest, I found it intoxicating. Another thing they always told me was, "Don't get cocky, kid, or we—or someone else—will knock you down." This was nothing new. My parents had been telling me similar things my whole life.

However, there were some things Jon and Dom told me that I took to heart. Never discuss anything you hear here outside these walls with anyone. Be careful who you trust. Never let others know what you're thinking. This allows you to not show your hand.

Some of the earliest conversations, when I actually sat down with Jon and Dominic, were to discuss building their gang's political connections. And not just local politicians, but police as well. At what I felt was the right moment, I'd asked Jon for permission to ask a question like, "Isn't that the guy we kick up to's responsibility?" Jon would explain that, even though they were under Sanfilippo's protection, the Sicilian-led gangs may not totally have their back. The Sicilians' political contacts came through the Unione. Jon and Dominic were the only Calabrian-led gang in The Heights and knew they had to protect their own interests. I knew they aspired to be more than just a spoke in the wheel, and I wanted to be part of it.

But I also had Marie. Though I had been spending less time at my dad's shops, that's where I met the most beautiful thing I'd ever seen. I had been helping my dad stock shelves and literally backed into her as she tried maneuvering around the boxes in the aisle. I was utterly struck by her beauty and couldn't get "scusi" out of my mouth. She had long, curly black hair just past her shoulders and brown eyes; the biggest, most beautiful round eyes God had ever given. She smiled at me immediately, causing my heart to beat out of my chest. I finally managed to get words to pass over my teeth and asked where she lived. She had recently moved about five blocks from where we lived.

"Can I come over and call on you?"

Before she could answer, a lady stuck her head into the aisle behind us and told Marie it was time to go. Her mom had obviously been eavesdropping on our conversation.

Over the next few months, I went to her house and took her on long strolls. Marie was stunning in the moonlight. I'd get lost staring into her eyes, totally mesmerized. We'd hold hands the entire time and I'd occasionally stop to kiss her gently, cupping her soft cheeks in my hands. I always brought flowers for Marie and her mother when I showed up on her doorstep, trying to prove I was worthy of her courtship. Her parents were always polite but cold. Her dad somehow found out I was spending time working at the Lucky Lounge and assumed I was a racketeer. Which I wasn't. I mean, I was dabbling in that life, but it wasn't necessarily what I wanted. It was good easy side cash. I knew Marie loved me, but I could see how her parents were starting to create a divide between us. I took it personally.

God, I loved her.

I was almost eighteen when I started hinting at marriage on our walks. She'd go a little quiet, and I could tell something wasn't quite right. As we sat in her back yard one evening, I finally asked if she saw herself marrying me. She began to cry and told me she loved me, but her parents didn't care for me. I tried explaining away my time at the lounge as just hanging out with my older cousin and cleaning up for extra cash. She started sobbing, saying it didn't matter. Her parents wanted her to stop seeing me, and she didn't have the courage to go against their wishes.

"Don't say no just yet," I argued. "We can give it time. I will prove to your parents that I am worthy of you. You make me whole. I will dedicate my life to making you happy. I will treat you like the principessa that you are. I need you!"

Marie paused but didn't agree to wait, either. I'm not sure what came over me, but right then and there I drew a line in the sand.

"Marie, if you'll be my wife, I swear I'll be totally honest and legitimate. I'll take over the family stores and we can start a family.

But if you say no, I will go into that life because without you, I have nothing to lose."

She wailed into her hands, unable to look into my tear-filled eyes. "I love you, Sal, but I can't. I just can't."

I went straight to my parents' house and cried for hours. My parents and sisters were equally as devastated as I was. Mom had said she loved how I acted when I was with Marie, especially the way I catered to her every whim when she came over for family dinners. She could see that Marie was good for my soul. My sisters were hoping for yet another sister. As if they didn't have enough of those.

But I was true to my word and went to the Lucky Lounge every day and night after that heartbreaking evening, trying not to think about losing my true love. My parents weren't excited about the path I put myself on, but I'm not so sure they were surprised. I still didn't think this was what I would do for the rest of my life, and to this day I'm not sure if I committed to Jon and Dominic to spite Marie or myself.

I know I didn't think it all the way through. I wasn't considering the inherent dangers and stresses that come with the life of a racketeer. I wanted to be tough, like the neighborhood boys who fought for their family's honor. I wanted to be respected.

But mostly, I wanted to make big money to help my parents raise my seven sisters.

CHAPTER 2

New Friends

By spring of 1919 I was devoting my time to Dominic, who was a presence in The Heights. I figured I could learn a thing or two and maybe get some exposure to his connections around Chicago. Jon would accompany us on occasion, but if he was out with us, he was always the first one to go home. He was married and looking to start a family, and I never saw him messing with other girls.

Dominic and I, on the other hand, would burn the candle from both ends if we were not on business. We were cugini, for Christ's sake. Cousins. Family. And we had fun. Booze, gambling, and girls; what's not to like? It was also a decent distraction from my recent heartbreak. Anyway, Dom and I were starting to frequent some of Johnny Torrio's joints. We were there to check things out, maybe talk to some local talent or, if we were lucky, run into Torrio's new guy.

On an unusually warm afternoon in early spring, Dominic told me we were heading into Burnham that night to visit Torrio's Coney Island Café. Dom had heard that Torrio was going to be there to show the new guy around. Dom and I got there by mid-evening, I'd guess. We were sitting in a booth toward the back of the lounge where we could see who was coming in and out of the Coney Island, along with whoever walked in and out of the bathroom. Dominic always situated himself in a back corner. It's obvious why, and I began doing the same thing, whether I was with him or others. All the booths were decked out in a red fabric, the tablecloths were black, and the windows were adorned with long red velvet panels. It was pretty swanky.

It wasn't long before a barrel of a man walked through the door, followed by Torrio and a younger guy who walked with swagger.

"There he is, Dom." I couldn't hide my excitement. "It's the new guy."

Dominic casually turned his head towards me and winked. "We'll let them do their thing, then maybe we'll introduce ourselves to the gentlemen—if it looks like the timing's right."

Once again, we didn't need to wait long for an introduction. The big man, who was obviously Torrio's driver and bodyguard, walked up to our table. "Mr. Torrio wants to see you boys."

I was surprisingly calm, despite being eighteen and getting ready to meet Big Jim's right-hand man. Dominic had some swagger himself and walked with a quiet confidence that exuded power. As we arrived at the table, the driver pulled up two chairs.

"Please, gentlemen, sit down with us for a moment." Torrio opened his palms to the two empty seats. "Your booth will be ready with fresh drinks when you return, as I don't want to keep you from your evening,"

"What can we do for you, Mr. Torrio?" Dominic was suspicious but respectful.

"I wanted to meet you, Dominic. You're with Jon Allen in The Heights, but rumor is you've been hanging around my places lately. Something got your eye?"

Dominic relaxed his posture to help calm Torrio and his bodyguard. "Mr. Torrio, I'm a bachelor. I like to go out to nice places and have a good time." Dominic turned toward the new guy, extending his right hand. "Dominic Scalea."

"Al Capone. How are ya?" He seemed unimpressed but

accepted Dominic's gesture.

Dom turned back to Johnny. "Yeah, I'm with Jon. This is my cousin, Salvatore. He's with us, too. Salvatore Liparello, meet John Torrio."

I looked at Johnny straight in the eyes and extended my hand. "Sal. Nice to meet you, Mr. Torrio." I turned to the new guy and shook his hand. "Sal Liparello. Nice to meet you too." I tried not to cough as Al's cigar smoke wafted up my face.

"Al Capone, Sal."

"Now that we're all acquainted," Torrio said, aggravation in his voice, "Dominic, you want to tell me what Sanfilippo has you doing here or what?"

"We kick up to him but we don't take orders from him, and I've never been in one of your joints on his behalf. I think you should see it as me extending public relations for possible future collaboration."

"Are you unhappy in Chicago Heights, Mr. Scalea?"

"No, sir. Love The Heights."

Torrio seemed satisfied. "I don't want to keep you boys any longer. I'll have one of my girls bring over a few drinks. On me, of course."

We got up, shook hands, and returned to our booth. I asked Dominic why he didn't tell Torrio about how the other Sicilian gangs treated us at times.

"What have I told you over and over, Sal? Come on. Never let people know what you're thinking. And I don't ever want to give the impression to anyone that we are disloyal. Got it?"

"Totally, cuz. I got it now."

And I did. It all clicked for me that night. It was exhilarating to meet Johnny Torrio and Al Capone, who all of the boys in The Heights were talking about. In fact, from that night forward, we were on a first-name basis.

Soon after, the boys in The Heights and people across the nation were following the developing support for Prohibition, which had gangs and bootleggers readying themselves for the passage of the Volstead Act that would go into effect by mid-January. I was busy driving and setting up meetings with Jon and various politicians, police officers, and the like. We really needed to cultivate deeper personal connections with public officials, which is critical when operating at that level. Jon's brother was a police officer in South Chicago, and he had become close with Mike McMahon, a powerful Bloom Township politician.

"You can never have enough political capital in your pocket, Salvatore," Jon would say. "You may not see the value in it now, when it appears you're making payouts for no reason. But when you need it, you'll be glad you have it. So, if it seems expensive … consider it cheap."

Must've been mid or late summer of '19 when Jon read a headline while eating Saturday breakfast with his wife. Prohibition Starts Mid-January 1920. He told Dom we needed to come over at two o'clock in the afternoon for a picnic.

"A picnic?" I asked Dom.

"Madone, lil cuz! When Jon says picnic, he means a friggin' meeting at some point during a real friggin' picnic, you strunz."

Jon's wife, a real doll, let us in the house that afternoon. "You know where to find him. I'll see you fellas when it's closer to dinner time. I'm in the kitchen if you need anything."

We walked through to the backyard, where Jon was sitting on the patio drinking an iced tea, his head tilted toward the sun. He spoke to us as we approached without opening his eyes. "We have a lot to discuss."

Jon laid it out quickly. "We came to this country to make big money. Well, boys, once the Volstead Act goes into effect, opportunities will be there for the taking. We need to build this crew, and fast! Bring in guys we know and trust. We cannot be an all Calabrese gang. It doesn't even make sense. Look for guys—even Sicilians—who may have issues with the power of Sanfilippo or the Unione Siciliana. We need to get our gang's bootlegging operation running smoothly before the end of the year. And more political contacts. This is how we take more control in The Heights and get some fucking respect."

I walked into my parents' house immediately after the meeting. Dad saw the urgency in my eyes. "Son, let's talk."

"That thing I'm doing with Jon and Dom, I need to help it grow … and fast. Before Prohibition starts."

I explained the strategy, and my dad reacted exactly how I expected.

"If there's something I can do to help, I will. In fact, I may have something for you already."

It turns out some uncles and cousins on my mom's side in Wisconsin were getting ready to bootleg, and they were looking to develop routes with us and our partners. I'd figured my dad would end up bootlegging, but I was surprised he'd already given it so much consideration. Dad also told me the Zingaros, who owned a confectionary, should be courted by Jon and Dominic. From one store owner to another, a Zingaro brother told him they'd be given more power based on their business—sugar, which is critical to making liquor. My dad also urged us to contact a couple other families who might be willing to show loyalty to Jon and Dominic for various reasons. Most had businesses in place that, once Prohibition kicked in, would be very well positioned for control and power.

I met with Dominic the next day for lunch and to exchange notes. I told him my dad would be bootlegging with my mom's family in Milwaukee, Kenosha, and southern Wisconsin. Dominic was elated to hear the families and their partners were already working on routes. I'd just given Jon and Dominic connections across state lines that would surely be a massive money-maker. Jon was as pleased as I'd hoped when he found out. He was appreciative of my father, but he also acknowledged my drive and loyalty. I wasn't even twenty yet, but with Jon and Dominic's vision, I would be high up on the totem pole soon. Dominic told me to set up meetings with the guys Dad recommended, and said I'd be sitting in with him unless told otherwise.

"There's one more thing we're going to do," Dominic said. "We're going to get to know Torrio and his new guy, Al, a lot better. A Chicago connection could serve us well and help position us better in The Heights."

I couldn't have agreed more. Jon and Dominic had believed for a while now that Sanfilippo and his lieutenants had gotten too comfortable. Jon was surprised there were no repercussions when Torrio started opening clubs close to The Heights. Torrio wasn't doing anything wrong, per se, though he was cutting it close. But hey, we weren't in charge.

"I think Torrio and Al are going to push on Big Jim," Dominic said. "I mean, if they're ever going to run Chicago, they'll have to hold off the powerful Sicilian factions. Al's from Naples. Torrio's not Sicilian, either. He's from Irsina." Dominic smirked. "The Unione Siciliana would love to have one of their boys in there instead of Torrio or Al."

"Capone, too? He just got in town."

"He may not jump ahead of Johnny T, but he's smart and hungry. He's got that look in his eyes. And you know what?"

"What do you got for me, cuz?" I shot back.

"Sal." He looked me dead in the eyes and leaned toward me. "I know another guy with that same look in his eyes … you."

A couple nights later, Dominic and I ran into Al at Torrio's Shadow Inn. Capone waltzed in as we were sitting at the far end of the bar, barely lifting his hat before smiling at us. It was like he knew we were there, waiting for his arrival.

In fact, I'm sure he did.

"The boys in The Heights. Business or pleasure tonight, fellas?"

"Both," Dominic replied.

"Love the honesty, Dom. Let's talk."

Al told the bartender Dominic and I were on the house the rest of the night and took us down a dark, smokey hallway to an office in the back. He sat in a black, buttoned leather chair behind a large mahogany desk and gestured for us to sit. "What's up, Dominic? How can I help you?"

Dominic nonchalantly laid out our plans and explained that we were looking to expand our political capital, even though that was supposed to be Sanfilippo's end of it, which was part of our kick-up. Dominic had me detail my family's routes in and out of Wisconsin, and I told Al that he should let me know if I could ever help him out.

Capone told us that Big Jim Colosimo was hesitant to push into bootlegging. He was afraid of the heat it would bring, but Torrio and Al hadn't given up hope that Jim would change his mind. In so many words, Capone told us that with or without Colosimo's blessing, he and Torrio were going to move forward when the timing was right.

"If there's anything you need, Al, just let us know," Dominic said as we left the office.

"I like what I see between us. Good night, Dom. Sal."

Dominic had just ensured that if Torrio or Al wanted help from The Heights, we were their guys. But we had to be careful. If Sanfilippo or his lieutenants found out the Chicago bosses were circumventing the boss of The Heights, we'd be dead.

A couple days later, I had two of the Zingaro brothers over for a sit down with Jon and Dominic. I was there, but off to the side, standing next to the door. Angelo, the eldest Zingaro brother, immediately asked Jon why he'd called the meeting.

Jon didn't hesitate. "I want you and your brothers to join Dominic, Salvatore, and me. I'm sure we could become quite powerful during Prohibition."

"Jon, Dominic, no disrespect, but what's in it for us?" Angelo asked. "With our sugar connections, why should we work with anyone?"

Jon calmly laid out his vision for his combined gang. He went through our interstate bootlegging routes and explained how we were building political connections that would be imperative with Prohibition on the horizon.

"Why are you worried about paying more for protection than you already are? You don't trust Sanfilippo?"

Jon answered. "It's not mistrust, per se. It's more that we believe we can't have enough protection, and we like having some of the guys looking after our interests actually know who we are."

"Listen, Jon," Angelo said. "I just don't think we need you right now. I appreciate that you want to work with us, and I more than appreciate your vision for The Heights, but the Zingaros are going to pass for now. Believe me, if something changes, I will reevaluate. Are you guys talking to anyone else?"

"I'm waiting to meet with the Stefanos, but I wanted to tell them you were on board when I met with them."

"Not yet, Jon. Take care."

Angelo Zingaro walked out of Jon's office, his middle brother following him.

"He'll be back once Sanfilippo lets him down," Jon said as soon as the door closed behind them. "Get the Stefanos in here, Sal. Even if they say no like Zingaro, they'll know we like them and want to work with them. The seed has been planted. Capice?"

A few days later, Jon gave the Stefanos the same sales pitch, but we got the outcome we were hoping for this time.

The Stefanos were three brothers, and they were mean. Really mean. But also really loyal, from what Jon heard around The Heights. They also had some bootlegging routes ready to go. The younger Stefano spoke a bit out of place and made it quite clear that they didn't trust Sanfilippo or his lieutenants, Lambretta and Pacenti. They told us flat out they were thrilled to join up with some fellow Calabrese and were wary of the power the Unione Siciliana held. They thought Sanfilippo was the Unione Siciliana's puppet, not the other way around.

Jon explained that he was uneasy over the Unione. He did say, however, that we couldn't be an anti-Sicilian gang. We couldn't get stuck in that clan mentality. He was trying to bring in the Zingaros, even though they were Sicilian, because they would control and hold the sugar used for bootlegging operations through their candy company.

My family knew the Stefanos pretty well. They went into my dad's store regularly and were always kind to my mom and sisters. Dad was pleased to hear the Stefanos were joining us and knew they would bring a lot to the table.

"Stay close to the Zingaros, Sal," my dad advised. "They'll come around once they feel disrespected by Sanfilippo. It may take months or years, but they'll come back to us. I'm sure of it. Now, if you have a little bit of time for your family, I could use some help getting our stills set up in the basement of the store on Shields. A basement that big is perfect. Plus your mom and sisters miss you, so get your eighteen-year-old culo home for dinner tonight!"

CHAPTER 3

Prohibition Begins

The headlines read Prohibition Begins Tomorrow, January 17, 1920 as bootleggers prepared their stills. My dad was up and running already. We'd done some dry runs with Mom's family in Wisconsin, and Dominic made a couple trips to Connellsville, Pennsylvania, to visit a Scalea cousin who was bootlegging in that region. They were mostly exchanging recipes and notes, from what Jon and Dominic told me, but they were also talking about the possibility of opening an east/west route.

It was early that same year that I was first scared for my life.

Sanfilippo called for Dominic and me. We had no idea what we could have done wrong. It didn't matter. All that mattered was what they thought we did. I mean, we were trying to bolster our gang by bringing in smaller crews but never under the pretense to knock off the boss. We walked into Sanfilippo's headquarters, and my palms were sweating. Was I about to get assassinated at nineteen years old?

No, I wasn't.

"What do you two know about Torrio's new joint?" Sanfilippo growled, a half-smoked cigarette pinched tightly between his index and middle finger. "I know you're hanging around his joints. This time he's gone too far."

You see, Torrio had opened a place in Chicago Heights. A sign of total disrespect toward Sanfilippo, and a message that Torrio was going to do whatever he wanted. He knew The Heights was booming and the kind of business we were doing. The fact was, Dominic and I knew Torrio had opened the Moonlight Café on Lincoln Highway. Dominic and Capone both were seen going in and out of there frequently, among the other Torrio-owned roadhouses.

Sanfilippo turned toward me. "How old are you, kid?"

"Almost twenty," I shot back, looking Sanfilippo dead in the eyes. He leaned back in his chair, taken aback by the look I delivered. My confidence grew that very instant.

"You run with some rough company, son."

"Dominic's family, sir. Are you saying I shouldn't be spending time with mi familia?"

"I'll call your cousin whatever I want, Salvatore! You boys are hanging out a lot with those Chicago guys. What the fuck are you up to?"

Dominic remained calm. "Boss, we go to those places to keep an eye on our competition. That's it. We make good money for you. We aren't disloyal. Honestly, we don't know Johnny T's motivation."

"Well he's definitely pushing me to my limits, Scalea! He opened a roadhouse in my fuckin' town!"

"Are we here to plan retaliation?" Dominic asked.

"I want you two to stay close, and if you think they're going to make a move against me, you let me know. Capice?"

As we walked out, and I was breathing a sigh of relief, Dominic turned to me. "He'll be the last one to know when someone's making their move against him. That strunz!"

"That's for sure. He won't see it coming. He's weaker than I thought."

"I'm not exactly sure what came over you in that moment, Sal, but it's like he flipped a switch. I knew you had it in you. Let it out, cousin!"

I had thought I was going to be dead at nineteen. Instead, I went to sleep that night thinking about how Jon and Dominic were going to take over The Heights, and I was getting in on the ground floor. Maybe Dominic was right. Maybe I did have a future in this business. I'd found my edge, and I liked it. It was like a wave of confidence crashed over me. I'd just looked the boss in the eye, made him push back in his seat, and told him what was what. Actually, I don't think I even slept that night. The adrenaline was still running hard. I was almost twenty, Prohibition had just started, and I was feeling lucky. But luck had little to do with it. As my dad loved to tell us, "Luck is when preparedness meets opportunity."

Later that year, Dominic's brother, Gaetano, arrived unannounced in Chicago Heights from Sambiase. My parents were ecstatic. It had been years since we'd seen him. Gaetano told us about his experience as a stowaway over coffee and cookies. Dom had surely called him over as reinforcement for our growing crew, and it wouldn't have been difficult to convince him. The promise to make big cash allowed Gaetano to leave a wife who was three months pregnant. Once again, my parents were a bit dumbfounded by my cousins' willingness to leave their young families behind. They'd also crossed illegally. Were they running from responsibility, or were they honestly here to make money to send back to Sambiase?

"Let's reserve our judgment," my dad said. "We don't know what's going on. It's between them and the wives they left behind. Obviously, the Scaleas are not Liparellos."

A few days later, we discovered his wife refused to come to America, but Dominic promised his brother so much cash that Gaetano decided to come anyway and send money back as often as possible.

Gaetano said he wanted to go by the name Guy while here. I didn't foresee how closely Guy and I would work together in the decades to come. I figured out fast, however, that Jon had just gotten himself another loyal soldier. The Scalea brothers were reunited and a force to be reckoned with, two bulldogs. Though Jon didn't want his gang to be too clannish, it was. And for now, that's the way I liked it. I was young, and I was working with my two cousins and Jon, a good friend of my dad's. I felt comfortable. Safe. Invincible.

There was a learning curve during the first eighteen months of Prohibition, though. We lost a handful of shipments on both sides of the Wisconsin/Illinois border. Some to busts. Some to mechanical breakdowns. Sometimes the drivers could get the word out for help, and we would send a truck in the middle of the night to swap out the load, but sometimes the police would see the trucks broken down and investigate. This was exactly what Jon meant when he spoke about paying for police and political protection. And while we had many of the police along our routes on payroll, it was obvious we didn't have enough.

Meanwhile, the Lucky Lounge began serving as a sort of booze clearinghouse. Bootleggers from all over the Midwest would show up to make purchases and arrange deliveries. Of course, gambling and girls were still available at the Lucky. That was a given. Jon had acquired a lot of land around his home and the lounge. He'd just finished building a fueling station across the street from the Lucky, where he set me up as manager. I now had a legit job in the eyes of the authorities. It seemed like the Lounge was always bustling with locals blowing off the day's steam or out-of-towners conducting booze business. Either way, we were making big dough. At twenty-one years old, I had a nice car, beautiful clothes, expensive jewelry, and I was out with showgirls regularly. I had the world by the cogliones.

I also hit the point where I was in too deep. And even if I could, I wasn't sure I wanted to change my life's course. If I left, I could only make a fraction of the cash I was making back when I was nineteen, let alone what I was bringing in at twenty-one. Besides, I was able to slip my parents cash to help provide for my sisters, who I planned on taking care of as much as I could. They looked up to me, and I didn't want to let them down.

Not long after Guy joined the gang, Jon and Dominic called me into a meeting that was unlike any other. Its purpose was to retaliate for services Jon felt were paid for but not rendered: providing protection in Blue Island.

Jon was pacing his office when I walked in. "This alderman from Blue Island, Arnie Myer, he must think we're chumps or idiots. Well, he's going to find out that we're neither."

"This is about the raids there?"

"You bet your ass it's about the raids! Not only is part of our kick-up to Sanfilippo supposed to go to Blue Island, our gang is also paying them just to make sure our boys aren't getting pinched! Dominic and Sal, did you deliver all the envelopes intended for Myer?"

"We most certainly did," I answered.

"Then this cocksucker needs his bell rung!" Spit was flying from Jon's mouth as he yelled. "These guys should know damn well that if they're going to take our money, they can't renege on their duties. This strunz definitely needs a reminder!"

This was the angriest I had seen Jon. I wasn't surprised he reacted the way he did, though. These raids were costly to the gangs and the bootleggers themselves.

"Jon, can I recommend we try a peaceful resolution to this situation?" I asked. "Maybe make sure someone didn't just fuck up by accident?"

"There's been three raids in Blue Island in ten weeks. That isn't a fuck-up. One raid is a fuck-up. Not three! But I do think we should arrange a meeting with Arnie to get a feel for his demeanor. I want to read him. Sal, set it up. Dominic, I'm going out with you on this one. Sal, I want you watching the lounge to keep an eye on things there. It's busy twenty-four-seven. I know you can handle it. Make sure the gas station is open. These guys gotta fill up on their way home or outta town. Twenty-four-seven, Sal."

"Understood, Jon. I'm on it. And thanks for trusting me with setting up the meeting."

This was another step that would make changing careers a bit more difficult. Once word got around that I was setting up meetings, every big shot would know I was moving up in the organization and had the authority to speak for Jon when asked to.

A couple days later, I set up the meeting through Arnie's son, Alex, who was Arnie's voice and hands if Arnie didn't want or need to show up. Next, I had to talk with Jon and Dominic and go over all possible scenarios and escape routes. Jon called Dom and me to the house for a picnic to go over all the details.

Jon answered the door, cheeks flushed. "We all set, kid?" he asked before the door was fully open.

"All set. Dom here yet?"

"No. Let's have a chianti while we wait. Come on in."

We made our way to the back of the house and Jon set us up in the shade. We sipped our wine, trying to relax before the intensity of the meeting began simmering.

Dominic showed up before we finished our first glass. "What did I miss? Am I late?"

"Not late at all, Dom." Jon lifted his almost empty glass. "All you missed was the first pour."

Dominic filled his own glass with what was left in the bottle and sat down, tucking his chair beneath him.

"What do you have for us, Salvatore?" Jon asked.

"Arnie Myer is supposed to meet you face to face with Dominic tomorrow night. I insisted, since you and Dominic felt it necessary to be present and that Arnie, not Alex, also be there. Alex agreed. I felt some arrogance that I wanted to rid him of, but I stayed very composed."

"What the hell, Sal?" Dominic asked, frustrated at my aside about Alex's demeanor. "Stay focused. Details."

"Alex wanted it in Blue Island, so I picked the location. I drove the area around Western Avenue scouting for easy on and off. We want dark and isolated, so if things go wrong, you should have time to jump onto Western and be gone. I think the place that meets our needs best is under the Rock Island viaduct at Western Avenue. I'll have a couple guys there before looking for a setup."

Jon asked, "Is there anything we should look for that would put me and Dominic on high alert?"

"The only people who are supposed to be there are Arnie, his driver, you, and Dom. If Arnie isn't there and his son is, I would be suspicious. I'm telling you, there is something about that Alex that I don't like or trust. I'm not surprised our money hasn't gone toward our protection. It's probably not leaving that prick's pussy hands. At 12:20 a.m., you guys will pull under the viaduct, lights off. Arnie and his driver should roll up at 12:25. One of our guys will give the all clear to Arnie's driver at the station a block north, and the other guy will guard your exit once you pass him a couple blocks south. There shouldn't be a cop within two miles in either direction on Western until 12:45. That's what I could secure."

"Sal, you did good," Dominic said. "Real good."

"Save it for when you get back and we drink to a successful meeting. Keep in mind, I have a bad feeling about Alex's attitude. Be alert."

Jon folded his hands around the stem of his empty wine glass. "Sounds good to me."

Later, when Jon and Dominic were on their way, I was keeping an eye on the Lucky Lounge. That meant taking and filling orders for bootleggers from all over the Midwest, not just the areas south of Chicago. We had a secret bar and rooms with girls. The Lucky had a lot going on at once, and I loved every minute of it.

But soon it was almost 1 a.m. and Jon and Dominic weren't back yet. I was just starting to wonder what was taking so long when they walked in, stone-faced and headed straight for Jon's office. Jon barely turned his head in my direction and nodded for me to follow.

"What happened?" I asked as Dominic closed the door behind us. "What went wrong?"

Jon put up his hand to stop me. "You're right, Sal. Alex is a fucking strunz."

"I fucking knew it. He wasn't supposed to be there. That was not what we agreed on, Jon. I swear!"

"Relax, Salvatore," Dominic said. "You told us to be wary of him, so we were ready."

"Okay." I took a deep breath and cleared my throat. "Now, someone please fill me in on what the hell happened out there."

Jon began. "I shot that disrespectful little shit. I'm pretty sure it was just in the arm. He'll be fine. The police would already be here knocking if he went to the hospital. Dominic and I were lucky we got out of there in one piece, though. Dominic, tell Sal what happened. I'll pour us some scotch."

"Let me back up a bit," Dominic said. "The spot was perfect, Sal. Right off Western, but you felt isolated under the viaduct. We showed up when we got the signal it was clear and left the car running with the lights off. The car was lined up for a quick hop back onto Western. Then Arnie's car pulled up coming towards us, lights off, just like the driver was supposed to do. Jon and I waited for Arnie's driver to get out and open the door for Arnie, then we got out of my car."

"You were both armed?" I interrupted.

"Yeah. Revolvers under our coats." Dominic swung open the left side of his jacket to expose the gun resting in its shoulder holster.

"Let him finish, Sal," Jon added as he sipped his scotch. "Keep going, Dom."

"So, lucky for us, there was just enough light that when Jon and I met at the front of my car we could see that it was Alex, not Arnie. We double checked our guns before we left, and Jon said to be ready for anything right as we were meeting in the middle."

Then Alex walks up and says, What's this all about? You guys upset about something that involves my dad? I couldn't believe those were the first things out of that prick's mouth. Jon said that with all the money his dad is getting from Sanfilippo, and us on top of it, there's no excuse for our operations being the focus of any raids. There were plenty of other bootlegging operations to bust. Jon told him it's like some of the money wasn't getting spread out as far as it's supposed to be. Then he asked Alex if we should bypass his dad in the future. Well, Alex gets defensive, turns unpredictable.

"Bypass my dad? Alex asks. How? I swear the kid's eyes were bugging out. So, Jon casually puts his hands on his hips so he's ready to draw his weapon. Alex is all over the place, erratic. Then Jon says, Well, if our money isn't getting past your pockets as promised, then this arrangement is a waste of our money, and we'll find protection elsewhere.

"So Alex starts yelling, My dad doesn't owe you shit!

"Like hell he doesn't, kid! Jon says. Does your dad even know you're here representing him? There's no way he would let an imbecile embarrass him like you are right now. We pay way too much for your shitty protection, and we won't anymore. Go home and tell your dad the cash isn't coming anymore; you piece of shit."

Dominic took a sip of scotch before finishing the story. "At that moment, Alex opens his jacket and tries pulling a revolver that was shoved down his pants. Jon and I both pull ours and start shooting at the driver, who had also pulled his gun. We had to shoot backwards as we ran toward the car. Thank God they had terrible aim. I swear, everything slowed down once shots were fired. I could hear the bullets whizzing by our heads. Jon hit Alex in the arm or shoulder, I think. I saw the driver throwing him in the backseat. We hit the gas, got onto Western, turned our lights back on, and made our way home three miles over the speed limit."

Jon interjected. "Dom, we need our story straight. And we need to find out if this kid went to the hospital because if he did, I'm sure the police interviewed him. He went in with a gunshot wound. We need to be ready for the police to come knocking."

It wasn't more than sixteen hours after the bungled meeting when Jon's prediction came true. The cops visited Dominic's and Jon's houses at nearly the same time. But Dom and Jon knew they were coming. We were tipped off three hours prior from one of our guys at the station—a perfect example of the political capital we invested paying dividends.

Jon and Dominic cooperated with the police and went to the Blue Island station to have their statements taken at the same time but in separate rooms, which had two metal chairs on opposite sides of a six-foot metal table. The rooms had a window with blinds that were drawn open so they could see each other across the station. It didn't matter that they were kept apart the whole time. The boys had their story straight.

The cops asked them the same questions, but they already knew it was their stories against Alex's.

"I'm telling you," Dominic said, "we were driving down the block when we saw this car pulled off under the viaduct. We thought these two fellas were having car trouble, ya know."

At the same time, in the other room, Jon was telling the exact same story: "We pulled under the viaduct to see if we could help these two guys with their car. If not, we thought we could drop them off somewhere. We pulled up, got out of the car, and approached them. When we got within twenty feet, they walked toward us, pulled out their guns, and tried to rob us. As soon as I opened up my jacket and showed my gun to, ya know, get these guys to back off, they started to shoot. So Dominic and I ran back to our car. I only fired my weapon to give us time to make it back. I wasn't even aiming, just shooting in self-defense. I had no idea I hit one of them."

When the cops asked, Dom and Jon acted like they didn't know Alex or the driver. It was a random attempted armed robbery gone wrong. A week later, they were contacted by the authorities and told there wasn't enough evidence to press any charges. But one thing was certain after that: Jon and Dominic were on the local cops' radar. I had just participated in a conspiracy by aiding and abetting, and I had no qualms about it. I did what I needed to, and I'd do it again.

We didn't have any more problems with operations in Blue Island after that. Arnie had gotten the message—make sure your son falls in line, or he'll fall into a grave.

CHAPTER 4

In Cahoots

By early '23, Chicago Heights was flourishing as a hub for illegal booze throughout the Midwest. Soon they'd be coming from even farther distances to do business through the Lucky Lounge and our bootleggers. What helped The Heights during Prohibition was Lincoln Highway. It was a major thoroughfare before the interstate system, and it gave us access to railroad yards in The Heights. About this time, Jon and Dominic started giving me and Dominic's brother, Guy, even more duties. After the Myer incident in Blue Island, Jon decided to step back from some of the day-to-day dirty work.

Dominic and I still went out a lot together. Sometimes for fun, but mostly to solidify our ties with Capone. The three of us got along great, and it seemed like we were building a genuine friendship based on trust. One night, we ran into Al at Torrio's Moonlight Café in The Heights and settled into our regular corner booth, the three of us puffing robusto cigars and drinking scotch whiskey. Capone went on about how their gang had been taking pressure from the Unione Siciliana on different fronts. He said Moran and his ally, Joe Aiello, were leaning on them on the Northside, the Genna brothers were causing them trouble on the Westside, and the Chicago Heights Unione chapter was also helping the Sicilians push against Torrio and Al.

"Al," Dominic said, "you need to know Jon, Sal, and I are getting shit on in The Heights."

"I believe it, boys. The money's big, and the Sicilians want it all. That clan mentality is dangerous. I'll do business with anyone as long as they're loyal and reliable."

I jumped in. "Jon says the same thing. In fact, the Zingaros are Sicilian, and we're trying to recruit them before Sanfilippo sways them against us."

"Those are the confectioner guys who control most of the sugar, right?" Capone asked, scratching his stubble.

"Yes," Dominic said. "We want those brothers in our camp."

Al smiled. "No, you need them in your camp. They'll make you the most powerful gang besides my own."

After hearing Capone's opinion about how powerful we'd be with the Zingaros, I made it my mission to woo them.

But I wanted to consult my dad before going to Jon with my new plan. I stopped at my parents' place to see my mom and sisters. Mom was rolling out gnocchis and already had a pot of gravy simmering on the stove. She must've had three dozen meatballs resting in the gravy pot, too. There's not much in this world that smells or tastes better, so of course I was going to stick around. I also figured I could get some advice from my father before dinner.

Dad and I brought a bottle of chianti outside to sip on while he helped me find the best way to get the Zingaros to join Jon, Dominic, me, and the others we had brought into our fold over the last year and a half. They had to have noticed our growing power and influence in Chicago Heights and beyond. Dad told me to find out if they'd taken any hits in raids that they thought they were protected from. If so, it was time to scratch off that scab and get them worked up against Sanfilippo. Let them know that combined operations would increase everyone's take. He also told me to find out if the Zingaros thought Sanfilippo was weak for letting Torrio open the Moonlight Café with no pushback. It looked weak to us, and we were sure others saw the same thing.

The next day at the Lucky, I asked Jon and Dominic if I could reach out to the Zingaros for a sit-down. Jon asked what my angle was, so I went over the stuff I'd discussed with my dad.

Jon was on board immediately. "I was just thinking it's about time to reach out to them. Set it up, Salvatore. I want Dominic there with you. And make sure you don't end up with the opposite results. The last thing we need is to piss off the friggin' sugar kings of The Heights. We could easily go to work for them, but I don't think they have the vision to rule this town when the right time presents itself. We'll be ruthless when we need to."

I had never heard such talk from Jon. Ruthless? Jon thought I could be ruthless? He thought we were all capable of being ruthless? I knew Dom had it in him, but me? It was like he could sense an impending gang war, and he was going to be ready for the battles ahead. He obviously saw violence on the horizon. I was surprisingly unafraid, filled with confidence. Was I overconfident? Probably. I left the meeting energized and wasn't going to let the Zingaros turn me down.

A few days later, Dominic, Guy, and I met all four Zingaro brothers in the back office of their candy store. Dominic and Jon wanted some of the other families to get to know Guy better, as he was ready to take on more responsibilities in our organization.

"Thanks for taking the time and consideration to meet with us on short notice," I started.

"What brings you boys here?" Angelo Zingaro asked.

"We'd like to start working closer together," Dominic said. "Maybe partner up on some stuff, or maybe the Zingaros integrate their organization with ours."

"We went over this a couple years back," one of the younger brothers said. "What's in it for us?"

I wanted back in this negotiation. I loved my cousin, but I wanted to be the one to bring the two organizations together. "I totally appreciate that, gentlemen."

"Appreciate what?" the youngest brother asked.

I shot him a look that said Strunz, shut your out-of-place mouth! Then I turned my head to make sure I was only directing my thoughts toward Angelo, who made all the decisions. "Like I was trying to explain, I think things have changed a bit since we last spoke on this subject."

"What's changed, exactly?" Angelo asked.

"Well, specifically—and I'm putting my neck out there by saying this—Sanfilippo has changed. I don't know where all the protection money lands, but we don't think it's getting to everyone it's meant for. Our group has been subject to raids in areas where we have paid protection, so we've started paying for protection on top of what Sanfilippo is supposedly paying them. We're also bringing a lot of police into our fold. Have you guys had any raids you thought shouldn't have happened?"

The Zingaros looked at each other.

"Yes," Angelo said. "We've been busted when we should've been tipped off."

"Exactly! And have you heard about anyone being surprised or even concerned about Sanfilippo letting Torrio open the Moonlight inside The Heights?"

"We have, and we also have concerns over these issues. So, what's your point, Sal? Dom?"

I knew Dominic wanted to broker this deal, but he was going to let me try. "Point is, fellas, our organization is growing. We're trying to consolidate as many Chicago Heights bootleggers as we can. Honestly, if we combined our efforts, we wouldn't cannibalize each other. I believe we would both profit much more. You'd have no competition from other sugar suppliers trying to sell to the bootleggers in The Heights. Sure, some of those profits will get split up, but your increased sales would make that split look like nothing. More importantly, our gang is taking protection into our own hands. We'll answer to Sanfilippo for now, but in the meantime, it's best if I, Jon, Dominic, and all our partners make ourselves as strong and powerful as possible. Bottom line, gentlemen: We really want the Zingaros to join forces with us."

I wanted to leave them with that thought. We all shook hands and Angelo said we'd have our answer in twenty-four hours. I thanked them for their time, and we filed out.

Dominic was beaming as we climbed back into his car. "Salvatore Liparello, you're a natural. I mean it. You have a way with people. You read them so well. You read the tension in the room, too. Plus, I see a ruthless drive. You need that to be a leader in this game."

There was that word again. Ruthless. I figured I better get used to it. Sounded like it would be essential for growth and survival.

"Really, Sal, that was impressive," Dominic continued. "The Zingaros are going to join us. I was watching Angelo. He was eating it up, and every point you brought up he agreed with. I think you may have just made us the most influential gang in The Heights, and we're not even Sicilian. I love it!"

"Let's see what they say before you give me a big head."

That's what I said, but my heart felt like it might burst out of my chest. Granted, this praise was coming from family, but Dominic was tough as shit and didn't take any from anyone. He was also hard to impress and one of the most driven guys I knew.

That night was the first time I really thought I had a knack for this racketeering thing and, honestly, a part of me wasn't sure how I felt about it. I wondered how my life might be different if Marie's parents had approved of me and we'd gotten married. I'd have a legit job. Maybe we'd have three or four kids always creating lovely chaos throughout our house. My eyes welled up and I pushed such thoughts out of my mind as best I could. I had to put Marie in the darkest recesses of my memory.

It was too painful to think about her.

The next day, Angelo Zingaro stopped by the Lucky Lounge unannounced. We were more than a little surprised he hadn't made contact before just showing up.

"Is Jon around?"

"Yeah," I said. "He's in the back."

"Dominic?"

"No, but he should be here soon."

"No worries. Can we go talk to Jon?"

"Follow me, Mr. Zingaro."

As I led him back to Jon's office, my palms had started to sweat, the anticipation unbearable.

I knocked on Jon's door.

"Come in." Jon put the papers he was studying into his top desk drawer as we entered.

"Hey, Jon, we have an important guest," I announced, opening the door wider.

"Jon, how are you?" Angelo asked as soon as he set foot inside Jon's office. "How's the family?"

"All great. Thanks for asking."

"I have to say, your protégé here is an impressive young man. He came up with some compelling arguments that made good business sense."

Jon was expressionless as he leaned back in his chair, hands folded. "Thanks. That's good to hear."

"Our contacts in town tell us they like dealing with you much more than the other gang leaders. You're a man of your word, and you treat all your partners with respect regardless of what part of Italy they deserted. You aren't clannish like Sanfilippo and most other Sicilians in power. We think that kind of mentality won't work here in America in the long term."

Angelo paused, and I thought I might scream the tension was so thick.

"We're in," he said, finally. "Let's do this."

"This is fabulous news!" Jon said joyously as he stood up. "Thanks for coming here so soon and in person."

The three of us exchanged handshakes and kissed each other on the cheeks.

"Let me show you out, Mr. Zingaro," I said.

"Call me Angelo, Sal. You've earned that right."

Closing the door, I glanced back at Jon. He winked.

I had done it.

After sending Angelo on his way, I raced to my dad's store to share the terrific news. Dad had one last thing to say to me after I kissed him goodbye. "Sal, keep your head up and eyes open. You're building quite a reputation. Remember there will be people looking to knock you down and take your place. So be vigilant. Love you, son."

The word spread like wildfire all over Chicagoland. Of course, when Sanfilippo found out, he couldn't believe a Sicilian family as powerful as the Zingaros would join a Calabrese-led gang. And the Unione Siciliana was incensed beyond belief. They came down hard on Sanfilippo, which made us wonder even more if Sanfilippo really was in power or if the Unione was Sanfilippo's puppet master. To us, it wasn't clear enough to be comfortable. Our new partnership was also a big deal for those Sicilians who thought they were still on their little island. Another example of the clan mentality being bad for business. Welcome to America, strunz!

Jon called me back to the Lucky the next day. He couldn't have been more proud and excited.

"We have a lot of work to do now, Sal. We just grew a lot, so we need to reevaluate all our bootlegging logistics and make sure we're doing things the most efficient and profitable way possible.

Minimize our growing pains. We also need to keep the Zingaros happy, and we need to protect ourselves. Sanfilippo will be watching us closely. He has to be threatened by our size and influence."

Dominic came into the office soon after. "Sal, let's go into the city tonight. I want to tell Al the good news. Plus there's a singer performing at Colosimo's that Al wants me to see. I'm feeling lucky. Aren't you?"

"When am I not? Who's driving?"

As we walked towards the entrance of Colosimo's, the doorman greeted us by name. "Welcome, Mr. Dominic and Mr. Salvatore. Mr. Capone is waiting for you at his table. Right this way, please."

Al stood up and greeted us, then motioned for us to sit next to him so we could see the stage. He had a big cigar hanging out of the side of his mouth, which was normal when he was enjoying himself. I lit one up with him as soon as I got comfortable in my chair. The club was filled with thick smoke mixed with the sweet aroma of the flappers' cheap, over-sprayed perfume. It was enough to give me a headache.

"Dominic, wait until you see Rio." Al grinned. "She's a real knockout!"

We drank and laughed and enjoyed the evening. When it was time for Rio to take the stage, the crowd started whistling and applauding. Al looked at Dominic and gave him an upwards nod as if to say, "Here we go. You're in for a treat."

She came on stage in a white sequined cabaret bodysuit and an ornate, matching headdress. Her voice was like silk and her body flawless. She captivated everyone in the room, even the women. Throughout her hour-long performance, she would look over at our table and smile. She definitely knew Al. After the show, she got a rousing standing ovation. About ten minutes later, she made her way into the club area. Men were flooding her way, but she made a beeline for our table.

"So glad you could make it tonight, Al."

"You know I hate missing your performances. Hey, I want you to meet two good friends of mine from Chicago Heights. This is Dominic Scalea and Salvatore Liparello. Guys, this is Rio."

We stood up to shake her hand. Dominic was like a schoolboy, red-faced and speechless. She sat down to join us for drinks.

"Rio, we're celebrating tonight!" Al said.

"What's the occasion?" she asked with a lilt.

"The boys here made a really big business deal this week. They're gonna be big time in The Heights and I couldn't be happier for them. Saluti!" Capone raised his glass.

The four of us drank and laughed all night at that table. Dominic couldn't keep his eyes off Rio. Al and I were making fun of him all night, and Rio seemed to be interested as well.

"Looks like you're a matchmaker, Al." I laughed, but Dominic and Rio were engaged in their own private conversation, as if they were a world away.

"I'm here to serve, Sal!"

At closing time, a few of the other showgirls came up to the table, struggling to keep their balance. "Can we steal her away from you, gentlemen?" one of them asked between giggles.

"I think I'm needed." Rio rolled her eyes. "I can't thank you boys enough for having me as your guest, but I need to take care of these girls."

Dom, Al, and I stood to wish her a good evening. She kissed me and Al on one cheek. Dominic got a kiss with an extra soft touch on his other cheek. Al motioned over one of the club's security guards.

"What can I do for you Mr. Capone?"

"I want you to get all these girls home safely. And I mean safely.

Capice? This should cover any cost and then some." Al discreetly handed the security guard some cash.

"I'll make sure they are all home safe and door locked behind them, Mr. Capone."

The girls left, and Al, Dominic, and I strolled outside.

"I cannot tell you enough how huge this was, for you to get that deal done with the candy guys," Al said. "Between Jon, you, Dominic, and this natural born leader"—he pointed his stub of a cigar my way— "you guys will be running the show there eventually. And I may help you do it."

Al laughed as we parted ways, and as we neared Dominic's car, I took the keys lightly out of his hand. "I'm in the mood to drive and I feel fine. You can sleep if you want."

"Sal, I'm in love."

"Your culo is in love, cuz," I laughed as I gently biffed him upside the head.

Dominic could only think about Rio, and I could only hear Capone calling me a natural-born leader. If that was the word going around Chicago's upper echelon ... holy shit. I couldn't believe I had a reputation outside of Chicago Heights. And not just any reputation. They saw me as a leader. That's respect. My future with Jon and Dom was looking bright.

Over the following months, Dominic got Rio as many regular gigs as possible in his and Jon's establishments. They were nuts over each other. I'd never seen this side of my cousin. He couldn't stop smiling when she was nearby, and her presence seemed to soothe him. He was gentle around her. It was nice to watch. I'd only seen his dedication, determination, and desire for success, money, and power.

In April of '24, Dom asked for a sit-down with me and Jon, and he wanted his brother, Guy, present. We met at the Lucky Lounge later that night.

"Thanks for coming. I have some pretty big news."

"What's up?" Jon asked with a cautious grin.

"Rio and I are getting married! We want to do it in a couple weeks, and we're hoping you guys will be there. Of course, we'll invite more friends and family, but I won't set the date until I know you three can make it."

Jon stood up. "Of course we can be there. In fact, we'll have it at the farm, if you're okay with that? Hey, another round over here!" Jon turned and motioned to his bartender.

"Jon, that would be wonderful. Rio will love that. I will love that."

I gave my cousin a bear hug. "I'm so happy for you, Dominic. We need to go home and tell my parents. They'll be so happy for you."

Guy was choked up, holding back tears. "Brother! I couldn't be any happier for you. God bless you two."

"Thanks, Gaetano. That means so much to me."

No one made a peep about Dominic's family back in Sambiase. We wisely kept our opinions to ourselves. I, for one, thought it was terrible. I could see him messing around while he was in the States, I suppose. But to get married when you already had a wife and kids seemed crazy.

A few weeks later, Jon threw Dominic and Rio a beautiful ceremony and party at his farm. It was a fairly intimate gathering. Of course, all of us Liparellos were there. Capone showed up, as he introduced them. In fact, Dominic told an abbreviated version of how Al had him "come downtown to see this girl" during one of his two speeches. The weather was great, the food and wine were homemade, and the booze was Canadian whiskey.

It really was a perfect day, and we all thought Rio was a doll.

CHAPTER 5

And So It Begins

Soon after New Year's 1924, Sanfilippo was assassinated by his lieutenants, Pacenti and Lambretta. He was found in his car, still running, up against a tree on Seventeenth Street with four gunshot wounds to the back of the head. He knew and trusted whoever was in his car.

For weeks we'd been hearing that Sanfilippo's horrible handling of security for the town's bootleggers was finally bringing down heat on Pacenti and Lambretta. Sanfilippo hadn't been respected for a few years, and it was a prime opportunity for his lieutenants to knock him off and take power. This was good news for our gang. Pacenti and Lambretta were currently on top, but Jon, Dominic, and I had plans for them. As far as we were concerned, it would be business as usual to benefit the Sicilians. This was one of the reasons we were so aggressive in trying to consolidate as many of the Chicago Heights racketeers as we could—so when the opportunity presented itself, we would be ready to assert power.

With Sanfilippo gone, it was just a matter of when and how we were going to take over The Heights and run it the way it should have been.

Over the next few months, Pacenti stepped in as the new boss, with Lambretta as his number one and Nick Martino, the political fixer, as his number two. Pacenti and Lambretta had used their affiliation and connections within the Unione Siciliana to muscle their way in. Pacenti was best known for his two nightclubs, the

Milano Café and the Derby Inn in Homewood, across from Washington Park racetrack. Pacenti immediately sent someone into Torrio's joint in The Heights to deliver a message: "You'll not make another business move within Chicago Heights or South Chicago Heights."

When it came to guys from The Heights and Chicago, Capone, Dominic, and I were only a handful of guys who got along. We were more than just good business partners. Al and Dominic were practically best friends, and I guess Al and I were, too. We had fun and, above all, trusted and respected each other. Al and Dominic were both driven, with shared visions of becoming the bosses and joining forces.

"I'll make you a lieutenant, Dominic," Al would say.

Dominic would always joke back. "That's only if Jon, Sal, and I deliver The Heights. We could just keep it."

Though it was said in jest, we all knew it was true, and we loved every moment of it. It wasn't so funny when Pacenti and Lambretta started making the same mistakes as their former boss. Raids that shouldn't have been happening were happening again. Obviously, some of the cash for protection wasn't getting to the guys it was intended for. The Chicago Heights bootleggers were disappointed with the protection they got from Sanfilippo, and now Pacenti's protection was spotty at best. The bootleggers wanted more for how much they were paying. Who could blame them? In the meantime, they needed to insulate themselves from growing pressure coming from federal agents.

One winter, my dad started stocking white paint in his store. I was confused until he explained how a still could produce enough heat to melt the snow off the roof of a house and law enforcement had started doing flyovers. After the first few busts, bootleggers came up with the idea of painting their roofs white in the winter.

In addition, some made boys in the neighborhood would place

themselves strategically around the block to act as lookouts for agents. Between that and helping paint roofs, some of these kids made decent change. One freezing January day, there must've been ten guys painting roofs. Local cops turned a blind eye, but federal agents were out to make a name for themselves.

Agents also employed what was known as the smell test, walking neighborhoods sniffing for fumes they could detect from the street. There was no early warning system for the smell test. Once the odor hit the air, there was no way to prevent agents from catching a whiff. That same year, ingenuitive Heights bootleggers created a still that didn't produce fumes. It was so successful that a contingent from our Wisconsin connections came, and Detroit's Purple Gang sent members to learn how the stills operated.

The Heights's bootlegging operations were running on all cylinders and the illegal hooch was distributed to the whole Midwest. They used three fermentation methods that produced 160 to 190 proof spirits. The highest-quality was produced by the seven-day method, a natural fermentation process that yielded thirty to forty thousand gallons per run. This method was also the most labor-intensive and required round-the-clock monitoring. Due to the scale of the seven-day method, these stills were usually located on farms or in large warehouses. However, a few motivated bootleggers in The Heights placed these huge stills in their basement, with holes cut through the first and second floors of the house.

The three-day method used stills that could fit inside a garage and used a chemical process to speed up fermentation. This was the method my dad used in a backroom basement, concealed by a false wall, at one of his stores. The process that produced the lowest yield, the sixteen-hour method, also used a chemical process to speed up fermentation. We called it bathtub gin.

The Stefanos were masters of all three styles. They had the

infrastructure and stills running for months before the Volstead Act even went to the floor for a vote. This was the reason my dad recommended Jon approach them. My father explained to the Stefano brothers why they should go with Jon, other than the fact that he was from Cosenza, Calabria, like them. They were pros. There were three of them. They were within seven years of each other. The youngest Stefano was probably about twenty-five back then. The brothers were fierce when it came to protecting their interests. They would also be very loyal to Jon for years to come. They believed in Jon's long-term vision for The Heights, and it paid off for them.

It was a little odd, engaging in illicit activity with my dad. I didn't know he had it in him, but he sure did. Well, he was just making booze. The entire nation considered prohibition a joke except for the overzealous. It was one thing for him to know what I was doing. It was another for me to tell him about it, then actually engage in those activities with him. I felt extra pressure to make sure I kept an eye on him. Though I knew he was capable of taking care of himself, I still felt responsible for protecting him, so it was another thing to stress over.

I want to say it was around November of '24 when Al called for a meeting with Dominic and me. Dominic told me Al seemed serious.

"You think he wants our help with something?" I asked.

"If he doesn't ask now, he'll be laying the groundwork for something in the future. Regardless, he called. We're going."

"Where are we meeting him?"

"The Four Deuces."

There were three entrances in the front of the building at 2222 S. Wabash. The southernmost led to a storefront Al would eventually turn into a pseudo furniture store. The other two led to a saloon. Behind a partition and to the left was a staircase, and on the second floor you could find benches along the sterile hallway in between the rooms. Men would be waiting for the twenty to thirty girls working on any given night.

When we stepped inside the Four Deuces barroom, a mountain of a man greeted us by name and directed us back to Torrio's office. We were meeting Al but at Torrio's headquarters.

"What's up?" Dominic asked Al. "You sounded concerned."

"You fellas aware of what's been going on between Torrio and O'Banion?"

I chimed in. "We assume it's reaching a boiling point."

Al nodded. "Basically, Torrio got scammed. He paid five-hundred thousand bucks for O'Banion's brewery, and as soon as he took delivery, the place got raided. A total set-up. Johnny's in the process of arranging O'Banion's ... permanent exit. This will lead us into full-blown war with the Northsiders."

Dominic replied. "Let us know if you need any guns or manpower."

When we were heading back to The Heights, I asked Dominic why he thought Al called us to the meeting.

"He wanted to look us in the eyes." Dominic seemed surprised I had to ask that question. "He wanted to know if we were with him or not."

"Well, of course we're there to help him. With the way things are changing in The Heights, we may need his help soon."

"Exactly."

O'Banion was shot dead outside his flower shop the next day, and word spread quickly.

The Beer Wars had begun.

It was quiet for a month or so, but in late January of '25 we got called to another meeting with Capone. This time he was going to The Heights and asked to meet at the Lucky Lounge.

"Torrio's out. I'm in," Al blurted out as soon as he sat down with Jon, Dominic, and me.

"Johnny's dead?" Jon asked.

"Close to it, but no. I just left his hospital room. They got to him yesterday at his house after running errands with his wife. Shot up the car in his driveway. Torrio was hit in the jaw, lungs, groin, legs, and abdomen. Johnny said Weiss tried to shoot him in the face, but the gun jammed, so Weiss kicked him repeatedly in the stomach and then Moran hit him with a billy club. He passed out and woke up after emergency surgery. Lucky to be alive, for sure. That's probably why he told me he was handing over everything to me. Torrio said he'll probably go to jail for violating his parole and will probably head back to Italy or New York.

"I'm in charge now, boys."

Dominic responded first. "Sorry about Johnny, but we're happy for you. What can we do?"

"I'm not sure yet, but I won't hesitate to ask when the time comes. I'll be fighting the Sicilians and the Northsiders at the same time, so I'll be spread thin for a while."

A few weeks later, Al's brother, Frank, was gunned down in Cicero by police. Some say he was mistaken for Al and he drew a gun on them, but Frank wasn't carrying a gun. Most of us believe Frank *was* the intended target, killed to punish Al. It was one of the few times I saw Al upset. Jon and Dominic sent a massive floral arrangement to the service. Jon made sure it would be the biggest and most beautiful one there. On the bottom, in flowers, it read, From The Boys in The Heights.

From that day forward the rest of the crews in The Outfit referred to us as The Boys in The Heights.

Meanwhile, we had our own power vacuum. Pacenti and Lambretta were pushing on us hard. We were hearing from our bootleggers that Pacenti was trying to undermine the alliances we had in place. He knew we had the best routes and controlled the sugar with the help of the Stefanos and Zingaros. The Unione Siciliana in Chicago Heights was also telling Pacenti to cut off any possible revenue streams Capone may have had in the area. They wanted Capone out and their guy, Aiello, in.

And as gangs in Chicago and The Heights prepared for the upcoming power grab, our business was booming. Bootleggers from Iowa, southern Illinois, Wisconsin, St. Louis, and Kansas City visited the Lucky Lounge daily to make purchases or pick up for distribution.

The Heights was such a lucrative and strategic location for Prohibition activities that we hoped Capone would jump at the chance to support us if we decided to go to war against The Heights's current leadership. Pacenti appeared to be dropping the ball on payouts, just like his predecessor. The Cosenza family recently joined our bootlegging alliance because of it. The Cosenzas had proven themselves ruthless in protecting their routes and relationships. The youngest brother, Joe, had spent some time in New Orleans establishing distribution networks. He was a hothead who would pull the trigger if needed. That kind of muscle was going to be handy, so Joe—Coz, we called him—was called in as vital reinforcement. Muscle with a money-making operation behind it was always a win.

Jon and Dominic decided to go up against Pacenti, Lambretta, and the Unione Siciliana when the time was right. They consulted with Capone to see if he would back us with guns and men if needed. He was one hundred percent on board with our plans.

You absolutely need to know who you're in the trenches with when the shit blows up.

ON NEW YEAR'S Eve 1926, we were hanging out at the Lucky. Everyone coming in and out seemed to be smiling and optimistic about the new year. Jon and Dominic were getting ready to go home to freshen up before the party their wives were dragging them to. They acted like they didn't want to go, but I could tell they were looking forward to it. I was going to head downtown with Guy and Coz. Jon walked by Dominic and me and told us to meet him in his office before we left. Jon and I looked at each other, knowing he meant now.

"Salvatore, Dominic and I have been discussing the current situation regarding the leadership in this town," Jon began. "We aren't so sure we're getting any more protection for the dollars we kick upstairs versus what we pay on top of that. We also have others showing a greater discontentment for their boss and his lieutenant."

I knew where this was going. I could hear the war drums in my head. My heart rate soared.

"The time is now, Sal," Jon continued. "This is the year we begin making moves to take over The Heights. It's time for Pacenti, Lambretta, and the Unione Siciliana to take a back seat. We're the most powerful and biggest earners in The Heights. There is no reason for us to answer to anyone else. We'll spend more money on protection than ever before and eliminate anything that gets in our way. We're gonna be in charge."

"What do you think, Sal?" Dominic asked with a grin.

"I'm ready to go right now."

Jon laughed. "Relax. Go enjoy New Year's. We'll talk in a few days."

Before I went out, I stopped at home to see my parents and sisters for New Year's hugs, though I mostly wanted to tell my dad the news. I knew he would worry when I told him, but at almost twenty-five years old, I wasn't expecting a lecture.

"Sal, sit down."

"Dad, look, I'm sitting."

"Sorry. Listen, you are fully aware of what this means, right?"

"It means war, Dad. I get it."

"Sal, it means people will be looking to knock you off before you win the war, and if you win the war, others will always be looking to take you down. When I say you need to stay vigilant, I mean all day every day. You will never rest easy. You'll need eyes in the back of your head, and you won't sleep without a gun within arm's reach."

"Yeah, Dad ... but I'll be sleeping on a pile of money!" I laughed, trying to lighten my dad's mood.

"Salvatore, I may have a large family, but I only have one son. Capice?"

I felt confident—maybe overconfident with Capone's promise to back us—but I understood my father's concern.

"Capisco."

THE WINTER OF '26 was fairly uneventful. I headed downtown to see Al a few times a month, either with Dominic or on my own. I'd give him the rundown on the action or lack thereof. Unlike us, Al had his hands full. He was catching heat from every part of Chicago, so Dominic and I would tell him we had plenty of family in The Heights if he ever needed to disappear for a while.

In Early spring, Jon and Dominic called me away from the service station kitty-corner to the Lucky Lounge. I walked in, and Joe Cosenza was sitting at the door. Jon was starting to give Coz more responsibility in our thing outside his own family's alky business. Like I said earlier, the kid had those eyes. Cold, deep, probing. Coz sent me back to Jon's office, where he and Dom were waiting.

Jon told me to sit down and poured a scotch as he started talking. "Sal, the war chest is built up. You're delivering more and more protection money every week. As of now, we're no longer paying up to Pacenti and Lambretta. Fuck that. Fuck them. We are done."

Dominic nodded his head as Jon sipped, paced, and talked.

"Pacenti only worries about what the Unione Siciliana thinks. He doesn't think past his own nose … that strunz! Dominic is getting word out to all The Heights's biggest and smartest bootleggers to consider working together. Consolidate, cut costs, increase everyone's profits, and hopefully reduce risk at the same time."

My palms were sweating. We were getting ready to walk off that precipice. "What can I do?"

"You should tell Al today, tomorrow at the latest, that we're planning our first move next week," Jon said. "We want him abreast of our doings so if we need his help, he won't be caught off guard. Capice?"

I nodded as Dominic started speaking. "Listen, Sal, there's another thing we want you to do for us once this war heats up. If Jon or I can't drive our families somewhere, we need you to be our driver. It's not an insult. It's that we trust you with our most precious cargo and we know you'll do anything to keep them safe. Anything."

I didn't hesitate. "It's my honor to protect your family when you can't."

I was ready for anything. I had a cold side I could turn on when needed. It didn't define me, but it was there. Dominic had it and could turn it off, too.

But not Jon. At least, not after that close call with the kid in Blue Island. Jon was a cutthroat businessman, smart with money and brilliant in investing in political protection. Never enough. No matter the cost.

"Salvatore, we need to be vigilant. I can't emphasize that enough …"

I must've smirked because Jon snapped at me.

"What's so fucking funny?"

"Sorry, but my dad told me the same exact thing. You're both men I look up to, and you both said the same thing. I wasn't insulting you, believe me. I'm listening."

"Good. Our lives depend on it."

As we were leaving, Dominic asked me one more time about my new responsibilities. "Are you sure you're all right with driving Rio when I'm not around? I don't want you to feel disrespected."

"Relax, Dom. My honor. She's in good hands."

"Thanks. She likes you. She calls you my good-looking cousin."

We both laughed our way to our cars.

A WEEK OR so went by, and my dad asked me to stop at the family grocery store. His message seemed benign, so I took my time.

"Salvatore, como se va?"

"Not much today. Jon's having a picnic this weekend to start planning our move."

"Sal, Lambretta came into the store this morning asking some questions."

"What kind of fucking questions?" My heart was pounding.

"He says, You're Luca Liparello, are you not? Friggin' strunz knew exactly who I was. I hate questions like that. So I say, Who wants to know?"

"What the hell, Dad!"

I was enraged. Not scared. Not in the least. I wanted revenge for their bullshit tactics. Don't threaten my father over my business. As far as I'm concerned, if you're threatening my father, you may as well be threatening my mother and sisters. My family was all I had.

I'd show no mercy in retaliation.

"Told you, Sal. It's time for your head to be on a swivel."

"What did he ask next? What did he want?"

"He wanted to know if you were my son and if you kept

company with Jon Allen and Dominic Scalea. I told him you're twenty-five, and I can't keep track of what kids you're running around with."

I rolled my eyes. "I'm sure he loved that."

"He wanted me to tell you that he knows our group isn't happy with the current leadership. I told him I don't know what he's talking about, and if his feelings are hurt, he should go talk to Jon or Dominic. Listen, Sal, I'm not afraid of this guy. I will put him down if he ever considers making a move against me or our family. I am telling you because you need to tell Jon that word is out. You're gonna need to move soon or fall back into line. Capice?"

"Thanks, Dad. I'll let them know today. Love you."

My dad had just told me it was time for war, and it sounded different coming from him versus Dominic or Jon. I also couldn't get past the fact that Lambretta showed up to intimidate my father and told him to deliver a message to me. "Fuck this guy," I told myself over and over. "I'll take care of him,"

I called a meeting at the Lucky Lounge. It was time to start planning before we got left in a ditch.

CHAPTER 6

No Turning Back

Spring was in the air, so Jon hosted a picnic at his house. Dominic, Angelo Zingaro and another brother, Joe Cosenza, a couple Stefanos, and I were in attendance. The air was charged, tense. I knew there would be no accidental smiles tonight.

"Thanks for coming. Let's eat, then talk, okay? This could go long. I want you guys to relax before that."

We had homemade angel hair pasta that night. The gravy was made with meatballs and neckbone and had been simmering for hours. In addition to the pasta, Jon cooked some chicken over his outdoor fire pit as we unwound. He knew we couldn't enjoy such wonderful food after meetings like this. You relax and bond, then you focus on the darkness. It's hard to go the other way around, you know? No, you probably don't.

The food and company were so good we almost forgot why we were there. But that darkness lurked under the surface. Maybe it was our way of coping with the knowledge that we were conspiring to murder people. But this was the life we chose. And honestly, after Lambretta showed up at the family grocery to send a message to me and intimidate my dad—which was impossible—I was ready to do whatever needed to be done to take The Heights away from those short-sighted Unione Siciliana puppets. We had talked about it for months and considered it for years.

It was now about to happen.

We moved inside with a bottle of Canadian whiskey. Jon's wife and baby were visiting some of his wife's family in Michigan, so we had complete privacy in the dining room.

"We're at that point of no turning back," said Jon, who was again sipping and pacing. "We need to make sure this is done right. We need to make it look natural. We also want to hit Lambretta and Pacenti at the same time, cut both heads off at once so the remaining gangs will fall into line as easily as possible."

"May I, Jon?" I asked.

He lifted his glass. "Please."

"Until we get this figured out, we all need to keep our eyes open. You guys all know that strunz, Lambretta, showed up at my dad's store insinuating a threat. The Unione Siciliana knows we're done with them."

As I spoke, a wave of intense chills flowed from my legs to my head. I felt invincible. "If they feel remotely threatened by us, they'll try to strike immediately. We need to be ready when the right opportunity arises."

Dominic addressed the room. "Any ideas floating around in your heads?"

The oldest Zingaro offered a plan. "Pacenti is finishing renovations on the Derby Inn. He keeps telling me I'll need to come check it out. When he invites me, that's the time to do it. He won't be suspicious. We just need to plan it out before the invitation comes so we are prepared at a moment's notice."

"That's it," Jon blurted as he swallowed the last of his whiskey. "It's perfect,"

Because Jon's family was not around, we conspired until almost three in the morning. The blood was flowing along with the wine and whiskey. We were finally doing it.

The Heights was going to be ours.

But we had to do it wisely. We needed to make sure our political capital was happy and make a concerted effort to get many more on the payroll.

Dominic drove me home that night. "We got another late night tomorrow," he said as we pulled up to my house. "We're eating dinner with Al at the Hawthorne. I want to fill him in. Keep him up to date, ya know?"

"Sounds good," I said as I shut the car door.

The next evening, Dominic and I arrived at the Hawthorne Inn to fill Capone in on our plan for the Pacenti-Lambretta gang.

We were greeted by name as we entered. "Al is waiting for you gentlemen at his table. May I show you the way?" the doorman asked as he gestured toward our table. We made our way down the long room with beautiful terracotta tiles on the floor. The length of the restaurant walls were adorned with huge mirrors that were framed by ornate wood moldings. The middle of the room had four-person tables with crisp white linens and red velvet chairs perfectly placed around each one.

Al stood immediately, a big stogie hanging out of the corner of his wide grin. He greeted us with hugs and kisses on the cheek. "My boys in The Heights! Sit down. Let's eat and drink. Sit. Sit."

After the drinks came, Dom stirred the ice around in his glass, getting ready to fill Al in on our plans.

Then the bullets started flying.

THE LEAD TORE through the restaurant windows, sending shards of glass flying. Everyone in the room was screaming, ducking under tables, or crawling to the back. I'd say two-hundred shots were fired from a car passing on the street. Shockingly, no one was hit by the bullets intended as a dire message to Al.

When it was all over, Capone was still in his seat, slowly sipping his drink.

"Salvatore, Dominic, you guys okay? No one hit, right?"

I answered. "We're good, Al. You?"

"Yeah. I need to end this war before it ends me."

Dominic wiped debris from his clothes as we walked toward Al's suite. "Actually, that's something we wanted to talk about tonight. We're ready to make our move for The Heights. We want you to know what we're planning."

"I got your back," Al said as he opened the door. "Men, cash, guns—whatever you need."

After we sat, Dominic continued. "It would be great if someday we can work together."

Al leaned forward on the table. "I have been saying for years that I see you as a lieutenant."

"I know," Dominic said, his voice steady as he looked Al dead in the eyes. "But this time it's different."

I jumped into the conversation. "I think it's clear that we'll both be waging war at the same time. I think we should help each other however and whenever possible."

"Al, we'll help you when possible," Dominic said. "You help us when possible—"

"And when it's all over, you bring Chicago Heights into my Outfit?" Al asked.

Dominic nodded. "Jon and I will deliver The Heights to The Outfit with your support and blessing."

"Okay, Dominic. We're going to do great things together." Al hugged and kissed us goodbye. "You ready for this, Salvatore?" He was grinning.

"More than ready."

"With the cold I see in your eyes, I believe you."

We'd just committed to waging war and there was no turning back once the declaration was made.

It was time to move full speed ahead.

In the car, I immediately asked Dominic the question I'd had in my head since we stepped foot outside the recently shot-up

Hawthorne Inn.

"Does Jon know we're being folded into Capone's gang once the dust has settled?"

"Absolutely. Think about it for a second. We won't be the men on top. I mean, we'll be in our territory, but we won't take the heat as if we were running The Heights and its surrounding territory independent of Chicago. We'd eventually end up at war with Chicago, and that is a war we don't want. Capice, Salvatore?"

"Yeah. Makes sense."

"We need to get more cops and politicians on the payroll. You have any meetings lined up?"

I nodded. "Next week in Calumet City. It's a small town with a matching police force, but I think they have potential. I'm also making sure Jon's brother isn't having any problems in South Chicago Heights."

"Sounds good. Hey, I got some stuff to take care of tomorrow. Can you drive Rio to her appointments?"

DOMINIC WAS ALREADY gone by the time I arrived to pick up Rio the next morning, so she answered the door.

"Good morning, Sal. Can I offer you a coffee and some cookies before you drive me all over creation?"

"Actually, I was running late and would love some coffee. Thanks."

The next time I checked a clock, it was noon and we hadn't left the kitchen.

"We better get your errands taken care of. What do you think?"

"I think you're right," Rio laughed.

First she got her hair done. Then I took her to a few stores. All the while, it was near impossible to keep my eyes forward. She was stunning.

But she was my cousin's wife.

I wouldn't.

I couldn't.

I swear I caught her looking at me, too, though. I got her back home in time to get dinner started. After walking her packages into the house, I made a quick coffee-walk around to make sure no one was inside waiting for Dominic. Then I said goodbye.

"Thanks for taking care of me today, Sal."

"No big deal," I said. "See you soon."

I left that night wondering if by choosing this life I would end up alone. I wanted a family. I loved kids. But it was hard to find someone when I was out all the time doing the things we did. Then there was my cousin who had a family back in Italy and another wife here. He was juggling two families when I felt apprehensive about starting one. I guess I felt guilty about bringing a wife and kids into my lifestyle.

The next morning, I woke up with Dominic standing over me.

"Rise and shine, sleeping beauty." Dominic laughed as he shook me gently.

"What the hell, Dom? Did I miss something?"

"Not yet. Jon wants us at the Lucky. Angelo Zingaro and Joe Coz are gonna be there. We might be on for today, so get washed up. I'll buy breakfast, then we gotta go."

I tried shaking away the cobwebs as Dominic continued.

"Oh, and by the way, it was that Weiss character and his crew who unloaded their machine guns on us at the Hawthorne. He'll be gone soon, now that Al knows who was responsible."

"Oh yeah. He'll be extinct before the first of the month."

I was showered, dressed, and out the door in less than fifteen minutes. Dominic and I ate, but I can't remember what we talked about. He was trying to keep the conversation light, I think. He knew what the coming months would bring. I did, too, and that's why I couldn't stop wondering about our upcoming meeting. War was imminent.

Jon was already at the Lucky Lounge. He sent Dominic and me to his office as he waited for the others to arrive. A few minutes later, Zingaro, Coz, and Guy filed in.

"Thanks for coming on short notice," Jon said. "Angelo called us here to tell us something."

"Thanks, Jon. I saw Pacenti and Lambretta last night. I was making small talk when Pacenti invited me to see his joint tonight. I'm not sure what time yet, but this is our chance. I think we can get both of them at the same time. This would be ideal, no?"

"That's exactly what we want," Dominic said. "Their place on their terms. They'll be half in the bag and their guard will be down."

"I'll let you guys know before dinner when we plan on heading to the Derby Inn. I'm meeting them at the Milano Café early. I'll send my brother once we have the time so you can be ready. I'll walk outside just before Pacenti and Lambretta are getting ready to come out. When you guys see me walk out, that should be the driver's cue to slowly pull up, headlights off."

Jon started doling out responsibilities. "Sal, you're driving. Coz, you're gunner. You guys good with that?"

"Absolutely," I replied.

"You bet," Cosenza answered.

"Guy, I want you across the street. If our marks get that far, walk up and finish the job. Okay?"

Zingaro wrapped up the plan. "The rest of us will wait here for your return."

After the meeting, I thought about going to the family store and filling in my dad. But he would just worry, so I went home to get some rest.

THAT NIGHT, DOMINIC picked me up in a car I had never seen.

"Like your new ride for the night?"

"It'll do."

It was a warm night for the first week of June. I couldn't get my heart to stop racing, either. It was doing somersaults, like the night the Hawthorne got shot up.

"The bartender at the Milano told me that Zingaro is heading to the Derby for after hours," Dominic said. "Unfortunately, there will be a couple gals there, so we need to be careful. You ready for this?"

"I'm just driving, Dom. I'm ready."

"Yes, you're driving, but all signals need to be interpreted correctly. You have to get Coz into proper position. So it's more than just driving. Capice? Tell me what the signals are."

"We're waiting about a half-block up. Lights off. I make sure I can see Guy because his eyes will be on the entrance. Guy's signal will be the same as Zingaro's, making sure I don't get confused. If Zingaro walks out and puts both hands in his pockets, then the marks should be exiting together shortly. If he exits and continuously runs both hands through his hair, then we should abort."

"Perfect. We're dropping me off at the Lucky, then Coz will join you. Okay?"

"Yeah, Dominic. It's all good."

Dominic pulled up a block from the Lucky and jumped out. "No reason for anyone to see this car around here. Good luck, Sal. You guys are all set."

I nodded as he shut the door. I slid over to the driver's seat and waited for Joe Coz to jump in.

"Hey, boss," Coz said as he opened the door.

"You set? You checked your piece?"

"Absolutely. I'm ready."

We had a couple hours, so I decided to drive around and get to know Coz, who was a few years younger than me. "Let's go grab a bite somewhere real fast. You hungry?"

"Yeah, I can eat. Maybe coffee and pie?"

After eating, we pulled up a couple hundred feet from the Derby. I kept the car running with all lights off. It was 12:40 a.m. I couldn't believe we had to wait another twenty minutes or so. It would feel like an eternity.

"So how was New Orleans?" I asked Coz, trying to distract myself.

"It was good. I kept things in line and made some good connections."

"Yeah, Dom said you did some good work down there, which is good. You never know when we'll want to call in that marker. Dom has a lot of good things to say about you. Your family is from Cosenza, right?"

"Yeah, we're practically Dominic's cousins having come from the same area of the old country."

"I guess that makes us practically cousins, too. Maybe we can get back sometime soon to visit family and family friends."

That little bit of casual conversation helped keep us relaxed. Talking about anything but what we were about to do seemed to quell our anxiety. But just before 1 a.m., Coz brought the conversation around to business.

"Don't worry, Sal. I'm not going to miss. Whoever is in that vestibule is going to get his."

"I haven't a doubt in the world. And when we're done, we'll go get a few whiskies."

"I'm probably going to need them."

A few minutes later, Angelo Zingaro walked outside, just beyond the vestibule at the entrance. He clearly had both hands in his pants pockets. I glanced quickly at Guy, who was standing kitty-corner from him. I immediately put the car into gear, lights off, and idled toward the Derby. It felt like a lifetime before I saw a couple figures exiting after Zingaro.

"Now!"

I sped up, and Coz unloaded all six shots from his revolver.

WHAT HAPPENED NEXT had been impossible to account for. Zingaro looked back, then pulled his hands out of his pants and furiously rubbed them through his hair.

It was far too late.

I sped away as soon as I counted the sixth shot, and Zingaro and Guy ran off to Guy's car on the back side of the Derby.

Coz and I were back at the Lucky twenty minutes later. As soon as I parked, a young guy I didn't know told me Dominic had instructed him to burn the car.

"Make sure it's done correctly," I told the kid. "No mistakes, or you'll regret it. No shortcuts! Capice?"

Coz and I walked into the Lucky and headed straight back to Jon's office and told him about the signal mix up.

Zingaro and Guy showed up thirty minutes later.

"What the hell happened out there?" Jon asked when we were all sitting.

"It was too late when I realized it was a gal with Lambretta, not Pacenti," Zingaro said. "The girls wanted to use the bathroom before we left. The bartender was told to lock up. I saw the girls go into the ladies' room. Then Lambretta, Pacenti, and I stood up. I told them I'll see them outside and I saw them a few steps behind me, so I went outside to signal we're good to go. I don't know when the girls came out or why Pacenti waited inside with the other gal."

Jon wasn't as upset as I'd feared. "Unfortunately, this is the price of war. Sal, Joe, you guys did real good. Real good. You executed your orders as instructed. Period. Okay?"

He stood and poured a whiskey, then remained on his feet. "We know Pacenti will be on high alert with extra security. We need to get him quick while he's on his heels and finish this war in a few months tops. We can't give the Unione Siciliana too much time to organize against us. They're also helping fund the war against Al downtown. Dominic, keep in regular contact with him. Sal, if Dominic is busy, I want you to go downtown and represent us. Dominic said Al is fond of you, so let's make sure you keep up that relationship."

Dad showed up in my kitchen the next day as I was having a late-morning coffee.

"So, it's started?"

"Yup. Listen, Dad, I know you're going to worry. But try to keep it away from mom and the girls for me, please."

That was the last we spoke on the subject that morning. For the next hour, we talked normal family stuff. It was a nice distraction from the previous day's stresses.

The following morning, the murders hit the papers, which said the responding police doubted robbery was the motive, as one of Lambretta's pants pockets held $3,700 in cash and $10,000 worth of diamonds were folded in a handkerchief in his other pocket. The girl who was inside with Pacenti at the time of the shooting ran and hid in a nearby cornfield until 5 a.m. to wait out the police and dark sedans crawling around. Smart girl.

Besides needing to take care of Pacenti, we had another four to six loyalists with Unione Siciliana's backing. We needed to make sure our gang was the only one to fill the power void we'd left in The Heights. Dominic, with the help of my dad, was doing pretty well at consolidating the Chicago Heights bootleggers under our umbrella. Most saw and heard how we were expanding our political influence throughout the growing towns around us.

However, before we could implement the options we'd been discussing, we had to redirect some of our resources to help

Capone. He was in the hot seat for killing a twenty-six-year-old assistant state's attorney, Bill McSwiggin.

A few days after our Lambretta job, Dominic came to find me in my dad's grocery. "Zio Luca, is Sal around? I can't find him, and I thought he may be here helping out."

"He's around here somewhere," my dad said. "You look nervous. Is everything okay?"

"It's that obvious, huh, Zio Luca?"

I peeked out from around one of the aisles, where I'd been listening. Dominic was breathing a little heavy, his muscles tense. "It's about Capone today." He said. "Al's getting heat for this McSwiggin thing. Did you see the papers?"

My dad answered first. "How could I miss it? It's national news. The article said he was shot outside a club in Cicero with some friends. A car pulled along theirs as they approached and shot up three or four guys, McSwiggin being one. How could Al think this wasn't going to blow back on him? Especially because it happened on his turf, Cicero."

"It is blowing back on him," Dom said. "I promised Al we'd hide him until the heat from this McSwiggin thing dies down."

"Dad, what about Marie's?" I suggested.

My dad hesitated. "I'll talk to Marco to make sure he's okay with doing this."

"I'm going to hide him for a week with me and Rio," Dominic said. "If Marie and Marco can hide him for another seven to ten days, that would be great."

"Dad, we need men for a lot of things. See if Marco is looking for additional work."

A few days later, I was at Dominic's house to meet with him and Al.

"Sal, I cannot thank your family enough. You know McSwiggin was hanging out with some guys from the Northside, and he was just in the wrong place at the wrong time, like when we were eating at the Hawthorne and you and Dominic almost got shot."

"Things happen," I said. "What are you gonna do? My family is happy to help a friend in need. It's no problem."

"Thanks, Salvatore. You're good people."

Rio walked into the kitchen and began preparing lunch as we talked about how much longer Al would need to lay low. She didn't pay us much attention, making our plates then vanishing somewhere in the house. After she left, Al helped Dominic and me plot against this strunz Piazza and some of his loyal soldiers, who would get backing from the Unione Siciliana. They were all backing the Genna and Aiello brothers in Chicago to push into Capone's territory.

As I was walking outside to leave, Rio came running out. "Sal, you have a second?"

"Yeah, what's up?"

"The other morning when I was cleaning house, I went into a closet to get some supplies and noticed a knapsack that I'd never seen before. Sal, it was full—and I mean full—of guns. Is everything okay? I'm worried about you and Dominic. Very worried."

"We'll be fine. There's a lot going on at once. That's why Dominic has me drive you around when he can't. My advice: Act like you never saw that knapsack."

"I can try, Sal, but it's not easy to unsee something. And I can't stop being scared when Dominic goes out at night. I'll worry about you guys no matter what."

"I know. Just try to relax. This is all going to blow over by the end of the year."

I gave her a kiss on the cheek and drove away.

Later that day, at the service station across from the Lucky Lounge, Dominic pulled up and asked me to be in Jon's office. His face was stony, mouth tight.

Something was brewing.

I walked across the street immediately. Jon sat behind his desk as Dominic laid it out for Guy, Joey Coz, and me.

"We've heard from our friends in the department that Nick Camora has been pinched. From what we know, he was picked up on suspicion of murder. Supposedly, while authorities were in his home, they discovered his still. I asked our contacts if they thought Nick would keep his mouth shut or spill. First, he's loyal to Pacenti. Second, he knows we're trying to consolidate the bootleggers in The Heights. He's become a liability we had not foreseen."

"Do you think he's an immediate threat to our thing here?" I asked. "Should this be addressed before Piazza?"

Jon stood up and began pacing the room, whisky in hand. "I don't trust this guy at all. I can only assume he's turned over some information to get out of this murder rap. He needs to be dealt with now. Not later this week. Now. I want you four to take out this guy one way or another. Capice?"

The order to kill Nick hit me harder than I expected. I knew it was coming, but it still felt like someone smacked a palm against my forehead. I couldn't show any visible emotions that might be interpreted as weakness.

"I'll find out where he's hiding or hanging out," Dominic said. "We'll put him in a car and leave him somewhere. When he's found, it will send a message.

"Those who talk don't walk around for long."

Coz nodded and lowered his head. "Okay."

"Sal and Joey," Dom said, "stay close and be ready to move at a moment's notice."

DOMINIC CALLED ME at the service station a few hours later. "He's at the Milano Café. When he walks out to his car, grab him. Got it?"

I picked up Coz, and we swung over to Guy's place. "You guys know how Lincoln Highway gets really isolated as you head east?" I asked Guy when he got in the car. "I think we leave him over there."

We all agreed, so I parked in the shadows of the Milano lot with a clear view of Nick's car and the club's exit. About a quarter to midnight, Nick came stumbling out, staggering toward his car.

"Go grab him," I ordered.

Joe and Guy flew out of the car and hustled toward Camora. Nick was fumbling with his keys when Guy came up behind him and put him in a bear hug while Coz gave him an uppercut to the gut. As soon as Nick bent over, I pulled up, and they all filed into the backseat with Nick in the middle.

No words were spoken as I headed east on Lincoln Highway. Joey and Guy had guns on Nick, who knew he was finished. I got to a dark section of the highway, turned off my lights, and pulled off the road.

Guy opened his door and slid out. "Let's go."

Nick inched out of the car with Coz behind him, the muzzle of a revolver in his back. They walked about twenty feet from the car to the bottom of a ditch. Coz raised his gun to the back of Nick's head just as Guy began to walk back toward the car.

Coz didn't hesitate. Nick dropped to the ground and Coz proceeded to put two more into his chest.

That took care of one potential informant. Pacenti had to be next. We didn't want to give him too much time to build up defenses or go on the offensive. I went to sleep that night surprisingly easily. No guilt or remorse, like I expected. Nick was a racketeer. He knew the risks of our lifestyle.

You make a decision; you live with that decision.

Period.

CHAPTER 7

Lines Leapt

Jon called another meeting the following day to go over what happened and how we should move forward against Pacenti. I was the last one to walk into his office at the Lucky—after dropping off a girl I met the night before—but Jon wasn't upset. He knew I was reliable.

That didn't keep him from busting my balls a little as he started.

"Okay, now that lover boy has graced us with his presence, let's get down to business. We need Pacenti dealt with before the weekend. The Unione is trying to build up some weak Sicilian-led gangs that they can manipulate behind the scenes. They're doing the same in Chicago against Capone. We need to destroy their networks, leaving us the only game left in The Heights." Jon leaned forward, fidgeting with his hands.

"So we probably have four or so after Pacenti to take care of before we can breathe," I said.

"Exactly," Dominic answered.

"Sal and Coz ... Pacenti doesn't see the weekend," Jon ordered. "Capice?"

Coz nodded. "Consider it done, Mr. Allen."

"Joe, please. You can call me Jon."

"Okay, Jon. I just wasn't sure, you know?"

"Well, I think you've more than earned that right recently," Jon said with a wry grin.

"Thank you, sir. I mean Jon."

Dominic laughed. "Finally, a smile outta this kid."

"Alright. Alright," Jon said. "Go finish off that stunad." Jon waved his hand to shoo us out the door, locking eyes with me. The message was clear:

Get this done right. And soon.

Jon had put me on notice. It was my responsibility to ensure this went off without a hitch. No mistakes.

TWO NIGHTS LATER, I got a call from a friend who worked inside Pacenti's Milano Café. Pacenti was there, strutting around, full of himself.

"Keep him there by any means necessary," I said. "You'll know when you can stand down."

I drove over to the Lucky, where Coz was waiting for my call. Then I swung over to pick up Guy, who had a car for us to ditch after the job.

"Three of us tonight, Sal?" Coz asked.

"Guy is driving," I said. "We walk up, spray him down, and run back to our car. We get up close, so it's only Pacenti who gets it. I don't want any more innocent mistakes. Know what I mean?"

"Loud and clear, Salvatore."

I pulled someone I knew from the Hill over to the car. "Tell the bartender you saw a beautiful full moon this evening."

It was pouring rain. No moon. My phrase was a signal. If Pacenti wanted to leave, the barkeep didn't need to stall him any longer.

Must've been thirty minutes later when Pacenti emerged. Joe and I jumped out of the car and walked briskly toward him, lifting our coat collars and lowering our fedoras to hide our faces. Guy threw his stogie out the window and drove around the corner so we could run directly across the street to him.

We were about ten feet away from Pacenti, just a few feet from the entrance, when he turned toward us both.

Each of us fired four shots. Then we sprinted across Sixteenth Street to the car and dove into the back seat. Pacenti's brother raced outside, and Guy was driving us away as we saw the brother holding Pacenti in his arms as blood gurgled from a shot that pierced his throat.

That was it. We'd taken out the two-headed monster.

I crossed a line that night. Actually, I leapt over it, easily. Too easily.

I didn't have much of a choice. If you want to move up and be respected by your soldiers, you must get your hands dirty. Lead by example. I wasn't quite sure how I felt about that, but I sure as hell knew I didn't want to mull it over.

After all, we still had to take care of a few others thinking about running The Heights. The three of us scrambled back to debrief Jon and Dominic. Guy, Coz, and I filed into Jon's office, where we were greeted with whiskey, cigars, hugs, and kisses on both cheeks.

Jon was ecstatic. "We're one step closer to running this thing!"

"Thanks, Jon," I said. "Not to ruin the celebration, but there is still stuff that needs addressing. Salvi, Lambretta's nephew, needs to be eliminated as soon as possible. He controls most of the vice on the East Side, and I'm confident that the Unione Siciliana will make a play to back him."

"That's why you are a future leader. You never lose sight of obstacles on the road to success. Any clue where Salvi hangs out?"

"Actually, I do. He's seen regularly outside of his cigar shop on East Fourteenth."

"By the middle of next week? You know what I mean?" Jon asked with that look in his eyes, laser-focused and unblinking.

"Not a problem." I turned to Coz. "I have a brother-in-law I can position across the street. He'll let me know when Salvi is smoking outside. Be around so I can pick you up at a moment's notice."

It had to be the first week of August, when it was nearly impossible to stay cool. It was dusk, still hot and humid as hell, and my brother-in-law called to let me know Salvi was outside his shop puffing on a cigar. Based on the size, he thought Salvi would be smoking for another thirty minutes.

I swung by Dominic's to pick up a sawed-off shotgun, but Rio answered.

"Where's Dom?"

"He just left for the Lucky. Can I help you with something?"

"Where's that gunnysack of guns you found a while back? I need something out of it."

She looked around, then ushered me inside. As we walked, she made small-talk. "Whose car is that? I haven't seen you drive it before."

"I'm borrowing the car from a friend."

Rio nodded as we entered an interior closet, where the sack was hanging in plain sight.

"Thanks, Rio. I got it from here." I pulled out the sawed-off, a box of shotgun shells, and closed the closet door.

Rio was standing right behind me. "Sal, are you and Dominic in danger? Don't lie to me." She rubbed her neck. "You know my feelings for Dominic, but do you know how fond I've become of you? I mean, you look after me more than your cousin does."

"Everyone is safe. Nothing's going to happen. You hear me? I gotta go, but I'll swing over tomorrow to check on you and take you wherever you need to go. Okay?"

I brushed past her and headed for my car. The drive to Coz's helped clear my head.

"Your piece is lying behind your seat," I said when Coz jumped in. "I'll turn off the headlights and coast past. He should be puffing on his cigar. You light him up. Got it?"

"Absofuckinlutely."

"Good. Anticipate where he's sitting and how quick we're coasting down the street. We don't want anyone getting hit but Salvi."

Coz picked up the shotgun. "With the spray from this sawed-off … I can't promise you that. But I'll do my best."

Ten minutes later, I was turning off my headlights and rolling down Fourteenth Street.

"There he is. Four storefronts up. Loaded and ready?"

Coz didn't reply. He was already in position. As we rolled past, he unleashed two blasts on Salvi. I looked in the rearview mirror and saw two fellas running to his aid.

We heard through the grapevine that he died a few hours later at the hospital.

A FEW NIGHTS later, Dominic and I headed downtown for dinner with Capone. He had just returned to headquarters after his stint hiding out in The Heights. I'd stopped over at my sister's house almost daily to check up on them and leave some money for my sister and Marco. I didn't want to burden them with the cost of hosting our special guest for over a week. They seemed to enjoy each other's company, always laughing, cooking, and playing cards when I came by.

Anyway, after surfacing, Al wanted an update on our war in The Heights. He also told Dominic he wanted to discuss someone else who was busting his cogliones. Two of Al's heavies opened the door to his suite at the Hawthorne so we could speak freely without fearing bullets would start flying through the windows.

"Thanks for coming, boys! Come here. Come here." Al poured us some red wine as he puffed his cigar out of the left side of his mouth. "Chianti's okay?" He nodded toward four high-backed leather chairs that surrounded a marble coffee table, a gorgeous crystal chandelier hanging from the coffered ceiling overhead. His two-bedroom suite also had a fireplace and a long dining table that ran across the bay window overlooking the street below.

"It's perfect, Al," I said. "Thank you."

"So fill me in with what's going on in The Heights."

"Pacenti, Lambretta, and the next in line are gone, but we probably have a couple more loose ends that need to be straightened out. Dom is actively consolidating the bootleggers in The Heights and thinks there's only a few holding out as independents." I looked at Dom. "Did I leave anything out?"

Dominic shook his head. "Just a couple more things, and The Heights belongs to us."

"Well, it seems like you guys are taking care of business down there. Well done." Al rubbed his chin. "Now, there's something else I need. Someone else. A guy. If he disappears, it would be good for the three of us."

I was glad we were finally getting to it. I didn't like thinking I'd missed an angle. "What's up, Al? Who's in our way?"

Al answered my question with one of his own. "Who does the Unione Siciliana in Chicago use as a go-between for Chicago and the Unione in The Heights?"

"Nunzio Nironi," I said. "Il Cavaliere."

"Yup. And the Unione, through Nironi, is supporting the Gennas to fight me in Chicago. He's going to help the Unione come after you in The Heights, too. He's gotta go."

Al stabbed the table with his finger. "Now."

"You want us to do it with you?" Dominic asked.

"Nironi spends a lot of time in the city and The Heights, so I want plans by tomorrow for both places. It needs to be done in the next two days. So, wherever he is, I want boys looking for him." Al leaned forward, eyes narrowed. "He doesn't see the weekend. Hear me?"

"You got it. Sal and I can have something planned by the end of the night. We'll fill our guys in first thing in the morning."

"Good. My guys here are already looking for him. I knew I could rely on you to be ready tomorrow. Our relationship has, as they say, blossomed in the last five years. Great things lie ahead." He turned to me. "And Salvatore, I cannot thank you enough for your family taking such great care of me during the McSwiggin fiasco. I'll never forget it."

And he didn't.

IT WAS AN oppressively humid August day, ninety-five degrees that felt like a hundred-twenty, and impossible not to sweat when stepping one foot outside. Nunzio "Il Cavaliere" Nironi's car came to a screeching halt in front of a barber shop at 454 West Division in Chicago. He'd been trying to evade a tail.

Nironi pulled his pistol as he leapt from his car to run down an alley, but one of the two gunmen fired first. Nironi got off two shots but took four. He died seconds later halfway down the alleyway and was identified by his Italian gun permit, the only form of identification on him. The son of the barber, Nicky Scardino, witnessed the crime and told the police he saw Aiello and another man he didn't recognize.

One of the Unione Siciliana's biggest yes men in Chicago Heights and Chicago was now eliminated.

We just had to take care of one or two guys affiliated with Nironi who may have been foolishly ambitious enough to try and fill his role. One of those guys was Frank Capello, a Nironi gunman. Dominic had a plan for him. Frank recently told Dominic that he liked his car, so Dominic offered to sell it to him. Frank accepted but said he wanted to drive it first. Dom knew this would be a good opportunity to eliminate Capello, who wouldn't see anything coming on his way to look at a car like his.

"We'll get him when he's on his way to the test drive," Dominic said. "We should think about getting him near 16th Street and State where it's quiet."

I nodded. "It's the best scenario to avoid screw-ups. Dominic accepts Frank's offer. We offer to drive Dominic's car back to Frank's house so he can drive his car home and not need to leave one behind at the Lucky Lounge. We get one or two fellas to ride along with Frank, you know, to keep him company. When they're around State and 16th, bam! We hit him, as long as there isn't any immediate car in sight. Whoever is following behind in Dom's car stops and picks up our boys."

Jon gave the orders. "Sal, tell Capello you'll follow in my car. Joey, you and someone will go with Frank. I want everyone here by ten-thirty tomorrow morning. Frank needs to feel relaxed and excited about getting a good deal on Dom's car. I want him to see guys relaxing and joking around. If we're running around all serious, it may trigger his defenses. Capice?"

JUST BEFORE NOON on August 29, Frank Capello parked his car across from the Lucky Lounge and walked inside looking for Dominic. I was closest to the entrance.

"I'm here to meet Dominic about the car," Capello said.

"He's coming. He's taking a piss," I said with a grin.

Dominic walked up a minute later, jingling the car keys between his thumb and middle finger. "Here ya go, Franky. Take her for a spin, and we'll talk when you get back."

"Sounds good. I'll be back in less than ten minutes." Frank took the keys out of Dominic's fingers.

"Just make sure you pay me in cash," Dominic laughed, winking at me.

After Frank pulled away, Dominic went over the plan. "Cosenza, I want you ready to ride with Frank. Take Nicky with you. Sal, you're following behind in my car."

Ten minutes later, Frank flew up to the Lucky and chirped the brakes as he came to an abrupt stop. He threw the car into park and popped out.

"Sold, Scalea! Dominic, let's talk numbers," Frank hollered as he walked inside the Lounge.

A minute later, Dominic and Frank left Jon's office. While they made their way to the front of the Lucky Lounge, Dominic set everything into motion.

"Frank, I'll have Sal drive my car behind you so you don't need to pick up the car later," he said.

I jumped in. "Joey, why don't you and Nick drive with Frank? I'll follow behind. We'll grab lunch after. Sound good, Frank?"

I was worried Frank might pick up on the fact that wouldn't have a ride after we were done dropping off the cars. It was a detail we'd stupidly overlooked, but Frank didn't seem to catch on.

"Yeah, sure," he said. "Whatever."

Then Frank perked up for a second. "You know what? That's okay. I don't need two babysitters driving me home."

Coz looked over at Nick. "That works. Obviously. Nick, I can take Franky on my own."

"Sounds good," I said. "I'll just follow you two."

I jumped into Dominic's car, following behind Frank's with Nick sitting passenger. Since Frank was driving and Coz was riding along, this would be interesting. How was he going to do his thing?

We were just about at the spot when I saw a flash inside Frank's car, which immediately swerved off the road into the ditch. Coz had to swing his leg over to reach for the brake and throw the car into park as it careened off the road. I pulled up where Joe had just jumped out. The new guy, Nick, was puking next to the car. He'd caught a bit of brain splatter and lost it.

"Hurry up," I yelled. "There's someone behind us, and in ten seconds they'll be able to identify Dominic's car and possibly us. Let's get the fuck out of here!"

Coz jumped into the car, and I sped off, leaving Frank dead in the front seat with the car running.

"How'd you manage that?" I asked Coz, who was gasping for air.

"I knew I'd need to get my foot on the brake and slam the shifter into park. Bing, bang, boom. I guess I'm a little lucky we didn't slam into a tree first."

I drove back to the Lucky Lounge and casually tossed Dominic's keys onto the bar.

"I guess the deal fell through."

IT COULDN'T HAVE been more than a couple days later when Dominic came flying into my dad's store, spitting bullets about some bootlegger. I was helping out that day, so I walked over to see what had him so upset.

"Zio Luca, what has that strunz been saying?" Dominic asked my dad.

"When I told him it was in his best interest to fall in line—to stop bad mouthing you and Jon and stop acting independently—he started foaming at the mouth," my dad said. "He thinks the Unione Siciliana is still in charge and is waiting to see what Sicilian gang will assert themselves."

Dominic's eyes were bulging. "Zio, does this guy not have an ounce of respect for me and Jon? For what we've built? For how we got this far?" He looked at me. "Sal, let's go. I'm going to straighten out this fucking strunz myself!"

Dominic stormed out, and I followed. That was probably the angriest I'd seen my cousin. The absolute lack of respect got to him. We hopped into his car and he started driving us to the Lucky.

"He's spitting in my face. I won't let this guy live another week.

Once I find him ... he's a goner, Sal. A goner!"

"So, who is this guy?"

"One of Nironi's buddies, Bruno Pellonino. They were tight, and he's been mouthy ever since Nironi left. Maybe he thinks the Unione Siciliana is going to back him. I can tell you this, Sal. He's delusional. He's out of line. He's dead."

"Okay, Dominic. I'll handle it."

Dom shook his head. "This one needs to be ugly and brutal. We need to send a message, make sure people take notice not to go against me, Jon, or you. I want you out of this one.

"It's gonna be messy."

TWO DAYS LATER, I heard three of our goons showed up at Bruno's house. He had a still in his basement and was usually there to keep an eye on things. Our guys didn't knock. They barged in and split up to find Pellonino. Two of them headed straight for the basement while the third went upstairs. They'd just watched his wife and kids leave the house, so they knew there would be no other family around except for Bruno.

"Who are you?" Bruno asked the guy upstairs, who was now standing five feet from him. "What are you doing here?"

"Down here!" the guys yelled from downstairs.

They ambushed Bruno, took him to the ground, and bound his legs and hands before carrying him outside and tossing him into the back of the car.

"Don't forget to grab some of his hooch," one of our guys yelled. "Run downstairs and bring up as much as you can carry in one trip. We gotta get outta here!"

The shortest one ran inside and came out two minutes later, arms filled with Pellonino's booze. The truck was open and waiting. He put the boxes in the trunk, slammed it shut, and jumped into the passenger seat. The men peeled away from

Bruno's house before anyone was the wiser.

"Where the hell are you taking me?" Bruno whimpered. "Is Allen or Scalea behind this?"

"Shut it," one guy said from the passenger seat. Another was in the back, pistol pointed at Pellonino's chest. The driver never said a word or took his eyes off the road.

"What's Dominic paying you? I'll pay you triple if you let me go. I'll disappear, and no one will see me again. Please, just let me out of this car," Bruno cried.

"Now you want mercy? You had months to fall into line, but you decided to be a tough guy. Fuhgeddaboudit! It's too late for pleading." The guy in the backseat hit Bruno in the head with the butt of his pistol.

"Here we go, boys," the driver said as they approached the intersection of Cottage Grove and Joe Orr Road. "People are about to find out what happens to guys who don't listen to Allen, Scalea, or Liparello."

The guy in the back put his gun away and looped a rope around Pellonino's neck, then the driver threw the car in park at the intersection and ran to the back to open the trunk. The passenger jumped out and opened the back door.

The guy in the back, with a tight grip on the rope around Bruno's neck, slid out of the car, pulling Bruno out with him, while the other guys grabbed Bruno's bound legs and dragged him to the middle of the intersection. Bruno was pleading and squirming until they punched and kicked him into submission.

The driver started dumping Bruno's own booze all over his body as the other two continued to pummel him. After all the booze was dumped and the bottles broken around Bruno's body, they set him ablaze.

Message sent.

CHAPTER 8

Close Call

About a month later, I was driving Rio to get her hair and nails done while Dominic was visiting a cousin in Connellsville, Pennsylvania.

"Are you excited for your naturalization ceremony at the end of September?" she asked.

"Absolutely. You and Dominic can make the party afterwards, right?"

"I'll be there, with or without Dominic."

I hoped she couldn't see me start to blush. "I'm not sure why you're getting done up today. You look stunning as you are. I hope Dominic tells you the same. I know how much he adores you."

"He tells me, but I feel like we're growing apart … I know we love each other, but it's different. The passion is gone. I mean, he sleeps with a fountain pen pistol next to him every night. All I do is worry. I feel like a prisoner half the time. I can't go anywhere without you or Dom."

"I'm sorry you feel that way. I appreciate you worrying all the time for Dominic, but he's fine. Nothing is gonna happen to him."

"I worry about you too, Sal. If anything happened to this gorgeous face"—she leaned over to caress my cheek— "I'd cry."

"Thanks, Rio. But nothing is going to happen to me, either."

"I hope you're right."

Rio leaned closer. I thought of Dominic and gently placed my hands on Rio's arms to keep her at a respectable distance. I'd had feelings for Rio, but I'd buried them. For years. She was my cousin's wife. Hell, he'd practically set us up, having me drive her around all the time.

But that wasn't a good enough excuse to cross such a nasty line.

"I'm sorry, Rio."

"You're sorry? I was the one who tried, Sal. I think about you now more than Dominic. I know it's wrong, but I can't help the way I feel."

We'd reached the salon, so I parked the car and turned to her. "Rio, this never happened. For both our well-beings. Capice?"

She got out of the car. "Fine. I'll be ready in two hours. Meet you here?"

"Sure. Two hours."

She winked and shut the door. My breath was shaky, hands trembling at the thought of what I'd almost done to Dominic. From there, I drove aimlessly, so lost in thought I couldn't retrace my route if I tried. I had to keep my feelings for Rio locked away.

Two hours later, I pulled up to the salon. Rio popped into the car with a radiant smile. "How do you like it?"

"Beautiful as always."

"I'm making dinner for you tonight. Cancel your plans, if you have any."

"No plans." Dominic was going to be in Pennsylvania for another two days. My pulse was racing from a combination of nausea and excitement, but it was too late to go back now. "Dinner sounds great."

"THANKS FOR KEEPING me company, Sal."

"Thanks for dinner. I'm a lucky guy."

"No. You're a great guy."

Guilt kicked in. I put a hand on her shoulder. "Rio, we should talk about what happened earlier."

"Not now, Sal. There's really nothing more to discuss. Let's eat and relax. Okay?"

"You're the boss."

You could tell Rio was married to a racketeer. When I said this never happened, she understood that there was nothing more to say. It had to be that way. Period.

After some chicken cutlets, salad, and a lot of wine, I began to nod off on the sofa.

"Sal, why don't you sleep over instead of going home and coming back at nine-thirty in the morning to take me to my doctor appointment? You had at least a bottle of wine yourself. You shouldn't drive. You'll hit a tree."

"You're sweet, worrying about me and all. I'll sleep in the guest room. Thanks for an amazing dinner."

"Good night, Sal. See you in the morning."

I remember stumbling into the bathroom to clean myself up before climbing into bed. It was probably fifteen minutes later when the door gently opened. Rio took a couple steps towards my bed.

I stood, groggy and still half-drunk. But I still had the wherewithal to fight my feelings.

"This isn't happening."

Rio slunk backward and closed the door. As soon as the latch clicked shut, I began to cry.

I dearly missed the feeling of being loved, something I hadn't experienced since my sweet Marie. I yearned for it, for the sensation of my soul feeling whole and at peace. Why did Rio have to be my cousin's wife?

The next morning, Rio was already out of bed and making breakfast in the kitchen, acting as if there was no more tension between us.

"Coffee and breakfast?" she chirped. "You have plenty of time before my appointment."

"It looks and smells great. Thanks."

The rest of the morning and afternoon, as I drove Rio from here to there, all I could think about was how our luck couldn't be any worse, and how once again it just wasn't in the cards for me to find the right gal. Even though I wanted it. Desperately.

But I was a racketeer. And as long as I lived that lifestyle, love would have to wait.

REMEMBER WHEN I said my luck couldn't get any worse? Well, a week later, there was a knock on my door.

It was the police.

"Salvatore Liparello?"

"Yeah, that's me."

"Sir, please come with us. You're wanted on suspicion of murder for the death of John Andrea."

I said nothing and let the officers bring me to the station, where they were holding Dominic and Jimmy Louis for questioning, too. I was nervous, but there was no way I was going to let this strunz John Andrea take me down from beyond the grave. How did this one come back to us? I took a few deep breaths and tried to focus.

We had to make sure this was taken care of. Now.

Andrea had been muscle for Sanfilippo, Pacenti, and Lambretta. He was looking for support from the Unione Siciliana and other small-time guys who thought the Sicilians would keep control of Chicago Heights and defeat Capone in the city.

Jon had heard that Andrea was looking to Chicago for support on eliminating me, Jon, and Dominic. We obviously had to move quickly. Our lives depended on it. John Andrea had a couple of local joints, and we had guys in place to keep their eyes and ears open for useful information. At the restaurants he frequented, Andrea liked to go in and out of the kitchens to engage the staff. He knew everyone by their first names and thought of himself as a big shot. We let it be known that if he was eating or drinking at one of those two places, we needed to know immediately, while he was still there. Our guys also needed to keep him there for at least thirty minutes.

It didn't take long for Dominic to get a call while Andrea was with our friend, Jimmy Louis, who told us to park in the back and opened up the door. We tried to blend in with the kitchen staff, but it wasn't easy. People were dodging each other like an orchestrated dance. Dominic asked a cook if Andrea had been back to the kitchen recently.

"He did once, but he usually comes back at least one more time before he leaves."

"Thanks." Dom stuffed ten dollars into the cook's shirt pocket.

"Not necessary, sir."

"Just be sure no one sees or remembers anything from here on out. Capice?"

I stood near the door to the kitchen so I could bear hug Andrea, and Jimmy or Dominic could finish him off. After a few short minutes, the kitchen door swung open and Andrea sauntered in, arms open, singing the cook's praises—the perfect position to put him in a full-nelson, exposing his belly and chest.

Dominic thrust a butcher's knife into his abdomen and ripped it upwards towards his heart. Andrea dropped to the floor with a thud, blood bubbling out of his mouth as he struggled to push back in his exposed intestines. A bus boy walked in from the dining area, but rather than call for help, the kid looked down in shock and scurried back out.

I felt nothing but hate towards Andrea during his last moments. I was a bit surprised by the amount of blood, though. Dominic must have hit an artery or something.

The three of us had stared down the cook and took off out the back. After that, I was acutely aware that I was capable of doing—and stomaching—anything. I wasn't impressed with this cold-hearted side of myself, though. Far from it.

But it was a necessary evil to survive the rackets.

And I had gotten in too deep to escape.

AS I SAT in the holding cell, I figured we had to find someone to locate the cook, who could lead us to the busboy before he talked to the cops. Jon got word to us that he was already on top of it.

Supposedly, the busboy had already told authorities that he saw Dominic and me in the kitchen with Andrea, which was why the cops arrested us in the first place. But Jon was in the process of getting the busboy to flip his story so there wouldn't be enough to press charges. All we had to do was sit tight and keep our mouths shut.

My dad came to visit and let me know that Jon was doing everything he could, and it looked promising. I asked Dad if mom knew I was being held. She did, but my sisters didn't, which was good. If they were aware of my predicament and scared for me, it would make it harder for my parents to deal with. More importantly, I didn't want my sisters thinking less of me.

The quiet and solitude was the worst part. And in those silent moments, my mind drifted to the negative. But I refused to let myself go down that rabbit hole.

It was mid-morning of day two when Jon finally came to see Dom and me separately.

"How you holding up, Sal?"

"I'm fine. Don't worry about me. How's it looking?"

"Made contact with the cook and the busboy. The cook isn't an issue. He never saw a thing and told the police the same. The strunz of a busboy, on the other hand, was a nervous wreck. We finally got to him last night and explained how he was mistaken about who he saw in the kitchen with Andrea, and that he actually only saw the backs of some guys' heads. He was told that if he didn't go to the police and change his story, certain things would happen. Our guy came back and said the busboy was very receptive. So, hang tight. They'll have to charge you or let you go by the end of the day."

"Thanks for coming through for us."

"It was nothing. Hopefully, we won't need to do too much more of this until we can run this thing our way."

CHAPTER 9

Into The Fold

Two weeks later, on September 30, 1926, I was awarded U.S. citizenship in Chicago Heights. My parents threw a huge party, and it was the most time I'd spent with my sisters in a while. Some of the older girls had boyfriends and were growing up fast.

It was a happy day. Dancing, great food, and—most importantly—no stress, despite the fact Rio was there with Dominic. She glanced at me across the room a few times, turning away with a smile. Dominic barely looked at her. They were drifting apart, but I needed to make sure I wasn't the reason for it.

Jon Allen and his family, the Zingaros, the Cosenzas, and the Stefanos were all there to show their love and support, which meant a lot to me and my parents. Our American dream included becoming citizens of our adopted country. It also gave me peace of mind knowing if I did get into trouble, I wouldn't be deported.

Things were quiet for months following my naturalization ceremony. We had taken The Heights, and Jon and Dominic were the bosses. Technically, Jon was considered Number One because he had the money to finance some fronts and operations. Dominic was his second, but Dom ruled like the top boss and Capone agreed. I guess that put me third in line, followed by Guy Roberto and Joe Cosenza.

It was time for a sit down with Capone to discuss bringing Chicago Heights into his Outfit, but Jon and Dominic wanted to have a meeting with just us Boys in The Heights beforehand. They wanted to consult with the Zingaros, Stefanos, and Cosenzas, who were an integral part of our success. Jon thought it was a good idea to show them some respect by getting their thoughts on folding Chicago Heights into The Outfit.

My dad had given me good advice for meetings like this. "Son," he'd said, "if you have doubts or reservations, don't express them during the meeting. Don't say anything that can be misinterpreted as dissension or disrespect. If you have a question, word it carefully, in private to your boss, and let him know you don't doubt his leadership or authority."

I had only one question going into this meeting, but I was confident someone would address it so I wouldn't have to. We gathered at the Lucky Lounge on a weekday morning before opening to the public. The energy in the room was electric, confidence oozing from every man there. We'd won the war against Pacenti and Lambretta, consolidated bootleggers, and were aligned with Capone, who was on the verge of winning his war in the city. We had few enemies left who were a threat, so everyone slept well—even if we kept guns within arm's reach.

And we were making a shit ton of cash.

Jon opened the bar before we got started. "Have a couple, two, three, and we'll get started."

We mingled, laughing and carrying on, for about forty-five minutes. It was nice, from what I remember. After all, we grew up together on the Hill or the East Side, and this was the first time in a long while that we felt free of the tension of our past.

"Okay, fellas. Let's get this meeting started. If you have any reservations about what we're going to discuss, this is the time for you to ask. Because after today, a decision will be made, and then that will be that. There will be no more discussion. Dominic, do you want to add anything before we open this up for questions?"

Dom nodded and stepped forward. "Thanks, Jon. We have not met or promised Capone anything yet. We really want you all to have knowledge of this beforehand so no one feels blindsided or insulted. Also, you deserve to have your thoughts or concerns heard so they don't fester, which could create future problems, ya know? Sal, you got anything?"

I was stunned. I wasn't expecting an opportunity to speak as a person of power within the crew yet. I would listen, at least until the end, before I would say a word. My parents always said you can't learn anything with your mouth open.

"Thanks, Dom, but I have nothing to add at the moment. Let's open this up to everyone else."

Angelo Zingaro slowly stood to address the room. "We are very proud of what we accomplished this year. Jon, Dominic, and Sal, you guys have delivered on all your promises. Your vision for how things could play out were on point. I think our family understands your reasoning behind bringing The Heights into The Outfit. There's plenty of cash to go around, and I don't think we would ultimately have the manpower to go to war with Capone. I understand that Dominic and Salvatore are close to Al, but that would change if it looked like there may be a brewing dispute. That being said, there are a couple things I'd like to address, if that is okay?"

Jon tipped his scotch on the rocks toward Angelo. "Please, continue."

"All of us here are fully aware that relations with the Unione Siciliana will still need to be maintained. Being that the Zingaros are the most important Sicilian family in The Heights now that we've taken the town from Lambretta and Pacenti, we feel like a Zingaro should remain the conduit for Capone, Jon, Dominic, and Salvatore when dealing with The Heights' Unione chapter."

"That should be an easy conversation for me or Sal to have with

Al," Dominic said. "I think that's an appropriate request."

"More importantly, the Zingaro family wants to continue to run our raw material distribution as we do now, and we'd like access to markets in Capone's Outfit, understanding that we won't step on any toes."

"We can make sure that isn't a problem with Chicago," Jon said. "We want that for you, too, and we think Al fully understands your contribution. So, access to some of his markets where there is a need should be possible."

Joe Coz stood up and spoke next.

"Thank you, Jon and Dominic, and Sal, for organizing this before you meet with Al. We appreciate the respect. Our family would like to increase its gambling interests in and around Chicago Heights, especially Cal City, as it blossoms into what we envision. We're also curious on how jukebox and pinball businesses will get divided up as we continue to expand."

Jon nodded. "Great points to address, Joe. There is room for the Stefanos and Cosenzas to expand throughout our territory. This obviously includes Calumet City, where we're continuing to deepen our political capital. In regards to who controls the girls we hire for our joints, that goes to the Cosenzas. The pinball machines will be overseen by the Stefanos. I'll let you know about the jukeboxes." Jon swept his gaze across the room. "Any issues with this?"

The Zingaros, Cosenzas, and Stefanos all shook their heads, so Jon continued. "Dominic, Sal, and I want to expand gambling operations quickly. Yes, we've been established in that racket since before Prohibition, but what happens when it's repealed? We need to be ready for that day because gambling will be a much more important percentage of our earnings."

"Are they talking about that?" Angelo asked.

"Not publicly, but our sources tied to Springfield and

Washington say that most government officials know the people view Prohibition as a scofflaw and think it should be repealed. If this is true, we would not be surprised if the Volstead Act was repealed a few years down the road. So, we need to plan for that now. Nothing lasts forever, and we need to position ourselves for the future."

"Great points," Angelo said. "But for now, I just need to make sure our distribution interests are protected. I'm not as concerned about growing our gambling interests so much at this point."

"That's fine. We'll address that like we said we would. All right? And just to be clear, as some of you open new clubs that provide gambling, you'll need to pay for the wire service results and kick up a percentage to us. If you think Dominic and I are fronting anything, you are mistaken."

After a pause, Dominic cleared his throat. "Any other questions about The Heights being brought into The Outfit? This is your last chance to air any concerns."

"I have a general question," Coz said, glancing nervously between Jon and Dominic. "But it's not a concern, I swear."

"What's up?" Jon asked.

"I would appreciate if you would explain your reasons for not staying independent from Chicago now that we're running The Heights and its surrounding areas?" It was obvious that Coz was being careful and didn't want to come across as questioning Jon and Dom.

Jon provided the answer. "The federal agents bother us, but they want the guy in Chicago who loves to be in newspapers. Dominic and I don't like the attention newspaper articles bring. And if agents want the boss, why should we have one in Chicago Heights to attract a slew of them to our territory? Let Chicago run it all and take most of the heat. There's plenty of cash for us all, even if we kick up to Chicago, which also has a lot of political clout.

Clout that reaches throughout the state to nearly every jurisdiction. Yes, we have some of it in our areas of influence, but to expand or maintain our operations, we need Chicago on our side. If we run into local resistance, Chicago can help out at the county, state, or federal level. Lastly, we feel like a war with The Outfit could be inevitable if our vision for gambling operations is correct. They would end up trying to muscle in on Cal City for sure. It would be less dangerous and possibly more profitable if we ran the whole thing and kicked up to Chicago versus battling to keep our territory from them. Yes, Al is our friend, but the money would be too big to keep him at arm's length for long."

Dominic took that as a cue to end the meeting. "Jon, Sal, and I are meeting Al tomorrow evening to tell him we're coming into The Outfit. We're also bringing our thoughts and requests to the table. If there's nothing more, we are done here."

The next night Jon, Dominic, and I headed to the Lexington Hotel in downtown Chicago to meet with Al, who had just moved his headquarters there from the Hawthorne in Cicero. He knew why we were coming and was silently ecstatic. He'd eagerly take the heat from federal agents in exchange for a percentage of our operation.

As soon as we entered the club, a bouncer corralled us into the back office, where a smiling, gregarious Capone was waiting. He stood to greet us, arms wide, lit stogie in his mouth.

"The Boys in The Heights! Welcome! How you doin'?"

Jon was first to greet Al, giving him a handshake that turned into a hug. "We're great, Al. Thanks."

"We're good," Dominic added, "but a little tired."

"That's more than understandable. It's been a stressful year, but look at you guys now. You're on top, running The Heights."

"We are," Jon said. "But it wasn't easy. There's never time to relax."

"Don't I know it."

The pleasantries over with, Dominic circled the conversation around to business. "It's time to discuss the future, Al."

"Okay then. What do you fellas have in mind?"

"We'll bring Chicago Heights and the territories we control into your Outfit," Dom said. "We and our main families also want to expand our operations in the south suburbs. In return, we'll need access to your politicians when things may not go our way. Obviously, we kick up to you based on what we agree upon—"

Al stopped Dominic mid-thought. "You guys get whatever you want. It's all okay with me." He motioned toward Dominic. "I'm excited to get the lieutenant I always wanted."

"Thanks, Al, but—"

"No buts, Dominic. You are my lieutenant." He looked at Jon. "No offense. But I said it years ago. Dominic's my guy down there."

Jon wasn't fazed. "No offense taken."

"Good," Capone said. "Let's figure out the details later, gentlemen. Right now, it's time to celebrate! We're gonna be massive. A true force. New York will be shocked and impressed by what we'll accomplish together. They'll need to show some respect moving forward. We're nobody's little cousin anymore. We are THE Chicago Outfit!" Al was yelling as he raised his drink in a toast to our newfound power.

We relaxed for a bit and discussed a few details here and there, but it was mostly a jovial evening. Al introduced us all night as his Boys in The Heights, referring to Dominic as Lieutenant Scalea.

On our way home, I made a suggestion. "We should buy Al a gift for his new office. What do you guys think?"

"Al does love gifts," Dominic said. "Good thinking."

"It has to be grand, but what do we get the guy who has it all?"

Jon grinned. "I got it!"

"Whatcha thinking?" Dominic asked.

"A bulletproof high-back chair. So it actually rises above his head as he sits in it. It won't be cheap, but it'll make a statement and be a good reflection on us."

"I love it," I said.

"Then a custom bulletproof high-back chair it is," Dominic said.

To say Al loved the gift would be a major understatement. He gushed over it, and everyone who entered his office was shown the throne given to him from The Boys in The Heights. Later, feeling grateful for his new position, Al decided to get Dominic and other associates extravagant Christmas gifts. So, he paid a jeweler $8,200 in cash to engrave thirty diamond-studded gold belt buckles with his friends' initials.

Dominic was grateful but told Rio he'd never wear it out in public. "Have you ever seen anything so gaudy?"

Weeks later, Dom showed up with a custom designed necklace made for Rio, featuring the diamonds taken from his belt buckle given to him by Capone.

Speaking of Rio, we understood that nothing but hurt would result if we had an affair. I would still drive Rio here or there if Dom wasn't around, and Rio still cared for Dominic. She just couldn't handle the stress of having a half-absent husband who is also a racketeer.

One day, the worry came bubbling up as I dropped her off at the salon. "Sal, I want to talk about that pistol on his nightstand that looks like a fountain pen. Is he in danger? I mean, a fountain pen gun? Is this what things have come to?"

"Rio, listen. A pen gun is easier to conceal. It's actually safer for him to carry that around, ya know? It's just a precaution. Hell, I keep a revolver in my nightstand. What's the difference? We chose the life of a racketeer, Rio, and that life includes you." I took her right hand, trying to ease her fears. "It'll be fine. Don't worry about it."

Rio smiled back, but her eyes betrayed her.
She didn't believe me.

CHAPTER 10

Bad For Business

One of Dominic's great accomplishments was consolidating bootleggers in The Heights, and in early summer of '27, Dominic and Jon wanted to throw a picnic to celebrate their union. Including myself and my dad, there were thirty-two of us. Jon set up the massive feast at Neroni's Grove on 22nd and State Street. No city the size of Chicago Heights had brought all the top bootleggers together, working for a common goal.

Jon, Dom, and I hated having our photos taken—we left that for the highfalutin guys in Chicago and New York—we only took one picture to commemorate the event. Why should we put ourselves out there for all law enforcement to see once the picture circulates? And yes, it always circulates. It makes no sense.

No sense at all.

Anyway, I was pissed because I ended up sitting on the ground in the first of three rows. I had to put down a newspaper so I wouldn't ruin my suit. I should've been in the back with my dad, but everyone wanted to get it over with so I just plopped my ass down where there was room.

Just after the photo was taken, Jon addressed the men. "The food is about ready, but before we break bread, there are a few things I'd like to say. Dominic, Salvatore, and myself want you to know that we're fully aware that our control of The Heights couldn't have happened without your cooperation and loyalty. We made you promises about more money and better protection. I think you all have seen those results, and we intend to only make more money and increase our political capital moving forward. If any of you have any issues—any at all—come to me, Jon, or Sal. Let's keep this family tight. It's family that keeps each other safe, and that is what I want. I want you all to think about The Heights as a family. We may now be part of Capone's Outfit, but WE ARE The Boys in The Heights!" Jon raised a fist in the air. "Our power and influence is felt throughout the entire Midwest and beyond!"

The men hollered and cheered. I was impressed and inspired right along with them. And I learned something about leadership that day. Power can be fleeting in the racketeer game. You must reward and show respect to those who fight and earn for you. You must keep them believing in your vision and leadership. If you don't, they'll do what we did to Sanfilippo, Pacenti, and Lambretta.

They'll replace you.

The comradery that took place over the next couple hours was satisfying. I've always been good at reading body language, and the guys seemed happy to be where they were, with no scowls or sideways glances behind the scenes. Some guys from feuding families even started to make amends.

After we all ate and drank, Jon addressed his bootleggers one more time.

"I just want to talk about a couple more things before you go back to your family … or your cumare," Jon said, getting a chuckle from the crowd—especially those with mistresses.

"Okay, okay," Dominic said, lowering his arms to try to quell the laughter. "Let Jon finish."

"Thanks, Dom. It's all good. Here's the last thing I want to address, gentlemen. Politics, police, and labor unions. We need to actively get our guys into positions to help our causes. If we have brothers, cousins, or friends who are looking for work, we can help them find open jobs or create ones that can protect our interests.

I'm talking about police officers, police chiefs, mayors, aldermen, union officials—anyone who has access or influence over the cash in the coffers. Keep your eyes and ears open. We need to place as many guys as possible who are connected to us into positions of influence. Okay? That's it for now, gentlemen. Thank you."

Joe Coz approached us after the picnic officially ended. "Hey, Jon. Got a second?"

"For you, I got five minutes." He put a hand on Joe's shoulder. "What's up, Joe?"

"I want to throw my name out there for when you expand gambling operations and need guys to fill important positions. I want more responsibility. You know I'm loyal, and you know I'm ready for whatever you throw at me."

"Joseph, when the time comes, you'll get a call. You're very high on our list of guys who are up for promotion. We'll have something for you for sure. Hang tight, okay?"

"Thanks, Jon. Thanks, Dominic. I appreciate it."

I THINK IT was the end of that year when I found myself in trouble with Johnny Law again. By now I had a bit of a reputation, so every time there was a murder or something, authorities loved to throw my name out there as a possible suspect. This time, someone said I was the last guy to see Tommy Bufallo alive. Did I know something about it? Well, it was part of my job to know something about everything happening around The Heights.

The police brought me in for questioning a few hours after Bufallo's body showed up lying near the corner of Ridge and Halsted. The Chicago Heights Star reported the murder as Another Booze Killing, which was an oversimplification. From what I understood, Bufallo may have been trying to muscle in on the Zingaro business. He was supposed to meet the Zingaro brothers for a sit-down that evening to iron out an arrangement, but the

Zingaros just wanted him gone. Jon and Dominic obliged their request and had Coz and a new guy take care of it. I was just there as part of the setup.

Bufallo thought he was going on a sugar pick-up downstate with me. I told him we were switching cars and picking up Coz for extra hands and cargo capacity. The ditch car was waiting a few blocks from my house.

"Ready for a little road trip?" Coz asked me with a devilish grin as he slid in behind Bufallo.

"Yup. Just need to swap out vehicles, then we'll be on our way."

We pulled up next to the ditch car, with the new guy already behind the wheel, and Joey C put his revolver to the back of Bufallo's skull. "Get out of the car really slow and get in the back seat."

Coz opened the back driver's side door, gestured with his gun for Bufallo to get in and slide over, then sat in the backseat, gun pointed directly at Bufallo's head. Our guy sped them away, and I drove back to the Lucky Lounge.

The rest of the story went like this: As soon as they got near that intersection, Coz capped Bufallo twice in the head, spraying a bloody mess all over the inside of the car. Coz reached across the seat to open the back passenger door and kicked Bufallo out of the car, and the driver hammered the gas as the body rolled into a ditch. They took the car to a wrecking yard a few miles away, where some guys were waiting to burn it to the ground.

Anyway, after a week of no evidence surfacing, the case against me was dropped. Like I told the cops, Tom Bufallo was still alive when I last saw him.

Things didn't quiet down much after the Bufallo incident, though. In this life, you go from one headache to the next, like when our trucks started getting hijacked. The last one was a huge sugar delivery meant for the Zingaros. Someone was looking to take a big shot at us and the Zingaros's grip on sugar distribution, but most of these idiots don't know how to keep a low profile or a shut mouth.

And almost none of them know how to avoid a camera's eye.

Anyway, because one of these hijackers couldn't keep his mouth shut, it didn't take long for the Zingaros to find out who ripped off the shipment. They came to see Jon, Dominic, and me at the Lucky Lounge to give us information on the trio who were stupid enough to brag about ripping off Zingaro and his scum Calabrese bosses. They were Sicilians with close friends at the Unione. Two lived in Chicago Heights, and the third lived in Chicago, all rogue bandits, small-time thieves who answered to no one. Their activities up to that point were on a much smaller scale. They'd never interfered with Outfit or Heights stuff, so they were almost never asked to kick up. When they had gotten a decent score, word got to the Lucky, and they always paid whatever was needed to be taken care of. Until this.

They knew where to sell a ton of sugar, perhaps from the Aiellos who were battling Capone, but more likely from Bugs Moran and his fellow Northsiders. They could have easily bought that much sugar and sold it quickly.

There was really nothing to think about. We had to get these guys for what they did, and we had to send a message that was swift and powerful. They also needed to be taken out at the same time so there was no time for word to get out. We didn't want one or two of them sneaking out of town.

It took a little bit of patience as we waited for word from the source who tipped us off in the first place. The trio was planning to gather for one of their weekly meetings, the location of which changed every week and was decided the morning of. Eventually, we found out they were meeting at a diner for lunch. We had a group of three shooters, watching and ready. As soon as they walked out together, our men cut them down in broad daylight.

Word spread quickly, and we had no more issues with hijackers.

Honestly, this kind of violence was bad for business. The public read about it in the papers and grew tired of it happening near their neighborhoods. Right after the hijacker incident, the Star began writing semiregular editorials about The Heights's corruption and racketeers, which may have been the motivation behind the paper's offices being bombed later that year. In fact, one editorial in '28 quoted the Cook County Highway Police Chief James Devereux.

"We have made progress in Cicero. Capone has left town and we have also been making it hot for the booze interests on the northwest side of Chicago. Chicago Heights has remained a sore spot. There are probably more than two dozen huge illicit distilleries in the vicinity of the suburb. Their owners have been getting richer and tougher and have come to believe that they are entirely outside the law.

"We intend to show differently."

CHAPTER 11

Not So Untouchable

Eliot Ness and his agents had it out for Capone, but The Heights couldn't be ignored. In the spring of 1928, Ness declared Chicago Heights "the second 'wettest' city in the whole country." It was impossible for the scale of our operation to go unnoticed at that point.

Of course, we saw a different Eliot Ness than the guy portrayed in the papers. Sure, he was out there doing his job, but he wasn't as innocent and pure as the country thought. He was seen drinking—even getting drunk—in our establishments. I had no doubt he was consuming the same spirits he'd taken an axe to twelve hours earlier. Ness was looking to advance his career, and busting Al Capone would take him to his perceived Promise Land. Sure, he had to work over The Heights, but at the day's end, all he really cared about was Capone.

Here's another example of how we knew Ness wasn't as untouchable as people thought. On a brisk night in late April, when you could just about see your breath, Ness busted a Sicilian gang's industrial still and was holding Joe Bushilli in Joliet. Bushilli did what he was told: say nothing, hang tight, and someone from The Heights will show up to get you. A few hours later, a couple of our boys spoke with Ness. They gave him four hundred dollars, and Bushilli went home. Yup, Mr. Untouchable took a bribe from The Boys in The Heights.

Untouchable, my ass.

Not long after, Dominic and I went downtown to meet Al for lunch at a greasy spoon near his HQ where he'd be safe. Al was going on about how the Aiello brothers were pushing hard on him with the support of the Unione Siciliana. Joe Aiello was aiming to become the Unione president, which would only cause more headaches for Al.

"Between Ness, the Aiellos, and the fellas on the Northside, I feel like I can't breathe. We may need to take this war up a notch to alleviate the pressure on me," Al said as he bit into his cheeseburger with extra tomato and lettuce.

"What do you have in mind?" Dominic asked. "Anything in particular?"

"Nothing at the moment. I'm just thinking out loud right now. But I know I want to hit them so hard they see no other option but retreat."

We told Al to keep us abreast of the situation and to reach out for assistance. Either Dominic or I was already meeting him at the Lexington about once a week to give and receive updates.

On the drive home that night, Dominic opened up to me on a personal level I hadn't seen in years. "Sal, has Rio mentioned anything to you?"

"About what?"

"About us. Our marriage."

I didn't like lying to my cousin, but I had no choice. "No," I said, "nothing like that. What's going on?"

Dominic sighed. "I think we're growing apart. I try to protect her from our life, but by doing so, I've created a gulf between us. We still love each other, but I'm not sure we're in love with each other. Know what I mean?"

"Yeah, I know what you're saying."

"Another thing, Sal. The feds are trying to throw me out of the country. There are too many eyes on me right now. Know what I'm sayin'? I gotta lay low for a while. It's time for you and my brother to take the reins more often for Jon. I am sure he'll talk about that with you, but it looks like you're getting ready for a bump in responsibilities. Honestly, Sal, it's a good thing. You can handle anything thrown at you. You're level-headed and think about all the angles. You'll be a great leader when the time comes."

"Dominic, slow down. You're not gone yet."

"Cousin, the feds are watching me. You know it's just a matter of time until I get tossed into jail or back to Italy. I'm realistic about things, and it's pretty hot for me right now. I just want to let you know so you aren't caught off guard."

There was no talking Dominic out of it. All I could do was be supportive.

"Okay," I said. "I hear you. I still think you're overreacting, but I understand where you're coming from. I do."

We barely spoke the rest of the drive. Dominic knew he wasn't going to last on the streets much longer. Meanwhile, I was thinking about Rio being available soon and wondering if I should pursue her. I was completely torn.

Two months later, maybe in May, Dominic and Rio divorced amicably. For the record, Rio and I met up a couple times when she wanted to tell me the news, but it was only as friends. She was done with being the wife or girlfriend of a racketeer. Who could blame her? I sure as hell couldn't.

Their breakup made me feel even more alone. How could I ask this woman to put up with the stress of being tied to another racketeer after I knew it was one of the reasons for the deterioration of her last relationship? I also didn't want to know what Dominic would do if he found out. He's my cousin, but I wouldn't put anything past Dominic when he's in a rage. No one escapes in one piece.

And how could I bring kids into the world with the chance their father would get shot dead in the street in front of their home? I wanted to find happiness. But I couldn't endanger people I loved because of the life I chose.

As far as taking a larger leadership role in Dominic's absence, I couldn't have been more ready. I had a feeling that Jon would be delegating more of his responsibilities to Guy and me, too. With the heat on Dominic, Jon would try to further insulate himself however he could.

By the summer of '28, Dominic was a nervous wreck, constantly on the lookout for authorities he thought were keeping him under surveillance. Around mid-June, he called Al to set up a meeting and picked up Capone at the Lexington, just the two of them—though he told me all about it later.

When Al got in the car, Dominic told Capone he was in the mood to drive to Lake Shore.

"Sounds good, Lieutenant," Al replied. "What's on your mind?"

"Well, you may not want me as your lieutenant in Chicago Heights."

"Nonsense, Dom. What the hell would make me want to replace you?"

"Al, I have a lot of heat on me. I need to get out of town or go back to Sambiase for a while. Maybe a long while. Rio and I split up, so I can leave when I need to."

"Dominic, try to relax. I have total faith in Sal and Jon."

"I know. I just don't want you to be disappointed in me."

"You guys in Chicago Heights have done nothing but have my back. I know where your allegiances lie. There's no way I could be disappointed in you, brother. Sal is always around. I'm comfortable dealing with him or Jon."

"Thanks, Al. I appreciate the vote of confidence. Obviously, Sal is just as capable as me, maybe more now. Sure, I brought him up, but he's a natural-born leader. He knows how to delegate responsibility, he identifies risks and is detail-oriented. Jon is already talking about being less involved in five to ten years and has expressed to me his full confidence in leaving all day-to-day decision making to Sal. Between Jon, Sal, and my brother Guy, if I happen to need to leave town, The Heights will remain in strong capable hands."

"I don't doubt it in the least. Like I said, I love Sal and Jon. It's all good. Just take care of yourself. Make sure you don't leave town without seeing me. Capice?"

"Absolutely, Al. I wouldn't think of leaving Chicago without saying goodbye."

Dominic drove up Lake Shore Drive north to Lawrence and was getting ready to turn around when Al said, "I'm not ready yet, but I'm going to make a major move against Moran and his leadership soon. And after hearing your praise for young Salvatore and with the guidance of Jon, I think I won't make a major move without getting their input. I mean it. I know The Boys in The Heights have my back. The way your family took care of me during the McSwiggin fiasco, fuhgeddaboudit. I'm not sure when, but when I'm ready to plan or execute, I'll reach out to Sal or Jon if you're back in Sambiase."

"They'll take care of you and make sure you've thought all the angles through. Not that your guys in Chicago can't do it, but maybe it's a good idea to leave some of your top guys out of it? You know what I mean?"

"Well, I think we've talked enough business for the evening. Whataya say you let my guys at the Lexington park your car for the night, and you get into some trouble with me? For old times' sake. Just in case you gotta disappear."

Dom smiled. "Let's park this son of a bitch and rip this city apart."

"That's my Dominic! To the Lexington for spirits and pretty girls!"

When they got to the Lexington, Al had the staff prepare a ballroom with a band and a buffet, making sure there were three or four girls for every guy. The booze was flowing. The cigar smoke was heavy and the men's after-shave was as over-applied as the dancers' perfume.

How do I know? I was there.

Al had Dominic call and invite me to an impromptu party he described as "so special you shouldn't miss it. Get your ass to the Lexington now!"

And when Al Capone has someone call to invite you to a party ... you show up.

ON A GORGEOUS September evening a few months later, I was at the family house for dinner. Just as my mom was sliding into her chair to join us at the dinner table, there was a rap at the front door.

I knew that knock. It was Dominic.

He walked in and gave my mom a kiss, then greeted my dad and sisters as my mom made him a place at the table.

"Dominic, pleasant surprise," my dad said, a hint of caution in his voice. He was protective and smart, and knew Dominic always had an angle. If I had good instincts, I got them from him.

"Thanks, Zio Luca. To be honest, I wanted to stop over to tell you guys something."

At that, all the forks hit our plates.

"Fifteen years ago," Dominic started, "you were the first people I came to see, and now you'll be the last."

"What are you talking about?" my dad asked.

"I am going to Sambiase. Things are too hot here at the moment, and I can do some business when I get there. I plan on coming back, but I'm not sure when. All I know is, I'm leaving town tonight, and I wanted you all to be the ones to send me off. After all, making the Liparellos my first stop brought me good luck. And I can use a little luck now."

I stopped eating and looked Dominic in the eyes. He nodded, then started eating.

We talked about family and friends back in Italy for a while. My mom gave him a list of people to visit for her, and Dominic promised he would. He knew if or when she saw him again, she'd quiz him over it. Besides, it was mostly family, and he'd see them anyway. Dominic stuck around for an hour or so after dinner until he stood up and said it was time to go.

I walked him to the door. "Need a ride somewhere?"

"No, I'm all set."

"When am I going to see you again?"

"A year or so, I hope. You'll hear from me directly or through Jon or Guy. Out of sight, not out of mind, Sal."

"Sounds good. Good luck, and be safe back in Italy."

"There's one more thing, cuz," Dominic said gently to me.

"What's that?"

Dominic reached deep into the front right pocket of his trousers and pulled out a watch.

A watch I recognized.

"Dom, I can't take this. It's the watch that broke when you crossed from Canada to Minnesota."

"I kept it to remember that fateful night. Now I want you to keep it to remember me and our adventures together. It's been a pleasure watching you grow into a man of honor."

DOMINIC'S TIMING COULDN'T have been better. In October 1928, Ness and his agents—including a brother-in-law, Alexander Jamie—started pushing harder. The Heights had such a tight grip on local law enforcement, and a reputation for being completely lawless, that the feds had taken offense.

The thing was, if they thought we were lawless at this point, what would they think about all that happened over the next year?

It was then I realized how imperative it was to increase our political capital. Whatever the cost, it was worth it. Period. Jon and I had to put out a lot more money trying to get more protection from the feds. It was also important that I talk with Jon about how to further insulate ourselves from Ness and his agents. We'd need to if we wanted to avoid jail time.

We had a really good talk in his backyard one evening after a wonderful family dinner. I was relaxing and gathering my thoughts when Jon walked out with two rocks glasses filled with ice and a bottle of Dewars. He poured us three fingers each and asked me what was on my mind.

"You and I relish our privacy," I said. "We don't want attention. We don't want our photos taken. We despise reporters."

"True. Where are you going with this?"

"We aren't Al Capone. We don't need to be known. We just need to get paid."

Jon raised his glass at that. "Also true."

"And we know who Eliot Ness is. We know what he looks like. We know he still lives with his parents. But he doesn't know Jon Allen or Salvatore Liparello. Let's try to keep it that way. Let's isolate ourselves as much as we can, while we can."

Jon poured another ounce into our glasses as I continued.

"I want to put guys in positions so Ness will get on their trail instead of ours," I said. "This way, when agents are asking around about who's in charge of the illegal stills, our names won't be mentioned. We can put some of our strunz troublemakers in positions where they think they're getting a promotion, but we're just transferring the bullseye from our backs to theirs. Only a few guys below us will talk to or see us from here on out."

Jon nodded. He was with me so far.

"We have some historical pain in the ass Siciliani, so we should elevate their perceived status. These longtime sons of bitches will become our decoys and scapegoats, Jon. We don't trust them, but we need to deal with them. And the more respect we appear to give them, the less likely they'll be to rat on us. And at the same time, when the heat comes asking about who's in charge of the Chicago Heights bootlegging territory, or who's behind all the bribes being paid to local law enforcement and federal agents, it'll be their names being spoken, not ours."

Jon took a sip, then smiled over the glass. "Brilliant, Sal. Brilliant."

"Thanks, but I've learned a lot from you in the last few years. My dad has taught me a lot, too."

We finished our drinks and Jon poured us another before getting even deeper into my plan. "So, who do you have in mind?"

"Martini and Basso could be elevated to handle the bribes. And I'm thinking that strunz Sorenzini from Blue Island, who thinks he's in charge of the still operators throughout the south suburbs, could be named as Dominic's replacement while he's away. Let all the guys on the streets drop these names when they get pinched."

"I love it. Let Capone and the others be the face of the operations. We don't want that following our kids and grandkids around some day."

My thoughts drifted to Rio—back to Marie, even—and how I wasn't close to having kids, let alone grandchildren. But Jon didn't want to hear about that, so I stayed focused on discussing the new power structure that would keep us from getting picked up by Ness and his henchmen.

THOUGH EVERYONE KNEW of Eliot Ness, I didn't have my first run-in with the man until the 1928 World Series. Jon, Guy, and I were glued to the radio in Jon's office at the Lucky listening to Babe Ruth hit three homers in game four when he and a stooge posing as crooked agents bellied up. Our guy at the front entrance sent a waitress to let us know about our special guests.

We weren't surprised. In fact, we were expecting them. The lounge had a reputation throughout the Midwest, so the agents were bound to hear about it. We snuck out the back while our bartender served the so-called undercover agents whiskey after whiskey until they were drunk. Ness was full of himself, but he was also tenacious. He and his goon tried asking some questions about the proprietor, but our bartender knew how to respond.

"You know, I just started here. I think the guy who hired me was a manager. He'll be back later. Sorry, I can't help you more than that."

Supposedly, Ness kept asking him the same questions in different ways until our guy behind the bar had enough.

"Listen, sir, I'm just doing my job here. If you want a full interview, you can wait for a manager or go dig up the public record for who owns this joint. Can I pour you fellas another round, or should I have that guy over there see you to the exit?" He pointed to the bouncer at the door.

Ness pulled back, sensing he'd already been made.

"Sorry. Another round for the whole joint. On me," Ness announced to diffuse the situation.

The next day, we got the lowdown from our boys and heard that Ness and his pal stumbled out of the lounge sometime after one in the morning, like drunken pirates. We all had a laugh in the Lucky's back office.

"Jon," I said, "should we tell Martini to try and get anyone of importance on the take if they appear susceptible?"

"That's a tough question. If we do, they'll have an easy case against Martini. If he gets indicted, we run the risk of him ratting us out."

"As long as we get to rats before they see the courtroom, it may be worth it. If he takes the cash and leaves us alone, it'll be worth every penny. But we'll definitely need to monitor our guys and the agents carefully."

"Sal, we need to put your plan into place tomorrow. Think about it. With federal agents in the lounge last night, indictments are an inevitability, right? So let's get further out of the limelight and promote some of those jamokes we talked about."

"I'll set up all the meetings and take Guy with me."

The next day, Guy and I met Martini at his favorite lunch spot, a well-known sandwich shop in the center of his neighborhood. He was a Sanfilippo loyalist who thought we were finally giving him the long-awaited respect and responsibility he deserved. I let him know he was now in charge of paying off police and politicians.

"If anyone's asking who you answer to," I said, "you let them think it's you. As far as anyone needs to know, you are the final say in who gets what. Capice? No one needs to know that you report to Jon and me. If anyone leapfrogs you and comes straight to me or Jon, I'll tell them I know nothing of such dealings. You're the man in charge of payoffs. That's it."

"Absolutely, Sal. I got this."

All I could think was, No, Martini, we got you. We got you right where we need you.

NESS MUST HAVE figured out he'd been compromised at the Lucky because he never attempted to pull off an undercover operation himself again. Over the course of a few nights, Ness' brother-in-law, Alexander Jamie, and a few other agents headed to speakeasies in and around The Heights's territory. They said they would provide protection for four hundred dollars, and after a few days of persistently asking who was in charge, the agents were told to look for Joe Martini, who knew where they'd be next.

The way Martini told it to us, when he saw two of them asking around as if they were looking for someone in particular, he approached the not-so-undercover feds.

"Good evening, gentlemen. Is there anything I can help you with?"

"Nice joint you got here," Jamie said.

"Thanks."

"I imagine you fellas pay for some kind of protection since you appear to be running speakeasies all around Chicago Heights with no police interference," the other agent said.

"Why'd you assume such things?" Martini shot back. "That's an insult to our local law enforcement. More importantly, who's asking, and who the fuck are you two?"

"Easy, guy!" Jamie said. "We're here to possibly talk some business."

"What business would I have with you two jamokes?"

"What if I told you that, for a sum of money, we could make Ness and his men look the other way?"

"I'd say that I'd be crazy to bribe a federal agent," Martini said. "You must think I'm stupid or something."

"You think we'd entrap you?" Jamie tried to act shocked.

"You better fucking believe you'd entrap me! Both of you need to leave now." Martini gestured to his bouncer to assist them in finding the exit.

After the agents left, Martini said he sat and thought about their interaction for a bit. What if they were serious about taking money for protection? No doubt it would be huge. However, if he was right and they were setting him up, he'd be indicted in no time. Then he thought about what an indictment would mean for him.

He would have given it more consideration, but he didn't have time. The same two agents continued to visit speakeasies in our territory, asking to speak to whoever was in charge. Just four or five nights after their initial meeting, Martini again found himself in front of the same guys.

"Excuse me, Mr. Martini," Jamie asked, grabbing Martini's arm as he tried to walk past. "You are Mr. Martini, aren't you?"

Martini shook the agent's hand off his arm with force, almost punching the fellow next to him.

"You obviously know who I am. And I know who and what you are. What do you want?"

"Relax for a second. I'll tell you what we want. Four hundred dollars. Each."

"For what?" Martini snipped back.

"For protection. Federal."

"Oh, so you can indict me for bribing a federal agent, or have some other idiot tell me we need to pay him because you guys are gone? You must think I am crazy."

"Well, Mr. Martini, you are a racketeer," Jamie said. "So, yes, we do think you're crazy."

At that, Martini walked away without answering any question. He knew their offer wasn't going away. The next day, Martini contacted me about the offer. I was highly suspicious to say the least, but I told Martini to feel them out. Ultimately, if we could get feds on the take, it would be money well spent.

Two nights later, the agents came to see Martini yet again.

"How about it?" Jamie asked.

"How about what, fellas?"

"Our offer of protection … for a nominal fee to each of us," the other agent chimed in.

"And what if I was to agree on said amount? What do I get? What do I have to do?"

"Your stills and your speakeasies run untouched, Mr. Martini," Jamie told him.

"For how long, agent? Does eight hundred dollars really buy my territory?"

"As long as the two of us are assigned to Illinois. We would, however, like to visit the stills we'll be protecting and the guys running them."

"I'll have someone find you. He'll drive you around to see the sights," Martini said, then walked away without a glance.

The someone Martini referred to was Tony Basso. The next day, Martini had Basso pick up the agents at a lounge just west of the Cal City limits and paid them each four hundred dollars. Basso took them to three stills over the next few days, and he couldn't help but blabber all over town about how he was driving around a couple of feds.

Let's just say Jon and I were not so excited.

"I don't think these agents are dirty," I told Jon. "Do you? If they really wanted to be on the take, they'd be happier knowing less, right? Smells fishy to me."

Jon shook his head. "Not dirty in the least. We need to clean this up before they rat."

"The strunz driver will be dealt with today. We'll keep a close eye on Martini for now."

I walked out of Jon's office and found a new, young trigger man to take care of Big Mouth Basso while walking to his car—the same one he was about to use for yet another federal tour of our increasingly less secret stills.

That sent shockwaves through our territory. Lips tightened, and Martini was rightfully scared for his life. The following day, Jon and I spoke in the back of my dad's store because the feds had been seen driving around the Lucky Lounge.

"Sit," Jon said. "Capone asked if he could have a meeting at my place, and you have to be there. He wants you to help him plan something big. If you're available on Saturday, I'll set it up."

"Do it. I'm around."

"One more thing. The assistant US district attorney announced they have a hundred witnesses from grand jury probes. They went beyond bootlegging and into gambling and corruption of police and politicians in Chicago Heights and South Chicago Heights."

"We'll beat this rap. Their evidence may disappear with their witnesses," I said calmly.

I believed it, too.

I had zero fear of prosecution. Sure, I knew it could happen, but I was twenty-seven years old and felt invincible. There was also a coldness to me now. A darkness that allowed me to talk casually about the permanent elimination of our headaches, like a shadow growing longer behind me as the years wore on.

CHAPTER 12

Meetings, Raids, and Loose Ends

Before that Saturday, Al had me drive down to Chicago for a meeting before the meeting. He was showing me incredible respect, and I have to say, I was quite honored.

Al was pacing with a lit cigar in his right hand. "Salvatore, you and your family took great care of me in the past. And you're a smart kid. Smarter than me. You consider all possible scenarios, so I'd like your guidance on something I need figured out before Saturday."

"Wouldn't say I'm smarter than you, and that other stuff was no big deal. You're a great houseguest from what I hear. Heard you can clean dishes as good as anyone." I smiled at my joke. "What do you have in mind?"

"Taking out Moran and his top guys in one fell swoop is what I have in mind."

"Shit, Al." Jon had said Capone wanted to talk about something big. I guess this qualified. "This is huge. It'll take a lot of planning and patience to pull off correctly. I'm honored you want my input on this."

"No need to thank me anymore. You've earned it. Capice?"

I nodded and waited for him to continue.

"I know you guys are dealing with a lot right now," Al said. "I hope no one gets pinched when these indictments come down."

"Probably just some petty fines. If we get some time, it'll be unfortunate, but I don't see it happening. Let's talk about what you need before the meeting at Jon's."

"I need names," he said. "I need guys who can finish what they were sent out to do. They need to be calm under duress and not rat if things go wrong."

"I'm sure you already have some individuals in mind."

"Indeed I do, but I want you to look 'em over. Make sure they're as capable as I think they are. I'm going to write some names of guys who will either shoot or be outside as lookouts or getaway drivers. If you scratch a name out, I want it replaced with one. Understand?"

"One hundred percent."

Al slid over the list of names. It was full of capable men, and not just from Chicago. Al was looking to pull fellas from all over the Midwest. I knew he wanted a revised version immediately, so while I was a little nervous, I felt comfortable with my quick decisions. I crossed off just three names I thought were not completely trustworthy and replaced them with guys who were solid.

I slid the list back as Al rocked in the bulletproof high-back we bought him.

Impressive," he said while scrutinizing my changes. "I like him and forgot about him. Good call." Al stood and extinguished his cigar in an ornate ashtray on his desk, so I stood, too. He walked around it and gave me a hug. "See you on Saturday. Tell Jon I'll have everyone show up around one in the afternoon."

"No problem."

"Salvatore, thank you again for looking out for my best interests."

"Of course. Your interests are my interests."

"I know, but you're different. I trust you. I like you."

Al Capone squared up to me and put his hands on my shoulders.

"Salvatore Liparello, until the day I die, I'll be coming to you for advice."

THAT SATURDAY WAS forever ingrained in my mind. I got there early to help Jon and his wife prepare for the picnic after Al's big meeting. I spent most of my time playing with Jon's ten-year-old daughter. That kid was full of spunk.

Al showed up at noon with bags of food and booze, plus flowers for Jon's wife. "I hope it's okay that I didn't tell the others whose house the meeting would be held at. I just told them to come to Twenty-Sixth Street and Chicago Road in The Heights."

"Perfect. Can I get you something? Make yourself comfortable. Sal is in the backyard playing," Jon laughed.

"Sal, you're going to scare the kid. Halloween isn't for two weeks!" Al yelled as he stepped into the backyard.

I told Jon's daughter it was time for grownup talk and turned to Al. "I have some ideas, but we'll probably need a few months for everything to fall into place."

"That's okay. When we pull this off, we'll be the undisputed champions in Chicago. We'll be giving New York a run for their money." Al flashed a devilish grin.

Guests trickled in over the next hour. Some guys were local, some from Chicago, and some traveled from as far away as Missouri. Al and Frank Nitti, his cousin and bodyguard, agreed that aligning with Egan's Rats in St. Louis would be smart. Jon and I had done business with them for years, so we knew their value.

Willie Heeney, Rocco DeGrazia, Louis Campagna, Claude Maddox, Nick Circella, and Jimmy Zingaro were the guests of honor that day. A lot of muscle and calculating minds had gathered for this meeting. We talked for almost three hours, going over details that would take a few months to pull together. Then we ate lunch and relaxed, enjoying the warm October afternoon. Before everyone left, Al asked Jon's wife to take a photo of the guys. He insisted that Jon's young daughter join them for the picture. She plopped herself right on my lap, with Al's right arm draped around her. It was monumental.

The calm before the storm.

As he was about to leave, before sliding into the back of his armored Caddy, Al pulled me aside. "Salvatore, veni qua. I want to say something."

"Sure. What's up?" I asked, hugging him goodbye.

"When we pull this off, I'll owe a large part of my victory to you. Dominic was instrumental, too, but he and Jon always told me how special you are. I've seen it with my own eyes the last few years. And after today, I'm impressed with your attention to detail. This move will make my Outfit the kings of Chicago and beyond.

"You're the most important man behind the scenes."

"Thanks, but I don't need any recognition."

"I know. That's why you'll be working for decades to come while I'm sitting in jail or dead."

BY MID-NOVEMBER, Martini had been indicted. He posted his ten-thousand-dollar bail within hours of his arrest and was back on the streets.

We couldn't risk him talking. This was why we put certain people in these positions.

Martini had to go.

And fast.

He thought the feds would take the cash and be our guys. That was foolish. It's the local political capital that works. They're there with you day in and day out. But the feds are climbing the ladder. They're here today and gone tomorrow. Martini should've known better. He was a relic, still on the street wishing his pals Pacenti and Lambretta were running the show.

I needed someone close to him to do the job, someone he was comfortable with, so I sent for his favorite guy and had Coz deliver my instructions.

On the thirtieth of November, Joe Martini was standing in front of his building at Sixteenth and Lowe, edged into the terra cotta cornice above the entrance. In fact, he was standing a mere hundred feet from where Pacenti had been killed. A nice coincidence. Witnesses said Martini appeared to know our triggerman, Martini's hands never leaving his coat pockets. He was shot in the head several times, and our gunman fired randomly to distract any witnesses as he ran away.

No one was ever charged for Martini's death.

Then another loose end reared its ugly head. We thought Larry Gilbert, the chief of police in South Chicago Heights, was with us. But word leaked that he was due to testify before a grand jury on December 7. This after his department busted a couple of our boys transporting around 50 five-gallon cans of our illegal hooch. We tried to reach out, but Gilbert avoided all contact leading up to his testimony.

We had no choice. At 10 p.m. on the sixth, as Chief Gilbert and his wife were relaxing and reading the newspaper in their living room, two guys rested their shotguns barrels on the windowsill a few feet away. Shotgun blasts exploded so close to the chief's wife that she lost part of a finger.

Needless to say, the chief never testified.

IN THE WEEK between Christmas and New Year's 1929, Special Agent Ness and partners raided the Lucky Lounge. Jon and I weren't there that morning, but from what I was told, about four revolvers and a couple of shotguns hit the floor when they barged in identifying themselves as federal agents. There was really no one there, just our barbacks, our bartender, and a few fellas from out of town relaxing upstairs with some girls.

In the following days, newspapers like the Herald and Examiner reported that the gang war casualties in The Heights had reached sixty, giving our city the highest murder rate per capita in the United States. Other newspapers labeled Chicago Heights the center for lawlessness and a municipal sanctuary for killers and bootleggers.

Not good.

The situation got worse when more than a hundred federal agents and detectives convoyed from Chicago and stormed The Heights. The feds took over city hall and relieved most of the police department of their duties, creating quite a scene in the station, from what I was told. Then they fanned out all over the city to deliver warrants and rounded up about thirty guys, including some Zingaros and Stefanos. Jon and I didn't need to worry about those fellas singing.

There were other things, however, that came to light during these raids, things that brought The Heights's importance to organized crime into the government's consciousness. A newspaper wrote that federal authorities found evidence indicating some of our guys had connections to or were operating a headquarters for a "mafia" syndicate in Chicago, Cincinnati, St. Louis and New York. One bust made their heads spin, though, and was one of the main reasons we would conduct a total audit of our political capital.

It happened at Oli Esti's place.

I've been able to look back and chuckle about it, but madone, the Esti bust was damning at the time. In Oli's garage on Chicago Heights's west side, agents found 434 slot machines, 55 gallons of illegal spirit, 15 cases of whiskey, and 45 cases of beer. He was eventually indicted for conspiracy—though he never gave up anyone—and did two or three years in jail. From what I heard, he lived happily ever after when he got out.

But what authorities found when they searched his house changed history.

That's where they discovered $400,000 worth of canceled checks. Oli also kept detailed records stashed in a few safes around his home. A ledger from 1928 showed that he took home a couple hundred thousand as his cut that year, and the other monies went to four unknowns. The contents of another safe showed returns for his slots that brought in $1.5 million that year.

That ledger showed payouts going all the way up the line to The Outfit.

And it was used to build the tax evasion case against Al Capone.

CHAPTER 13

The Fellest Of Swoops

On the fourteenth of February in 1929—after months of meetings, planning sessions, and stakeouts led by Al, Nitti, Campagna, and me—the Capone gang was finally ready to eliminate Bugs Moran and his crew.

Moran's men believed they would be meeting up at the SMC Cartage warehouse on Clark Street in Chicago, then driving to Detroit to buy some stolen Canadian whiskey from the Purple Gang, who did business with Capone and The Boys in The Heights. Most of Moran's guys arrived at 10:30 a.m., though Moran saw a police car and turned around. But one of our lookouts mistook a guy named Albert Weinshank for Moran and signaled that they all were in the warehouse.

Witnesses saw a black Cadillac sedan pull up to the garage and four men emerge. Two wore police uniforms and took their shotguns around the back of the warehouse, where they found two members of Moran's gang working on one of the trucks they thought they would be driving to Detroit. The uniformed gangsters told all the men to line up against the garage wall and signaled their accomplices in plain clothes.

Then Capone's guys opened fire with two Thompson submachine guns.

When the smoke cleared, the fake officers escorted the plain-clothed assassins out of the building, hands raised, and led them to waiting getaway cars. Seven of Moran's men lay dead, limbs amputated by bullets, the garage painted with entrails, brains, and blood. Heads laid open like busted melons, some faces shredded so wickedly they were unidentifiable. Police found seventy Tommy gun and two shotgun casings on the floor or in the garage wall.

The vicious scene triggered the beginning of Capone's demise. Though Capone decimated one of his biggest rivals and scared the other one, Aiello, into submission, the carnage would prove too much for the government or the public to forget or forgive. It took years for me to realize I'd been involved in something so legendary. We didn't see it that way back then, and I sure as hell didn't want anyone knowing I'd helped plan the infamous Saint Valentine's Day Massacre. I didn't want to see what kind of attention that would garner, and I definitely didn't want people telling my younger sisters what I was involved in. It would crush them.

But Al wouldn't let us off the hook that easily when it came to laying low after Valentine's Day. He was on Palm Island in Florida the day of the events, but because of the discrete care my family showed him with the McSwiggin thing, he reached out to us when it came to hiding one of the triggermen, Fred Burke. I was hoping not to put my sister and her family in another predicament, but my brother-in-law Marco was a rock. I could trust him and, quite frankly, he wanted the responsibility.

Eventually, though, my sister started meeting with me face-to-face to lodge some complaints. All of them were understandable, and I would listen attentively. "I know, sis," I would say. "But what are we gonna do? It'll die down soon, and it'll all be over with. I promise."

I encouraged Fred to move along to his contact's place in St. Joseph, Michigan, as soon as he could. But when said he was "comfortable where I'm at," I knew exactly what my sister was talking about.

I told him to get out within two days, or he'd disappear.

"Does Al know you're demanding this?" he asked as we stood in my sister's living room.

"Al knows that we do whatever we want to do within our territory, and not only are you under protection in my territory, you're a guest in my family's home." I took a step toward him. "And I'm telling you, you've worn out your welcome. I'm not saying we can't help you out again, but for now, you're gone within two days. Go ahead and get word to Al. Not only will he not care, he'll ask if I've removed you from his list of possible rats from Valentine's Day."

It worked. Burke took off the next day, leaving a nice cash gift for my sister and brother-in-law for their hospitality. And, though I didn't get to disappear him, that strunz got what was coming to him.

Burke was arrested for homicide in December of '29 after getting into a car accident and shooting the patrolman who responded. When police raided the St. Joe home where Burke was hiding, they found a trunk containing two Thompson submachine guns, two shotguns, thousands of rounds of ammo, a bullet-proof vest, and $320,000 in bonds that had just been stolen from a Wisconsin bank. A new police science called ballistic testing directly linked the Tommy Guns to the massacre. He got sentenced to life in prison and ended up dying in his cell in 1940.

I never liked that sonofabitch.

WHEN IT LOOKED like timing couldn't get any weirder—or perhaps more perfect—I could always count on Dominic to show up.

I heard his signature knock on my parents' door just as we sat down for dinner, and I stood up and gave Dominic a hug. "Let me guess, you came back because you couldn't wait for your indictment and Sambiase is just too comfortable?"

"Heard I missed quite a storm."

My dad was a bit more pointed with his sarcasm. "And what, you want to return to the destruction to try to be a hero? I'm confused, nephew."

My mom interrupted. "Not now, boys. You can talk about such things later when the girls aren't around." She gestured to the table, where my sisters sat staring at us.

After dinner, we men started cutting up peaches to put into our wine and Dominic explained. "You're right, Uncle Luca. My timing is suspect. But by the time I heard what was going on, between the raids in The Heights and Capone's move on Moran, I'd already booked my trips."

I'm not sure if it was comedy or tragedy, but indictments were handed down against us just days later. Charges were brought against Dominic, Jon, me, and the Puzzi brothers, among other gangsters. But they also included some public officials, like Chicago Heights Chief of Police John Costabile, and the city's former chief, Ed Cassidy.

To no one's surprise, the indictments lacked substance. We were charged with conspiracy to violate the National Prohibition Act, but not gambling or murder, which seemed crazy. My formal charge was allowing a still to operate. Jon's was possession of alcohol. In the end, we each paid a few hundred dollars in fines. What a joke.

What the indictments made abundantly clear was the scope and scale of The Heights's operations. They charged that from January 1, 1925, to April 30, 1929, three million gallons of alcohol were manufactured in Chicago Heights at a value of $36 million to go along with annual gambling profits of $1.5 million. It was now quite evident why Capone had wanted to bring us, and The Heights, into The Outfit's fold.

Big, big money.

Dominic left in June and returned in November but was

detained at Ellis Island for a pending conspiracy investigation, which ended up lasting until February 1930. He wanted to get back to Italy but was afraid the Italians would deny him reentry. He decided to try the naturalization process but was denied for making false statements on his application, which included lying about his past marital record under oath. He was convicted and sentenced to two years in Leavenworth.

Dominic's prolonged absence gave Jon more control and a rise in stature for Guy and myself. All of it was personally approved by Capone, who saw no difference between Dom being away in Italy or sitting in a Kansas prison.

CHAPTER 14

Unimaginable Loss

By 1930, the Great Depression had hit, and my own luck seemed to be running out. Pat Roche, a chief investigator for the state's attorney's office, raided Chicago Heights in October of that year. He rounded up me, Guy, Coz, Nick Soldini, Tony Moltesanto, and three others on suspicion so he could run our names through the Bureau of Investigation. Roche found nothing, other than that I was frequently seen hanging around Capone's headquarters. No shit. That's all these idiots had. Many wondered how long it would take for the feds to get their act together and gather real intelligence on us.

Capone's reign as leader of The Outfit also came to an end. He'd gotten pinched for carrying a gun in '29 and served a nine-month sentence. Nineteen months after his release, in October 1931, Al was sent back up the river for eleven years on the tax evasion charge aided by the Oli Esti raid.

About a year later, though the Depression hadn't hurt my pocketbook, the foundation of my world cracked open underneath me.

The saddest thing is, it had nothing to do with me or my participation in the rackets.

It really had been a pleasant November day in 1932. I met Jon for lunch to go over some things we wanted to start in Cal City, then showed up at the family store to help my dad unload a big delivery. Like always, he told me that my mother would like it if I joined them for dinner, saying my younger sisters were requesting my presence. And, like always, I showed up. When possible, I did everything I could to preserve how my sisters saw me. It was quite a special night, full of eating and laughing. Just before I was set to leave, my dad said he'd walk me to my car because he was heading to John Sposato's and might play some cards if any other fellas showed up.

Two-and-a-half hours later, I got a frantic call from my mother. Through uncontrollable crying, she told me to meet her at the city morgue.

We had to identify my father.

I have no recollection of driving to the coroner's office. Holding my hysterical mom as we sobbed over my dad's body was the only thing I clearly remembered from that day, and it replayed in my head for years.

Rage traded places with sadness when I finally got hold of the coroner's inquiry. My father had been shot twice in the chest. Mom made me promise, through our tears, that I wouldn't take revenge. My sisters "would really need their big brother now that their dad was gone." I cried harder and promised myself I would always do whatever I could to help my sisters.

Sposato was at my front door by six a.m. the next day, and I invited him in for some coffee. He was shaking, visibly upset over the tragedy that had unfolded in his home.

"When your father arrived, the family was finishing dinner," he said. "Luca was sitting in my wife's chair as she cleaned the dishes and the kids cleared the table. We were drinking wine and catching up, which was the whole point of your dad and Luigi Cianpini coming over. When Luigi showed up, Maria took the kids upstairs for baths and bed."

Sposato sipped his coffee, pausing before he got to the shooting. "We were having a really nice time until the subject of money came up. That led to discussion of Cianpini's unpaid grocery tab at your family's store. Cianpini made a casual comment about how his business was finally taking off. Your dad smiled and told him, Good, then you can pay off your debt to the store. Cianpini took exception, even though it was obvious your dad was only busting his coglioni. When Luca saw that Cianpini was angry, he got a bit more serious. Why brag about your successful business if you still have debts to your friend's business? he asked. Cianpini reached into his pocket and pulled out some money. Your dad told him if he wanted to settle up, do it at the store and keep business, business. Cianpini threw the cash on the floor. That was when I stepped in. They were chest to chest, and I could see Maria looking down from the top of the stairs. She wasn't happy. I urged them both to relax, to go home and forget about the whole thing. Cianpini grabbed his jacket and was heading for the door when your dad said something that just set the whole thing off."

Bile and anger swirled in my queasy stomach. "What did he say?"

"Well, after I told them to go home, your dad told Luigi to forget the debt to the store because he'd need the money to feed his family after his piece of shit business failed. At that, Luigi, who was nearly at the front door, spun around, drew his .38, and began firing shots off. Your dad pulled a .32 from his coat pocket, and the gun battle was on, right in the middle of my house with my family screaming upstairs. After ten shots were fired back and forth, your dad got hit in the chest and Luigi took a few in the stomach. Luca died almost immediately, and Cianpini died a few hours later." Sposato was fighting back tears as he finished. "I lost two of my best friends over a dumb argument about money."

I cried with him for a few minutes, then hugged and thanked him for coming to tell me directly so I didn't have to wait for the authorities. I raced to see my mother and said she didn't need to worry about me seeking revenge. As far as all the families were concerned, it was a tragedy that should be buried with our fathers. I told Luigi's wife that she didn't need to worry about the debt to the store or any type of feud as long as her oldest son let the incident go.

I spent at least half the week with my devastated sisters and mom. A cloud hung over the house for months as we tried to cope. I was busy selling the stores because my mom wanted nothing to do with them. I gave her money every week so she never had to worry and supported my sisters until they all got married off. Then I gave my brothers-in-law jobs when they wanted or needed them.

I BLINKED AND nearly missed Prohibition's repeal on December 5, 1933. I was so busy with my mom, sisters, and our various rackets that I barely remember the details. Jon and I had seen it coming, and I was surprised Prohibition lasted as long as it did. Unfortunately, our very lucrative booze business dried up, so keeping the Depression from hitting us meant reallocating our efforts into gambling and pushing into unions.

At about the same time, Dominic was permanently deported to Italy. It's ironic how hard Capone and Dominic fought for years to gain the control they had, yet they had to hand over the reins shortly thereafter. But Dom didn't retire. He set up shop in Sambiase and entrenched himself with Calabria's 'Ndrangheta crime syndicate, which worked like its most famous cousin, Sicily's La Cosa Nostra. There was also the Camorra, based in Naples and the Campania region. There were other organizations in Italy, but these three tended to dominate control.

From what I heard, Dom brought Chicago's ruthlessness to Sambiase when he muscled in on the action there. I would see Dominic when I went back to visit family, but that was only every few years or so during the '30s and '40s. Jon would also travel to

Calabria and Rome to go over things and see Dominic on every trip. In fact, throughout the forties, Jon and Dominic met with Lucky Luciano in Rome. What were they ironing out?

Things that our thing supposedly wasn't involved in. That's what.

Also throughout the thirties, my sisters all got married. The ceremonies were beautiful but always bittersweet because my dad wasn't there. And remember those Fazio boys from Hungry Hill? Two of them became my brothers-in-law. Tony Fazio married my sister Concetta and Aldo married my sister Angelica. Sofia married a nice medigan, Ben Thomas, and Lucia wed Joe DeCarlo. Gia, my youngest sister, married Joe Rosetta.

My last sister to get married was Valentina, who in about '43 ended up with a Fazio cousin in California. For Valentina, I threw two receptions. The first was in Chicago Heights, and the second was where they lived out West. I rented rail cars for family and friends who would be crossing the country to attend, two Pullmans for sleeping and a third retrofitted into an extravagant lounge where we could all gather and party while watching the miles zip away.

Let me tell you something, when it comes to my kind of business—where you need to trust people unequivocally—there is no substitute for family. And with the exception of Valentina's husband, all of these brothers-in-law, including Marco, did or would come work for me.

ALSO THROUGHOUT THE early to mid-1930s, Jon and I worked tirelessly on strengthening and expanding our political contacts. This was important, especially considering we no longer had Capone to rely on in Chicago.

The Outfit had several leaders after Al was sent to a pen in Atlanta and, eventually, Alcatraz. There was Tony Accardo, who liked to keep a low profile like Jon and me. There was Sam 'Momo' Giancana, who was a bit like Al and appeared to be fine in the public spotlight. They were a decent complement to one another, I guess. Then there was Paul Ricca. I knew Al liked him a lot. He was a Napoletano like Capone. I liked him, too. There were times I thought Ricca should just be the boss because he seemed to be a good balance between Accardo and Giancana. I can't forget about Joey Auippa, who took over Cicero after Capone left. He was a gentleman and the real deal. What about Nitti? Good guy, but I don't think he ever wanted to run The Outfit.

Anyway, those were the big four who led Chicago post-Capone. Jon and I had a good relationship with all the boys in Chicago. We had history with all four of those guys. As for the younger guys beneath them, I can't speak to that.

Besides getting our friends back in place in The Heights after those meddlesome raids, we had tremendous success in locking down Calumet City. We knew Cal City would be a main source of income for decades to come if we maintained our political capital there and didn't attract attention.

It was probably late in '35 when Jon called me over for a family dinner to discuss what we'd accomplished over the last few years and how he saw us moving forward. After a delicious meal—and offering to help wash the dishes but being rebuffed by Jon's incredible wife—Jon led me to his study, two cocktails in his hands.

"Your wife is a doll, Jon. She's always so attentive and sweet."

For a second, I was afraid I'd overstepped. I was a bachelor who wanted what Jon had—the ability to balance the life of a racketeer and the life of a family man. My hurt for a wife and children had shone through my carefully constructed armor.

But Jon didn't seem to mind. "She's definitely one in a million. And it's funny you should say that. Family is kinda what I want to talk to you about."

"Of course,," I said, relieved. "There's nothing more important than family."

"I've also been wanting to spend more time concentrating on my passion—horses and racing."

"Sure, Jon. No worries."

"I'm not stepping down," he said. "I am, however, handing the day-to-day reins over to you. I'll be in Florida for at least three to five months vacationing with the family and running at the tracks there. I'll also be running in Louisville, Kansas City, and New Orleans regularly. But while I'm doing all of this, I'll be networking. We need to establish or buy the wire services in Louisville and New Orleans. That way, we'll be ahead of the other families out east. This will only increase Chicago's clout nationwide and make The Heights that much more integral within The Outfit itself."

"I love it."

"I know we promised Joe Cosenza a joint to run in Cal City, and he will, but I also want him to be one of our point guys in setting up and helping us run these wire services in New Orleans and Louisville."

"I'm sure he'll be ecstatic when you tell him," I said. "But let me ask you something. What exactly does this mean for me?"

"Quite a lot, actually. Like I said, you'll be in charge of day-to-day operations in our territory while I'm out of town. But I want you to run all of Calumet City for us. Everyone answers to you and only you. If you want to run something past me, great. Otherwise, when it comes to Cal City, you answer to no one. Besides Cal City, you are now in charge of all slots and handbooks throughout our territory."

I nodded. "Sounds good to me. I obviously appreciate your trust in me."

"Salvatore, I cannot think of someone more ready for this. You're capable of running the entire Outfit. In fact, if you lived in

Chicago, Al may have picked you. He probably loved you and Dom more than his own guys. I know he trusted you more."

"Actually, I'm thankful I'm in The Heights. I wouldn't want to compete with Auippa, Ricca, Accardo, or Momo. I'm happy we get to work with those guys and not against them, and I think The Outfit is positioned to accomplish great things. Especially once we have control of the wire services."

"I'm thankful you're in The Heights, too. We both know Chicago will always control The Outfit. Honestly, we've always wanted it that way, have we not? You came to me a long time ago and advised isolation and to avoid media attention at all costs. Remember that? You were so right." He took a drink and smiled. "Hell, you remember when your dad first sent you my way for leadership? Look at you now. Look at us now."

I smiled back. "I do, Jon. I remember. We've come a long way."

I gave him a hug goodbye, and that was it. For all intents and purposes, Jon had made it clear.

I was in charge of The Heights.

WHEN JON STARTED to network nationally, I only spoke to him when I needed advice. New York and Accardo also reached out to him, which was fine by me. I didn't want a target on my back right after we'd dodged the last indictments with only a $300 fine.

Jon did want me to talk to Joe Coz before he contacted him with any specifics, and fortunately I bumped into him a few nights later at one of our joints in Cal City.

"Salvatore, que si dice?" Coz asked as we embraced.

"Let me buy you some drinks. You got a couple minutes to spare? I'd like to fill you in on some stuff if we can find a quiet corner."

We made our way to a back room of the club and settled in with drinks.

"Jon wanted me to touch base with you about some things we're looking to get into."

"Sounds good. I am eager to hear what you guys have in mind."

"Let's start with Calumet City. Jon and I are going to get you a gambling joint to run. I have no details right now, but I think I'll get you a new one so you can get it set up based on your own vision."

"Wait a second. You're going to get me a new joint?"

"Yeah. Jon has put me in charge of Calumet City because he's going to be on the road a lot."

"Congrats, Sal. That's great for you. I'm glad I get to work with you and I'm grateful to Jon."

"Your family has been loyal and hard-working for years. Especially you, Joe. You've given your entire self to this organization. Jon knows that and has even more in mind for you."

Coz looked like a man who'd just shed a thousand pounds. "Thank you. I'd been hoping this would happen soon. Can you tell me anything about what Jon's thinking?"

"Well, I'll tell you what I can tell you. Like I mentioned, Jon will be on the road a lot more. He'll be spending time in Florida with his family and his horses. He'll also travel to Louisville, Kansas City, New Orleans, where he'll be networking."

"Wow. Okay. How do I fit in?"

"Besides running your own joint in Cal City, Jon wants you to set up wire services in New Orleans and Louisville. Our wire results will be disseminated across the country, and the services will be huge in keeping Chicago Heights and The Outfit an integral cog in the national gambling machine, which is more important than ever now that booze is legal again. Everyone will need to come to us. New York is ignoring almost everything west of their noses."

Coz nodded and smiled. "This sounds huge for us and a great opportunity for me, Sal."

"It is. Jon is gonna have you set up, take over, and protect the interests he establishes. But when it comes to your joint in Calumet City, you'll answer to me and only me."

"Understood. Thanks again."

"You deserve it, Joe."

We both stood up, clanked our rocks glasses together, and put back the rest of our scotch.

CHAPTER 15

Vice Paradise

One of my other big projects in the late 1930s was working deeper into labor unions. Why? If you control the union and its officials, you control the dues. You have access to pension funds and good construction jobs. And let's not forget about the kickbacks. With control of the unions, we'd gain access to cheap loans so we could develop and expand our endeavors.

Whenever possible, we put our guys in positions of influence at the unions. Our selections came from families we knew well or guys who were already part of our crew in The Heights. One of those guys was Dante Fazio, who you may recall was the oldest Fazio brother and the brick-wielding kid who ran into the house of the bully who was harassing his younger sister.

Dante started off in the Local 5 of the HOD Carriers, which became the Laborers' Union, consisting mostly of bricklayers. He worked his way up to business agent when the Local 5 became the Laborers' Local around 1941. Nunzio Neroni, who served The Heights for decades, was a union representative in the Local 5 before he handed the title off to Fazio. Vince Pizzoli, who caught Jon's eye when he was a bookie at Balmoral race track, started off pulling weight in the unions and it was big-time for us. It was guys like that who took prominent roles within the unions, cultivating the power and political influence that The Heights and The Outfit have today.

We also had guys in the Common Laborers' Union, which

represented ditch diggers and asphalt spreaders. We steered away from the Barbers' Union, though. These sons-of-bitches were run by socialists, and my father was right in warning me to steer clear of the socialists and their ways. They're bad for business. In fact, Jon and I did everything we could to support political candidates who were running against socialists during the thirties.

Jon was tirelessly networking with politicians for the whole decade. One politician in particular, John Macky, had to be caressed. Macky was actually one of Dominic's best catches, and Dom even maintained the relationship while in Leavenworth before his deportation.

Macky was a successful construction contractor when Dominic first started dealing with him. When Macky decided to go into politics, Dom, Jon, and I always did what we could for him. Macky was serving as head of the County Central Committee for the Republican party in '34 and would eventually go on to serve as Cook County commissioner. It was crucial we kept him happy, which Jon ensured after Dominic wasn't around.

Let's also be quite clear about something. Jon and I may have voted Republican, and Jon was a member of the Republican order of Chicago Heights, but we contributed to plenty of Democrats, too. We contributed to whatever party was going to best serve our interests. That was my real political affiliation. I mean, we had to deal with that reform Democrat who got elected mayor of Chicago Heights in '35. Jon made sure he was happy so our vice and gambling interests could continue to operate unmolested. Jon and I had connections in Blue Island, Hammond, Harvey, Steger, Dixmoor, Willow Springs, Kankakee, South Chicago Heights, Calumet Park, and the ever-more lucrative Joliet.

However, what Jon and I accomplished in Calumet City was historic.

Sure, it was lucky for us Cal City was still as corruptible as it was during Prohibition in the twenties. By the mid-thirties, Jon and I had Cal City's police chief and all fifteen of the city's officers on payroll. You want to talk about owning an entire town with access to thousands of factory workers looking to blow off some steam? Fuhgeddaboudit.

With Prohibition over, Nitti was pressing his lieutenants to find new sources of income and to push harder into gambling, and we had the politicians in Cal City. Now, Jon and I had to consolidate all the joints under our control. So yes, we were The Boys in The Heights, but Calumet City was our cash cow. Jon and I had a vision on how to build a Vice Paradise, so to speak—a Sin City with a Strip of countless options. If things fell into place, Cal City would become a national destination, and it would all be run by The Heights.

Where do you think Las Vegas got the nicknames Sin City and The Strip?

BEING IN CHARGE of Cal City meant I was ultimately responsible when something went wrong. I wasn't going to let that happen, which meant I could only put into position of power those people I trusted wholeheartedly.

I put some brothers-in-law to work, but I also brought in Peter Banino. I'd known Pete for twenty-something of my thirty-something years. Back in 1928, the Sicilian racketeers in New York thought it would be a good idea to have a national meeting in Cleveland. Capone, who was still harassed by the Unione Siciliana in Chicago, came to The Heights for help. Back then, there were very few Sicilian gangsters who Capone, Dominic, Jon, and I trusted, but Peter was one of them. Al wanted him to attend under an alias to add a layer of protective insulation for everyone, so Banino attended that national meeting under the alias Tony Bello and Capone didn't have to worry about any Sicilian coup attempts coming out of Cleveland.

I asked Pete to open a legitimate business on the Strip to help us clean and move cash. He opened Jimmy's Pizzeria in 1934, I think, and it's still around today. Ultimately, Banino was trusted with large sums of money, which meant I really trusted him. Some can't handle the temptation to skim, and I don't want people to put me in a position where I need to discipline them. Then there's the guys who the thought of stealing doesn't even enter their consciousness. Banino was one of those. My brother-in-law, Tony Fazio, was another.

So, we had all the Cal City cops and politicians in our pocket. We just had to finish consolidating every joint in Cal City under our crew's control, just like we'd done with bootlegging in The Heights. Everyone was falling into place with zero pushback.

Well, almost everyone.

There was this one guy—we called him the Dutchman—who ran independently on the Strip around 1935. We had to give the Dutchman some respect, though. He knew Jon and I didn't want to attract negative press with violence, so he stood firm as long as he could. First, we had the workers strike against him. When that didn't work, I had Pete and Coz organize some of Jon's prize fighters to rip the place apart. That didn't work either.

But as one of Jon's boxers was giving him a once-over, the Dutchman coughed up some blood and—as he was spitting out some teeth—he felt the need to send me a message.

"Tell those fucking WOPS, Allen and Liparello, that I won't sell to them. Not ever. I'd rather die than give those fucks my joint. I'm not afraid of you greasy dagos! If you ain't Dutch, you ain't much."

That was the last thing he said before getting knocked the fuck out.

A couple nights later, I went to see the Dutchman personally. His disdain and lack of respect had painted me into a corner. Jon and I could not have guys like him talking that kind of shit without repercussions. That kind of thing can snowball into an avalanche before you know it, so I had to send a message to everyone—including my equals in Chicago—that Jon and I were to be obeyed or suffer dearly. Unfortunately, messages of torture and death were the only kind sunk in with most of these types, so torture and death were both headed the Dutchman's way.

I brought Joe Coz and two others on this mission, which was now personal.

"Coz, you know how you're gonna pick him up?" I said, fully expecting a prepared answer.

"He leaves his club at the same time every night. And every other night, he stops at his girlfriend's place before he heads home. We'll pick him up when he gets out of his car at the girl's place, and one of our guys take his car for disposal."

"Sounds like a start. How you gonna finish the job?"

"Still working on those details. Any ideas?"

"Make him feel it before he's gone," I said, envisioning what all Coz and the others might do. "Make sure you remind him of all the shit he said about me, Jon, and Italians in general. Make sure he's reminded he could have sold and made money versus being in the predicament he's in. And make sure when word gets around Cal City, The Heights, and Chicago, that no one will want what happened to the Dutchman to happen to them. I want people to know that when I ask for something the only answer is Yes.'"

"You got it, Sal. No reason for me to give you the details. Probably better if you don't know them, anyway."

"You trust these guys you're taking along?"

"One hundred percent. I wouldn't even have considered them if I wasn't positive. I mean, my life depends on it."

"Great. Have you heard from Jon about helping out with the wire services?"

"Oh, yeah. I'm really excited to get going on that. And If you have any ideas for my new joint, let me know. I mean, I'm open for suggestions."

"I suggest you make a lot of money," I started laughing before I could get all the words out.

Cosenza smiled back. "Yeah, yeah."

"Just kidding, Joe. If I think of something, I'll let you know."

"Sounds good. And I'll let you know when the Dutchman is taken care of."

TWO MORNINGS LATER, there was a knock at my door.

"Morning, Joe. Come in. I just put on a pot of coffee."

"Thanks. The Dutchman is no more."

"No loose ends?"

"No loose ends."

"How'd it go down?"

"We picked him up on his cumare's street. When we followed him, we had cars in the front and rear, and we converged as soon as he got out. Nicky grabbed him and tossed him into the car, where I was waiting. I kept a gun pointed to his head the whole drive. He knew he wasn't coming back."

"Did you move the Dutchman's car?"

"Yep. Nicky's brother took it straight to our wrecking yard for permanent disposal. That went off without a hitch. The car is burnt out and already dismantled."

I nodded. "What happened next?"

"He was treated like a hostile enemy and given no quarter. He didn't have much to say at first, but while we were driving to the vacant building, he actually got a little mouthy. He started cursing us, you, and Jon. Calling us stupid WOPs and greasy smelly guineas. I was so tired of hearing him spit bullets, I began pistol whipping him, but I made sure he never lost consciousness." Coz stopped a beat before continuing. "Once we had him tied to a table, arms and legs spread open and secured, he got a lot quieter."

"Whoa. You weren't messing around, were ya?"

"Well, you said you wanted a message sent. Once word leaks about what we did, I don't think you'll hear the word no much anymore."

"Okay. So how'd he leave us?"

"I told the Dutchman his mouth was a major source of his problems, so Nicky pulled his tongue with a pair of pliers, cut it out, and laid it across his face. He tried screaming, but he was choking on so much blood it came out as a wet cough."

I could see everything Coz was describing and motioned for him to continue.

"Then I told him we'd need to cut him into pieces to get rid of him easier. He let out a cry so loud I thought he'd wake the dead. Next, Nicky took an ice pick to his eyes. He was thrashing around so much I thought that big fucker might bust the table and break free, so we just stabbed him in the neck a bunch of times. After he bled to death, we cut him up and disposed of him nice and proper. No one will find him … well, what's left of him."

When I'd imagined what they would do to the Dutchman, I couldn't have pictured anything like that. "Christ, Coz, I have never heard of such brutality. Are you okay?"

He looked toward my face, but his eyes were focused on some invisible spot a mile past me. "I'm not sure if I can do another one of those for a while, Sal. I still smell the blood. Taste it, too. Just this lingering metallic taste, like I'm sucking on a fucking penny. And the images … it's all I see when I close my eyes."

"I understand. Get out of town for a while. Head down to Louisville and meet Jon. I'll tell him you need to lay low for a week and you can help with wire service setup."

He blinked, then returned to the present. "Yeah. Sounds good."

I gave Coz another attaboy, though I knew no amount of praise would help.

Time was the only thing that could.

CHAPTER 16

Expansion

The entire Cal City Strip was now under The Heights's thumb, and a couple weeks after we dealt with The Dutchman, Jon returned and told me we were going downtown for an important meeting the following night.

"Anything I should know in advance?" I asked as we sat in the Lucky's office. "You know I don't like walking into these things cold."

"It's about Cal City and opening a new joint. I want you there for all the obvious reasons."

"Sounds good. I'll have Toots Potenza drive us down. Call me tomorrow and let me know what time you want to get picked up."

Once we were on our way, Jon let me know we'd be having dinner with Accardo.

"So Tony wants some direct action on the Strip?" I asked.

"Can you blame him? He knows what we have created in Cal City."

"Whatever you think, I'm behind you. You know that. By the way, it obviously doesn't matter, but what restaurant are we heading to?"

"Ristoranti Accardo, Sal," Jon answered with a little chuckle.

"We're going to his house?"

Jon nodded. "Just the three of us at Tony's place." Jon leaned forward and put his hand on Toot's shoulder. "Sorry. You're going to have to wait for us in the car."

Toots looked back at us through the rear view mirror. "No worries, Boss. I don't need to eat."

"We'll send out a plate and some wine, if possible," I said.

At Accardo's driveway, we were greeted by two armed men waiting for our arrival and Tony came out to welcome us. We started with a pre-dinner cocktail in his study before diving into homemade veal scallopini and fresh angel hair. I was chomping at the bit, waiting for Tony or Jon to bring up business. Finally, as the table was being cleared, the new venture came up.

"Jon," Accardo started, "I have to say that I'm really excited that you returned my call about future partnership opportunities in Cal City."

"Absolutely. I don't think Sal and I will have any issues working with you."

"I trust you both. What do you have in mind?"

"We recently secured a building, but it's going to require thirty to forty grand worth of upgrades to get to our specifications. It's going to have first-rate entertainment and, of course, plenty of gambling. It'll be open until 4 a.m. and re-open at 6 a.m., practically 24 hours every day."

"Sounds impressive. Do you have a name for it yet?"

"No, but—"

"May I?" I interjected.

"By all means," Accardo said.

"How about the Owl Club? A night stalker. Up all night."

Jon smiled. "The Owl Club. I love it."

"You just come up with that on the spot?" Accardo asked.

"Actually, yes. Just now."

"The instincts on this guy! Capone was right. I see why you keep him close and happy, Jon. I'll take the max percentage on the

Owl Club."

"How about a fifty percent stake?" Jon offered.

"Done."

"Sal is my guy in Cal City. He runs the town, and all day-to-day decisions are his. The club should be ready early next year. Looks like '36 will be a great year for us."

Accardo stood and raised his glass. "Saluti, gentlemen. To the Owl Club."

"To the Owl Club!"

AS I WAS focusing my efforts on the Cal City Strip, Jon was networking for Nitti and the entire Outfit to take more control of the wires.

Publisher Moe Annenberg had been our point man since getting in on the service. But Al's guy, reporter and fixer Jake Lingle, was found shot dead in 1930 wearing his gold and diamond-studded belt buckle on his way to the Washington Park race track. Rumor was Lingle hadn't been able to secure a stake in the General News Bureau for Capone. Nitti knew Jon was deeply involved and expanding his racing interests, so he appointed Jon to continue pushing harder to procure independent wire service operations by any means necessary.

I'm pretty sure it was 1935 when Jon asked Joe Coz to visit some independent books doing decent size in Louisville, St. Louis, and New Orleans. Coz brought some muscle with him to persuade the independents to join in, get taken over, or get eliminated. Jon, meanwhile, was busy successfully brokering a deal to buy out a Countrywide Service minority owner for $750,000.

Everyone wanted in on wire control. Even Western Union and AT&T jockeyed for the sixteen thousand miles of wires, leased to over three hundred handbook locations across the country. AT&T

took over after Western Union had to abandon its lucrative relationship with the country's illegal bookies in 1935 due to reform pressures. At the time, Western Union was leasing those wire lines for $2 million a year. I think Countrywide paid AT&T half a million to lease the lines. They were the company's fifth largest client at the time. I know Lansky and Luciano were happy about what Jon and Humphrey accomplished.

All the way back in 1929, there was a conference hosted by Meyer Lanksy, Frank Zingaro, and Johnny Torrio in Atlantic City. It was at that meeting that they were educated on the value of a national wire service and encouraged to own one.

Well, The Boys in The Heights got it done.

With The Outfit's influence over Countrywide Service, they now controlled race wires stretching across the United States, Canada, Cuba, and Mexico. This actually started an interesting link between Jon and Lucky Luciano. Their interest in racing would lead to a long friendship and cooperation between New York, Chicago, and Dominic back in Italy.

In addition to controlling the wire service, we wanted to control the racing forms, which were huge for those betting on the ponies. This made ownership of the printing companies an important revenue stream to the racketeering families across the country.

Jon was always in communication with the families before he came to town if he was looking to run his horses. Many of these meetings were with Carlos Marcello in New Orleans regarding operations and splits. We got a piece of the NOLA Printing Company out of that. Jon would only be a minority owner with Carlos but it still gave Chicago Heights and the Chicago Outfit influence in New Orleans and the racing form racket. NOLA Printing acted as the primary distributor for the race results of Fair

Grounds Racetrack and Jefferson Downs Racetrack. NOLA would compile, print, and distribute The Sports Bulletin daily—except Sundays—for fifty cents at newsstands or for twelve bucks with a monthly subscription. These bulletins would be sent directly to the horse track bookies along with the line sheets, which NOLA also printed.

But The Sports Bulletin wasn't just for the New Orleans tracks. Oh, no. It contained listings of horses, jockeys, post times, and the track odds for races held at Belmont Park, Arlington Park, Suffolk Downs, Monmouth Park, and Detroit. At the time, most bookies offered maximum odds of twenty to one. So, to avoid confusion, The Sports Bulletin adjusted track odds from twenty to one downward. Brilliant.

WHILE I WAS getting the Cal City Strip consolidated, a little birdie told me something very valuable. The mayor of Calumet City found himself in some serious tax trouble. He owed a hundred thousand in back taxes, so I got a hold of Jon immediately to pitch the situation as an incredible opportunity for us. Jon said I was right and contacted the mayor, telling him to meet me for lunch at Pete Banino's place.

The next day, the mayor and I had our little sit-down. The joint was closed to the public but I still situated myself in the back corner booth so I could see the length of the restaurant to the front door. I wanted the mayor to feel my eyes on him as he walked past every red-and-white checkered plastic table cloth until he arrived at the booth I was situated in.

Then this strunz had the nerve to show up nearly ten minutes late.

Nothing pisses me off more than when people are late for engagements. It's disrespectful. Period.

When the mayor finally got there, it was just the two of us and Pete, though I'd do all the talking.

"Salvatore, good to see you," he started. "Jon said we should talk."

I sneered at my watch. "Sit down."

The mayor rubbed his neck and glanced around the room. "What's this all about?"

"We hear you have some tax issues."

"Rumors," he said, clearing his throat. "It's no big deal."

"Don't insult my intelligence." I said, almost spitting through my teeth.

"Okay, okay. I just didn't want you and Jon to be concerned."

"Mayor, here's how it's gonna be. You owe the Feds a hundred K. Jon is going to give you the money to settle your debt."

"Jon doesn't need to do that. I have it under control."

I slammed my palm on the table. "Listen here, motherfucker. God knows how long you haven't paid your taxes. How fucking dumb are you? It's obvious that you have absolutely nothing under control."

The mayor lowered his head. "I'm sorry, Sal."

"So let me tell you how this is going to work. Jon gives you the money to get the IRS off your back and, in return, we run Cal City wide open and unscathed. Got it?"

He nodded quickly. "Understood. Your businesses will never run into local problems, and if any agents ever ask questions, I don't know nothing about nothing."

"Now you're starting to make sense. Jon will get you the money this week. If I find out that any of this cash went to anything other than your tax debt, your tenure as mayor will end quite abruptly. Understand?"

"Yes." He glanced over his shoulder. "Tell Jon I'm grateful and looking forward to a prosperous relationship."

"I will. You can leave now."

The mayor scuttled out of there like a teenager who'd just stared down the barrel of his girlfriend's father's shotgun.

WITH CAL CITY organized and completely under our thumb, I looked to expand our slots territory in The Heights.

It wasn't hard.

Since the twenties, we'd created a red-light district by way of mutually beneficial agreements with The Heights's politicians to not operate in plain sight—unlike the slots in Cicero. So, we had to get creative about the locations of our machines.

Places where clubs and fraternal organizations met were perfect, and we did a solid job of finding them. We had our machines at the Catholic Veterans Club, the Loyal Order of Moose, the Christopher Columbus Society, the Polish Falcons, and the Military Order of the Purple Heart, just to name a few. Hell, I was even able to fill the garage of St. Agatha's church garage with slot machines. I gave them a 50/50 split.

It was also time to refocus on building the Owl Club. It had to be seen as the nation's premier gambling joint. I wanted guys in New York to drool over what we were building on the Cal City Strip. It had to be simple and efficient, so we constructed a wide open rectangle with betting windows along one of the walls. Racing results would be posted on another of the main floor walls. One of the smartest things I did was ensure there was always a stocked buffet. If we filled our customers' bellies and quenched their thirst while they were gambling, they wouldn't see the need to leave the establishment and their endurance to bet or play would increase by at least a few hours. There was also a section of the floor that accommodated craps, poker, and roulette tables. A back section of the main level was reserved for priority clients. No scumbags allowed. We had entertainment back there, with tables, chairs, and waitress service.

And yes, this was in the wide open. Remember, we had the whole city on our payroll. The club took on different iterations over two and a half decades, but this was the basic setup most of the time.

My dad had been gone for a handful of years now, and I missed his advice. He was the one who taught me how to recognize people's angles. Sure, I have a good radar, but nothing compared with a father's guidance. Now that I was in charge of a truly wide-open Sin City, there were plenty of times I wished I could've asked my dad for his thoughts. When building my team, I often asked myself, What would Dad say? He would offer opinions but, in the end, he'd always say the same thing. "You have amazing instincts. Better than me. Follow them. Your gut feeling is probably correct, son."

Eventually, Jon became the guy I went to with such questions. Even though he was my boss, I'd known him since I was thirteen. He knew my personality intricacies—the real me—better than any man alive, even Dominic.

Anyway, I started to put guys I felt I could trust into management positions—or onto the business licenses themselves—to insulate myself, give them responsibility, and show them respect. And respect works both ways. I wanted it as their superior, but I knew that if they felt disrespected, a knife in the back wasn't far off.

My brother-in-law, Tony Fazio, helped me manage the daily duties at the club, and I let him handle the money without a care in the world. He was one of the few who didn't have sticky fingers. He could also run a game like only a few could.

Joe Coz also had his place up and running. I helped keep an eye on things when Jon called him down south to help with racing and wire issues. Jon did that a lot, because he knew what I knew.

Coz didn't leave loose ends.

CHAPTER 17

World War

Things ran smoothly until World War II broke out. I enlisted in the Navy, and I wasn't the only one from my crew who signed up. My brothers-in-law Don Fazio and Joe Rosetta, for whom I had just found jobs, enlisted in the Marines.

I ended up as a cook stationed at the Great Lakes Naval Air Station in the northern suburbs of Chicago, and I loved spoiling the soldiers I was out with. I used my connections to bring in the best steaks from the Union Stockyards and fresh seafood from the South Water Market. I prepared large, elaborate meals, complete with pasta and cheese courses, wine, and homemade desserts from my connections at the Taylor Street bakeries. The boys ate like kings and deserved it for the sacrifice they were making.

I loved telling them about the cabaret places in Calumet City. Whenever I had a chance, I took a few with me to show them a good time. Most of the servicemen didn't have a means to get to the Strip, so I eventually arranged cabs for them. We'd pick them up in Chicago and take them to Cal City and back. Their eyes would pop out of their heads when they saw how I was treated whenever I entered a joint. When I pulled cash out of my pocket, their eyes grew even bigger. We'd be on our way back to the air station, and I'd give them a wink and say, "Remember, I'm just your cook." They'd always respond the same way. "Whatever you say, Sal."

The guys would then tell stories about how girls and gambling were in the wide open on the Cal City Strip. Well, I don't need to tell you how much G.I.s love girls, gambling, and booze. They weren't stingy with their cash, either. They saw and heard bad things but didn't hold back on having a good time when the opportunity presented itself. Of course, when they came with me, everything was on the house. I used these G.I. trips as a chance to check in and see how things looked at night while I was stationed away.

Despite my desire to maintain a low profile, there were always a few people who would stop by my table to say hello. Some people just didn't get it. I often excused myself to the bathroom when I wanted to talk to whoever I had left in charge. Sometimes I'd be gone for twenty to thirty minutes, and my innocent guests would say, "Sal, you okay? We were about to send a search party after you." They also loved to joke and say, "Sal, we thought you fell in!" Man, I loved setting those boys up with our best girls, too. The ladies would look at me, and I'd just nod to the boys I was sitting with. They'd give the young patriots the attention they deserved.

JOE COSENZA WASN'T in the war. Too old to enlist. I was eventually discharged because of my age, too, but Coz was one of my main sources of help while I was in the Navy. Guy was an invaluable pair of eyes and ears as well. Of course, Pete Banino and I were always communicating, and Tony always gave me unfiltered, straight-up answers and genuinely had my best interests at heart. I also liked and trusted Toots.

There was someone else who knew Ricca and had just gotten out of college—what we affectionately called prison—who was looking to hook up with a crew. Guy had heard good things about him from the boys in Chicago, and we needed a hard worker who could help out while I was out of pocket. This go-getter was known around town as Ricky the Bomber. Ricky got his start working for a Northside crew. His mentor, King of the Bombers Bellini, headed Capone's bomb squad throughout the twenties. Ricky got pinched for possessing a dynamite bomb around 1933, got paroled and was let out from Joliet State Prison in '42.

That same year, I pulled Tony aside for a quick chat when I had some G.I.s at the Owl Club.

"I think you're doing a knockout job for me here in Cal City," I said. "I'm looking to expand gambling into northwest Indiana, southern Cook County, and Will County. I'm looking for someone to find safe places to set up high-stakes poker games for the high rollers and regular poker games for the ordinary guys. This is something that would need to move around to avoid heat from authorities. I want that someone to be you. You think you can take this on for me?"

"No problem. I'll get started tomorrow. And I appreciate the vote of confidence."

"The high-stakes poker guys like and respect you. Word is, they feel safe if the game is run by you. Plus, I know I can trust you with the cash."

"Thanks, Sal. Your sister and I could use the extra cash right about now."

This was the first I'd heard of money troubles with them. "Is there a problem I should know about?"

"Oh, no. On the contrary. She's pregnant with number two!"

I smiled so hard my face hurt. "Holy shit! That's wonderful, Tony! Well, I'm glad you'll have the chance to make some more scratch."

"Absolutely. I got you covered."

I HAD MY guys in place, and things ran pretty smoothly and quietly while I was away. Like most Italian-Americans, I was happy to fight for my country. I don't think any of us could understand how

Mussolini ever came into power. He was an embarrassment, and I would gladly have killed him myself with a smile on my face.

Meanwhile, Cal City was running on all cylinders. Ricky the Bomber was pulling shotguns on any club owner who thought he was more important than he was and tried to deliver light envelopes. He was useful muscle, but we really had to keep an eye on him. Left unchecked, that guy would rob you blind. The Bomber loved the life; he'd would rather make $100 illegally than $1,000 legally.

By 1943, Jon was focusing on his horses and family down in Florida and meeting some interesting people along the way. Charles and Anne Lindbergh were actually the presenters of the winning bouquet when his horse, Snorky, won a race at Riverside Park in Kansas City. That reminds me, Capone was out of prison by then, but he was bedridden on Palm Island taking this new stuff called penicillin. What made me think of that? Most people who didn't know Al thought his nickname was Scarface. But it wasn't. It was Snorky. And Snorky means classy and elegant, in case you didn't know.

Anyway, the Lindberghs hosted a party that evening at the swankiest hotel in town, where Jon and his wife were the guests of honor.

Jon's horses were so well trained that they could hear him from the rail during a race. One day in 1945, Jon and I were spending an afternoon up at Arlington, a beautiful facility in the northwest suburbs of Chicago. Jon knew of all the horses, trainers, and jockeys, so we were doing pretty well and having a good time. His horse was going to run in the seventh race of the day, but Jon's mood began to sour as he saw the horse was now at even odds.

"How the hell did this happen?" Jon fumed.

"What do you mean?"

"I mean this wasn't supposed to happen. Something or

someone leaked," Jon said, trying not to draw attention to his disgust.

"That means it's both."

Jon looked me dead in the eye and nodded. "I'll fix this and then some. Let's go grab a scotch before the next race." He smiled and patted me on the shoulder as we made our way up to the Owners' Club.

When the sixth race ended, Jon pulled me aside and said he wanted to watch his race from the rail, so we made our way back outside. I was heading for a position near the finish line when he pulled on my sleeve.

"This way. I want to watch it from down there."

"Wherever, Jon. It's all good to me."

"Come on. I want to watch it just out of turn four, when they're getting ready to hit the final stretch." Jon had a shit-eating grin on his face.

"What's she going off at?" I asked.

"Even."

"So we sat this one out?" I always told Jon to put me down for whatever he was doing when I was at the track with him.

"Oh, no. Quite the contrary. We're all in on today's proceeds."

I immediately knew he was up to something. As his horse came around the turn in second place, Jon let out a whistle. The horse shook her head and kept running but dropped back to nearly last place.

"We're winners, Sal!"

"Dinner's on me tonight," I said as we sauntered back to the window to collect our winnings.

"I'm not done. This was part one of a two-part plan."

I laughed. "Why does this not surprise me?"

Of course, none of this went unnoticed. Some of the other players demanded an inquiry. Nothing happened to Jon, but his jockey had to serve a short suspension to make it look like the racing board was doing something about it. About a week later, Jon—out of nowhere—told me that he was picking me up the next day at four a.m.

"That's in five hours," I said.

"Is it?" Jon laughed as we stumbled out of Peter Banino's place.

"What's up? Do I need to know about something?"

"Not at all, Salvatore. All is well. Part two plays out tomorrow afternoon in Detroit, paisan."

Turns out, Jon was running the same horse he'd held back with a whistle.

"What race?"

"We're running in the fifth. We're currently going off at eighteen to one," Jon said with a sly glance.

I knew exactly what he'd done. His horse had performed so poorly the day before that he knew the odds makers would fade her hard the next time she ran. Oh, and she was also running up a class.

"Where are we watching from today, Jon? The rail?"

"No. Let's grab the finest table in the owners' box and relax."

"Sounds perfect."

After Jon's horse crossed the finish line first, Jon and I barely budged. We knew to always look like pros. Never get too angry or excited in public. Never.

I leaned forward to touch the bottoms of our rocks glasses. "Well, that was worth getting just four hours of sleep." I chuckled, thinking that was an easy eighteen hundred bucks in my pocket.

But when an eighteen-to-one horse takes it by three-and-a-half lengths, people take notice. Bookies were clambering all over the country. That's the kind of race that freaks them out.

There were some big payouts that day. A racing official at Arlington took particular interest and filed a complaint with the

Illinois Racing Board, arguing that Jon Allen was a detriment to Illinois horse racing.

Nothing ever came of it, but Jon and his horses were under a more watchful eye.

CHAPTER 18

Creating A Vending Empire

It wasn't long after the Detroit race in '45 that I had to deal with an unfortunate situation back in The Heights. Word had gotten back to me that our old friend and ally Angelo Zingaro was pushing back and doing some talking.

The Zingaro brothers made us tons of cash throughout Prohibition with their sugar operation, and apparently Angelo felt like his time had come. With Jon semi-retired, it appeared that my authority and future appointment as boss of Chicago Heights didn't sit well with at least some of the Zingaro clan. I arranged a sit down with Jon as soon as word got to me. Waiting too long to address this could endanger what Jon and I had built in our territory, especially on the Cal City Strip.

And it could cost me my life.

Jon and I met in the back office of the Owl Club. I was there early to process all the angles, which I liked to do before offering opinions or making decisions.

"Thanks for coming," I said. "Can I get you something to drink or eat? The food for the buffet just got delivered."

"No thanks. Sounds like this is urgent. Let's get to business."

"It's Angelo Zingaro. He's questioning my leadership and doesn't like the idea of answering to me when you're not around."

"Where did this come from?"

"I first got word from Ricky the Bomber, but it was confirmed by Tony Fazio, who heard from a good source. Pete Banino also said he'd heard rumblings that Zingaro thought he should be in line to replace you once you retire permanently from the day-to-day operations."

"Do you think the Zingaros are aware, given your current responsibilities and how much money you're making for the entire Outfit, that you're my obvious choice?"

"The Bomber heard that Angelo Zingaro said he'd push back on the order."

"Okay, so we have our—actually your—first coup d'état. You probably haven't slept since news got to you. I'm sure you've got an idea about how to … rectify this situation."

"You're right. I haven't slept. I have a rifle and a revolver loaded in my bedroom, a revolver behind the cushions of my living room sofa, one behind my family chair cushion, and one in a kitchen cabinet. As much as it pains me because of what Angelo Zingaro has meant to our crew over the years, his actions can threaten everything we've built. There's a complete lack of respect for me and your wishes, Jon. Not to mention, there's no way Chicago would want this, either. The Zingaros painted me into a corner, and I won't stand in it for very long. It only deteriorates my credibility within our crew."

"You have my backing," Jon said. "Just be smart and be safe."

"Well, Angelo has to go first. Cutting the snake's head off first is usually the path of least resistance. If any other Zingaros want to step up, then they'll be dealt with swiftly and harshly. I'm going to hit Angelo at his favorite bakery. He's there almost daily and it's run by one of his best friends. This should send the message to his closest allies as well, since their place is in our territory."

Jon nodded in approval. "Not only are you saving what we've built, you're probably saving your life and maybe even mine. Get it done."

I smiled. "It's happening as we speak."

Just before the meeting started, three of my guys had headed to the bakery on 22nd Street in Hungry Hill. The guy who walked in first immediately pulled his .45 and instructed the clerk behind the counter to call Angelo from the back room. We knew he was there. I made sure we had eyes on him before we sent in the three guns. My instructions were to leave the clerk unharmed, so as soon as he did as asked, one of the gunmen told him to get out.

As soon as Angelo emerged from the back, he got hit with the first of eleven shots. Four other men ran out from the back, including a younger Zingaro brother. A few of them, including the Zingaro, sustained minor gunshot wounds but later recovered.

"So it's done?" Jon asked as we stood to end the meeting.

I checked my watch to gauge the timing. "Supposed to be."

"Sal, I don't see anyone questioning your authority or future position in Chicago Heights for a long, long time."

"I hope you're right."

Sure enough, the other Zingaros fell into line after that. They were smart and the family was making good money.

There was no need to jeopardize that in exchange for more trips to the morgue.

NOW THAT ORDER had been restored in my territory, I focused on creating more revenue for The Heights and The Outfit. Slots were great, but I needed to get into every legitimate business I could. I called Guy to help brainstorm. Coz had his hands full, and Jon was out of town for another five to seven weeks.

Guy and I met for breakfast. There was something Tony loved ordering, and he kind of had me hooked: steak and eggs, over-easy. I was starving and couldn't wait, so I ordered and was halfway done when Guy arrived.

"That looks delicious," he told the waitress filling up my coffee. "I'll have the same."

"Thanks for meeting me so early. My sister just had a baby boy, so I want to get over there and visit my new nephew."

"That's beautiful! Which sister?"

"Concetta."

"I'll congratulate Big Tony when I see him next."

I nodded and swallowed my mouthful of breakfast. "So I want to have a casual conversation about creating new revenue outside of gambling and girls. The women don't bring in the money we're looking for. They're just a need we furnish. I'm thinking we need to form some legitimate enterprises that are a bit more mainstream."

"Makes sense. Do you have anything in mind?"

"Well, when I called you, I honestly hadn't given it a lot of thought yet. But now that you're sitting here, I have an idea or two."

"You saying I'm your muse?" Guy chuckled as he forked in a massive bite of steak dripping with egg yolk.

"I guess you are, Guy. I guess you are."

"So what are you thinking?"

"I'm thinking jukeboxes and vending machines. We can put up those in any restaurant, bar, nightclub … anywhere."

Guy stopped shoveling in food, his fork hovering above the plate. "Holy shit, Sal. It's simple but brilliant."

"Cigarette machines will be massive. Gum and candy bars will be huge, too, but we'll make sure every cigarette machine is ours. Every single one, in every town we control and beyond, will be ours. I'm not sure who I'll put where yet, but I'll want your help managing whoever's put in place."

"Shit. No wonder Jon and my brother want you to be the King of The Heights," Guy implored.

"Easy, Guy."

He dropped the fork and slapped his hands together. "That's it! Royal Vending Company. The name should be Royal Vending."

I grinned. "I friggin' love it, Guy! Royal Vending it is."

"So we got the vending angle. Any thoughts on the jukeboxes, Sal?"

"I think Co-Op Music Company has a nice ring to it. And you know what? Those music executives will be knocking on our door trying to get their records into our machines. They'll pay to get played, and they'll pay for placement."

"Friggin' fuhgeddaboudit, Cousin. You're a mastermind."

"I couldn't have come up with it without my muse," I laughed while cleaning my plate with the last piece of toast.

I GOT THE corporations set up before Jon returned from Florida. I thought he'd be pleasantly surprised.

That was an understatement.

A few nights after he got back, Jon told me Accardo was heading over to the Owl Club and we should let him know what I'd started. I made sure the club was cleaned from top to bottom and that the office was dusted and organized too. Impressions matter.

A few hours later, we were in the club's back office. Accardo was eager to hear the good news.

"Salvatore, it's always a pleasure. Jon, thanks for the invitation tonight."

"Pleasure is mine," Jon said. "Besides, I'm sure you were ready to check on your investment in person." He handed Accardo a whiskey neat and a cigar that he graciously declined.

"Of course. But with the fat envelopes that get dropped off every week, I haven't been too worried. You and Sal have quite a competent crew helping you with things in The Heights and Cal City." Accardo lifted his rocks glass to toast our efforts.

"Thanks," I said. "Glad you came down tonight so we can catch up."

"Jon said he came home to some unexpected good news. Said

you're working overtime."

"That's nice of you both to say, but aren't we always working?"

"Well, a lot of fellas get overly dependent on their existing rackets. Get too comfortable. But not you. Capone saw that. Sam, Paul, Joey, and I all see your drive and how you're always seeking an angle. Obviously, Dominic and Jon do, too. How is Dominic, by the way?"

"Dom is great. I'm actually heading there in a month with Cosenza and the bagman to discuss what's happening here, and possibly some new business ventures with families back home."

"See, Jon? Always working, this guy. I love it."

"All right," I said, trying to get back on track because I don't like attention. "Let's get to the point. While Jon was in Florida, I set up two new legit corporations that I think will bring in a lot of money for The Heights and The Outfit."

"Two companies? Do tell."

"Co-Op Music Company will install juke boxes everywhere. Every bar, restaurant, VFW hall, soda and ice cream parlor, and anywhere patrons can spin a record. Not only will they provide cash, there's a pay-to-play side to it, too."

"Pay to play?" Accardo knew what I was getting at but wanted to know exactly how I meant it.

"So, these record executives and producers want their records in our machines, right?" I asked. "Well, I don't care how popular your artist is. They aren't getting into a Co-Op jukebox unless they pay. They want their record toward the front of the records and not buried in the back, they pay. Pay for play. Pay for placement."

Jon sat back in his chair with a big grin. "What do you think?"

"It's brilliant. I love that it's a legitimate company and you can put it in any business that wants music for their customers. And you have another one of these ideas? What the hell can it be?" Tony leaned forward, eyes wide.

"We just set up the Royal Vending Company. We're going to offer gum and candy bars, but the machines I'm most excited about—which we can put literally everywhere—are the cigarette machines. If all cigarette machines are Royal Vending, it'll be a windfall for us."

"Told ya Sal had good news," Jon said.

"You weren't kidding, Jon. The guys back in the city are gonna flip over this."

I nodded and took a sip of my drink. "Glad you like it."

"Jon," Accardo said, "I know Sal always comes down to the city to meet a few times a month, but now I want to split the trips with him. He will still come to the city or River Forest to see me, Paul, Joey A, and Sam. But I'm thinking I also want to come to The Heights once a month." He turned to me. "Sal, you're obviously a busy man, and I appreciate how you just expanded The Heights' revenue streams. It would have been easy for you to rest on the gold mine you have on the Cal City Strip."

"I'm glad you're pleased," I said. "Really."

"Listen, I'm hosting a party for July Fourth, and I want you and Jon to come."

"I'll be in New Orleans," Jon said. "But I appreciate the invite."

Accardo laughed. "I should have guessed you'd be out of town again."

"I'll definitely be there," I said. "At the house?"

"Yeah. And tell your brother-in-law, Tony Fazio, that he's invited, too. I've talked to him a few times at the Owl Club, and I like him. I hope to see him with you in a couple weeks."

"Will do. I'm sure he'll come."

Accardo stood. "Perfect. I should get going. Jon, I'm happy you had me down tonight. This news made my week. When our guys hear me bragging about Sal's amazing ideas—not one, but two—I hope it lights a fire under their asses."

CHAPTER 19

Fireworks

A few days later, I was feeling burnt out and realized I needed a vacation. I planned to head to California to visit my sister and her husband, but not until after Accardo's Fourth of July bash. He had a full fireworks display every year, and you had to be careful driving out of his neighborhood because kids were all over the streets.

I also wanted to give explicit instructions to my managers and my eyes and ears. I don't like excuses and would rather have a calm five-minute conversation on the front end than get enraged by some numbskull on the back end. They knew that when I got back, I wouldn't tolerate hearing about how something got messed up.

For example, I had Marco—the brother-in-law who hid Al after the McSwiggin incident and Burke after that Valentine's Day thing—pick up a guy named Francis from Joliet and bring him to my new house for a meeting. I wanted Francis to know I expected him to stay vigilant and not hesitate to report something that was out of place in his territory.

I was sitting in my family room talking about the White Sox game with my bodyguard when Francis knocked on my door and made his way inside.

"Hey, Francis, sit down." I waited for Marco to follow him in.

"Thanks. You want to talk about stuff before you take off, eh?"

"Wait," I said, glancing at the door again. "Where's Marco?"

Francis shrugged. "Huh?"

"Don't fucking huh me. Where the fuck is Marco?"

"He's in the car."

"Why is Marco in the damn car?" I yelled, spit flying out of my mouth.

"I told him to wait there." Francis started getting fidgety. "Sorry."

"You told him to wait in the car? My guy picks you up and take you to a meeting at my house, and you think you have the fucking authority to tell anyone anything? To tell my brother-in-law to wait in the car? What kind of idiot do I have looking after my interests in Joliet? Holy shit!" I looked to my bodyguard and motioned toward the front door. "Go get Marco."

When Marco entered the house, Francis jumped to his feet and apologized. We smoothed everything out, and Francis did an excellent job of taking note of my expectations and his duties. And I think he figured out who'd be keeping eyes and ears on him.

Yup, it was Marco.

I still had to talk to Guy, Banino, Pizzoli, and The Bomber about The Heights, Cal City, and our other interests. But I had time. Accardo's shindig was still a few days away.

I LOVE THE Fourth of July. Something about a holiday in the middle of the summer is just fun. Maybe it's because I love grilling for friends.

I was in a good mood and on my way to pick up Tony for the big soiree. I flew into my sister's driveway, looking forward to seeing my nephew.

"How's Junior?" I asked Concetta.

"Oh, he's wonderful. Such an angel. Come see before you two leave."

I peered into the other room where he was playing with wooden blocks. "Look how handsome he is."

"Now just bring my husband home in one piece," she warned.

"That'll be up to him," I joked as Tony and I walked out the door. "I'm driving there, but he's driving home."

"I'm ready to have some laughs, especially with a crying baby in the house," Tony said as he shut the Buick's door. "Nice ride. You just pick this beauty up?"

I nodded. "Just yesterday for the drive out West."

"Well, it'll be a nice drive in this new boat, that's for sure."

"Listen, Tone. Let's talk business really quick before we start having fun. Get it out of the way."

He raised his chin at me. "Shoot."

"While I'm away, I want you to report to me anything you think is askew. Trust your gut. I'll have Guy managing The Heights and Pizzoli managing Cal City. Toots Potenza will be helping Pizzoli with whatever he needs, and he's also gonna be available to Guy. Everyone knows what I want them to do and how I expect it done. Your duties are the same. Run your games and help manage the Owl Club. But like I said, I want you to keep your eyes and ears wide open. If there's something you want to talk about, come straight to me with it."

"Not a problem. I got you covered."

"Outstanding. I knew I could count on you. Now let's go have a good time. Accardo will be happy to see you. He asked me to invite you specifically."

"You're making me blush," Tony said with his signature giggle.

Accardo's house was more like an estate. River Forest was full of beautiful homes, but his stood out. The stone work was amazing. As soon as you opened your car door, young go-getters were right there, ready to park your car. The fireworks were still hours away, but the streets were already filled with kids running around with sparklers and blowing off their stash of firecrackers. As soon as we got to the backyard, our host spotted us and made his way over to greet us, as he does with all his guests.

"Salvatore, you brought Tony with you. I'm so happy you could come." Accardo hugged us hello.

"We're happy to be here," I said.

Tony waved a server over to take our drink order. "Yes. Very nice of you to offer the invitation."

Accardo slapped my brother-in-law on the back. "You're good people, Tone. I'm glad to have you at my home. Please mingle, eat, drink. There's food and bars inside and out. Have fun, fellas."

"Let's blow off some steam," I said, patting Tony on the shoulder.

We had a great time. Tony was busy mingling with some of the fellas from Elmwood and Melrose Park and laughing it up with some of the guys running things in the northwest suburbs. Everyone loved my in-law. He was a happy-go-lucky guy, and everyone picked up on that. There was a genuineness about him that the smart guys in our line of work picked up on. He was also big in stature, so he could kick ass when needed. But he was even more valuable at organizing and moving big games around to avoid heat.

What was I doing at the party? Well, I was preoccupied with drinking scotch and introducing myself to the single ladies.

A handful of hours later, it was time for fireworks and our host made one last announcement before the big show.

"I want to thank all of you who made the trip to celebrate this great holiday," Accardo said. "If you're here, it's because I wanted you here. Thank you all for coming. Enjoy the fireworks, and please drive home safely when you leave. That's it outta me tonight. Saluti!" Accardo toasted his guests as they raised their glasses and let out a "saluti" in return.

The fireworks were absolutely spectacular. And that finale? Fuhgeddaboudit. It had to be close to two in the morning when my brother-in-law found me schmoozing a lady.

"Had enough yet, Sal?"

"Yeah, sure, Tone," I sighed. I wasn't getting anywhere with the gal, anyway.

"Come on. I'm driving."

We got back to The Heights in under an hour. Tony flew into his driveway and threw the Buick into park. "You're gonna love driving this thing out west! Nightcap?"

"I better not. You'll be up with the kids in just a few hours."

"Shit," Tony chuckled. "I forgot."

"Yeah. I'm going to be on my way."

"You want to sleep here? You good to drive?" Tony asked sincerely.

"If I can't talk my way out of a little traffic violation around here, I have bigger problems," I said, laughing as I backed out of the driveway.

What a night. It was time for a much needed vacation, and my bags were already packed. So, I crashed for seven hours, then hit the road a couple days early.

CHAPTER 20

Perfect Days Interrupted

There's something about California. I love San Diego, San Francisco, the farmland around Stockton and Linden, the Sierra Nevadas, and Lake Tahoe. All of it. Back in '45, the G-men did their best to follow me there, but I was able to insulate myself well when traveling. I paid cash for hotels and used an alias when checking in. I hadn't seen my sister, Val, in quite a while, so it was nice to catch up.

She and her husband, Vincent, were always gracious hosts and had a bedroom for me whenever I was in town. I stayed with her for three weeks before heading out to look into some new ventures. They were set up on a bunch of acres that Val's husband or family had bought. I didn't ask, and it didn't matter. I give my sister a lot of credit. She was doing her own thing out in California while myself and her six sisters were all in The Heights. She carved her own path with a great guy.

Days on their farm were relaxing and made me want to buy adjacent land, and I would have that chance a few years later when the land went for sale. Well, actually, I put a letter in the neighbor's mailbox with a cash offer if they ever decided to sell. Until then, I stayed with my sister and brother-in-law.

My vacation days pretty much consisted of waking up around eight o'clock to a glorious breakfast. Val made the best breakfast, and I know my breakfast. I rarely helped with the daily chores, but

I got my hands dirty once or twice a week. I should have done it more often. Working on the farm cleared my mind of the stress of Chicago Heights and Calumet City. Come lunch time, I usually settled down to a platter of freshly cut tomatoes or some kind of deli sandwich. Cocktail hour started around four or four-thirty every afternoon. After dinner, we'd sit on the patio, watch the sunset over the fields, and call it an evening sometime between ten and eleven. Perfect days.

After unwinding for a couple weeks, I was ready to check out the surrounding mining areas. I wanted to invest a good chunk of cash into those things, spread it around into gold, silver, mercury, and tungsten.

On impulse, I bought a cabin not too far from Nevada, near the Tahoe National Forest. I'd been driving around for pleasure when I stopped into a real estate office on Tahoe's north end and asked about properties. I found something decent, tucked away and off the beaten path. It was two stories, but the upstairs was small, basically just a bunk room for kids and a loft area. I couldn't wait to show my sister and her husband the unexpected purchase.

"Sal, this is beautiful," Vincent said. "But I hope you'll still stay with us, too. I like the company."

"I most definitely will. I always feel relaxed when I'm at your house. I'll just hide out here when I need to, on the front or back ends of my trips."

"This is pretty isolated. I think you'll be safe here, for sure."

We got back to my sister's place a few hours later, just in time for patio cocktails at sunset.

"So, Vince, tell me about your family's history out here," I said. "How'd the Fazio cousins end up in Cali?"

"My family worked the railroad west with Stefano Fazio, Tony's dad. In fact, I think Tony was born in Spokane. Eventually,

Stefano moved his family back to Chicago Heights when the kids were toddlers and my parents stayed in California and became farmers."

"Interesting. I love hearing these stories." I exhaled, signaling my exhaustion. "Well, that's it for me. Too much to eat and one too many to drink for me tonight."

FOR THE NEXT few weeks, I visited mining companies, investing in as many as I could to spread the money around and maybe hit it big with one or two. You never know. I really enjoyed being out there. Even when meeting with fellas in San Diego and Los Angeles, I felt less stress overall.

Then one night, my sister stuck her head out of the patio's sliding door. "Salvatore, telephone."

Her tone said it all.

Who had this number? What went wrong? Only two of my brothers-in-law, Tony and Marco, plus Francis, Pizzoli, and Guy knew to contact me here. If it was a family affair, my sister would've taken the call.

I walked straight to my bedroom and grabbed the phone.

"What is it?" I asked

"It's Francis. Sorry to disturb you, but there's something I believe deserves your immediate attention."

"What do you have for me?"

"You know those Irish brothers? The ones connected to Judge Wilson? The ones with the slots and vending business to the south and west?"

"The Smithes?" I asked, already agitated.

"Exactly. Well, one of them is saying if you're not going to be around, he's going to push into Cook County."

"When did you get word of this?"

"Four hours ago."

"Okay." I took a deep breath. "I'm going to stay here another couple of weeks. I'll call you in ten hours with instructions that you'll deliver in person to The Greek and The Bomber. Got it?"

"Yeah. I'll be waiting for your call."

I hung up and sat in the dark silence for a few moments. The Smithes had built up quite a racket with their company, Automated Music. They were rivals to Co-Op Music in the Joliet area, with both political capital and deep pockets. It had always been easier to coexist with them than wage war. However, if this was how one or all the Smithes felt, I couldn't wait around to see how motivated they were to push into Cook County, or even Will County.

I called Guy and Pizzoli to see if they'd heard the same. It appeared the rumors were true. And even if they weren't true, they were spreading, which is sometimes just as bad. But if the rumors were false, the Smithe family or their representative would have gotten word to me that no one was looking to break the existing territorial agreement.

A few hours later, I was eating breakfast at one of my favorite diners outside of Linden. It was time to call Francis back. I told the waitress to leave my plate and keep the coffee warm, then walked across the street to the pay phone at the service station.

"It's me."

"I'm here."

"Tell The Greek that The Bomber should drive him to the job. The Bomber will decide the right time and place, but it needs to happen within seventy-two hours. I want to get back home soon, but I'll stay out here while this happens."

"Understood. If that's it, I'll deliver the message to Ricky immediately."

"See to it."

I hung up and made my way back across the street. Lo and behold, my waitress had a new breakfast waiting for me.

"Doll, you didn't have to do that. You're too much."

She smiled as she poured me a new cup of coffee. "Just like your tips, sir."

Within thirty-six hours of my call with Francis, The Bomber had figured out which Smithe was plotting to push into Cook County and had mapped out his daily schedule. The next evening, as the middle brother pulled into his driveway, Ricky pulled in behind his car at almost forty miles an hour.

Before his loaner could even come to a halt, The Greek jumped out of the passenger seat and emptied all six shots from his revolver into Smithe.

Five weeks later, I took over Automated Music from the Smithes. Lucky for me and them, they decided to sell. I didn't want any retaliation or other trouble down the road so I made my cash offer quite favorable. And it was well worth it. I now had Automated and Co-Op Music, nearly identical companies servicing different territories. Automated probably brought in another $100 to $150K a year, which pleased Ricca, Accardo, Auippa and Momo and everyone else in The Outfit.

I brought Francis in as a partner in Automated. He deserved it. I mean, we had turned a threat into a windfall in less than a week.

Talk about making lemonade out of that lemon of a phone call.

CHAPTER 21

Behind The Scenes

I hadn't been back in The Heights for more than a month when Jon and I met about going to Italy the next time The Bagman was scheduled to head over there. It was another post-family dinner meeting at Jon's house, and the smell of ricotta slapped me in the face as soon as I stepped inside. After the amazing homemade manicotti and meatballs, Jon and I made our way to the back patio to talk.

"Why do I get the feeling there's more to this trip than normal, Jon?"

"Because there is. We're going to fly into Naples and drive down to Sambiase to visit Dominic during the first half of the trip. We have a lot to tell each other about what we've been accomplishing. And we haven't been together, the three of us, for quite some time. It'll be really nice to do that. Don't you think?"

I nodded. "I do. What about the second half?"

"Okay, let's back it up. Let me try to fill you in on what's been going on while you've been attending to … what you're supposed to be attending to." He looked down and shook his head, trying not to laugh.

I smiled. "What's so funny?"

"You're one tough sonofabitch, Salvatore Liparello." Jon chuckled as we clanked our Dewars-filled rocks glasses.

"Maybe. Now tell me what I should already know."

At that moment, I realized something. It was the first time I'd spoken to Jon like he was my equal and not my superior. If it was as important as Jon was making it seem, then yes, I felt I should know what's been planned. I'd been busy, but not too busy to know what the hell was going on. But there was no disrespect intended nor did he take it as disrespectful. I think he was more surprised that I had never used that tone toward him.

"Well," Jon started, "Dominic will fill both of us in on specifics, but he's made a lot of friends in Italy the last seven years. These friends have now extended into contacts in Rome, Milan, Naples, Taranto, and Palermo."

I thought about the last four cities and what they might have in common. "Shipping routes?"

"Correct."

"So, obviously New York is in the know."

"A few are. Meyer and Lucky are the point men, as you'd expect. Which leads to the second half of the trip. Dominic and I are supposed to meet Luciano in Rome a week after we arrive. I have a horse there that's scheduled to race. So, why not discuss future business with New York at the race track in Rome?" Jon smiled.

"I can appreciate why you kept this trip—well, the true reason for this trip—tight lipped. Even with me."

"The nature of this business is very controversial. The public and political backlash might be bad, but the profits will be out of this universe. If we don't bring stuff into America, someone else will."

"Agreed. We are racketeers. We sell vice. It's as simple as that. At the same time, I won't tell anyone else what's going on until right before they need to know something. I don't need the family involved in the revenue stream Dominic's cultivating between Italy, New York, and The Outfit via Chicago Heights. If my brothers-in-law eventually find out, so be it. As long as my sisters don't. And our crew can't be involved. I won't let my boys get exposed to scrutiny or lengthy prison sentences. The sentences on trafficking are long and make it much more likely someone will rat. A gambling charge is a walk in the park, comparatively."

"Exactly, Sal. Depending on how things come into Chicago, The Heights may never touch the stuff as it is. So I agree, there's no need for anyone in our crew to know any of this. This involves you, me, Lucky, Meyer, our equals and bosses in Chicago, Dominic, and our partners in Italy."

"Understood. Thanks for talking to me tonight. I appreciate it."

On the drive home, all I could think was wow. I was impressed with the clout The Heights crew was carrying around the country with the wire services, the heavy influence in the newly growing Vegas scene, but this would put the Boys in The Heights on the radar amongst international organized crime elites. Dom had obviously been quite busy building something in and beyond Lamezia Terme. He was always hard at work, and his projects were becoming more grandiose over time. I was excited to see him.

When Jon and I arrived in late 1945, I felt terrific. It had been about seven years since my last visit, and I always felt at home when visiting Sambiase and the surrounding region. The streets were bustling with smiling and friendly people. Locals rested and soaked up the therapeutic waters at the local hot spring. When I was a boy still living in Sambiase, people used to bathe in that grotto, but it eventually became used more for sunbathing. The olive groves that ran up and down the hills of the surrounding area were not far from the gorgeous beaches that lay at the bottom of cliffs. The sea was as clear and blue as the sky above. Being there made me question why I lived in the cold and dreary Midwest. I could never leave my mom and sisters, and Chicago was beautiful from June to

September, but being in stunning Sambiase planted such thoughts.

Jon took the opportunity to visit some family in and around Cosenza to the north. Dominic and I ran around Sambiase and all over Lamezia Terme. That area appeared to be the center of Dominic's newest operations. At least, it was where he spent most of his days. Dominic appeared more intense than he had back in the late '30s. I hadn't seen him like this since our run-ins during the Sanfilippo days and the Beer Wars that ensued.

We were eating prosciutto and cheese sandwiches on toast at an outdoor cafe on a sunny afternoon in Lamezia Terme when I brought up his new ventures. "Dom, you're hustling your ass off here, aren't you?"

"The same can be said about you. I heard you're doing some quick expansion with new companies that are bringing in hundreds of thousands a year. Well done, cousin. Word is that Jon is ready to spend more time away, and Accardo, Auippa, and Ricca are fine with it because they know he's within reach and you're the one steering the ship. Well done."

"Thanks, Dominic. But let's talk about you. You're building something that I haven't seen before."

Dom nodded while he finished chewing a bite of his sandwich. "I'm bringing some of the clans together down here, and I'm working with some very powerful people with deep political ties. We've recently worked our way into positions of influence at several key ports. Positions to hide things in containers and get them in and out of certain ports around the world. We're still working out a couple kinks, but we're on the verge of rolling out our new arrangements with some new and old partners."

"Anyone I know?" I laughed.

"If this happens, Sal, it'll make Prohibition look like child's play. The money will dwarf what we did back then. Gambling is good, but even you know that it can't pay for everyone's needs. That's why Jon and The Outfit are so happy with Co-Op, Automated, and Royal Vending. You understand the need to constantly find new revenue streams. This one will most likely never be legal, so it's paramount to build a powerhouse international syndicate. New York is sending their power duo. We're meeting with some new partners from Naples and Rome next week. Once we have that figured out, we'll meet with the fellas in Palermo."

"Wait, Are you getting once-warring factions to do business together?"

Dominic laughed. "That I am. Money is a great peacemaker. The key is to let the Calabrese, Sicilians, and Napulitano each think they're getting the best deal."

"What about the guys in Rome and Milan? They don't cause you headaches?"

"Sure they do. They have egos, but they're more cosmopolitan and don't care so much about what their old foes are getting. They're content if they think they're getting paid what they deserve. The reality is, with all these moving parts between countries and crossing oceans, there's someone or something always causing headaches."

"Impressive."

Dominic sighed. "It's been a long road. Getting the heaviest hitters in Italy to come to the table has taken years. The level of mistrust between the regions is something I underestimated when I got back here a decade ago. I've had to be really careful, too. I suppose I can't deny it at this point, but I was labeled 'Ndrangheta by the other leaders when I was trying to sell myself as an independent who's trying to bring The Outfit's organizational skills here. Over time I had success consolidating many of the clans in southern Calabria."

"When are you and Jon heading to Rome to meet the others?"

"We're scheduled for early next week. I'm waiting to hear from the Rome contingency when the location and security is in place. Naples is pissed because they think Rome is too hot and may be compromised by authorities. It took me a month and many trips to ease their fears. See what I mean? Managing relationships with the Camorra, 'Ndrangheta, and La Cosa Nostra is quite the challenge."

I had a hard time believing there was this much peace. "So there's enough money in play for all the groups to put aside a century of jockeying for control?"

He chuckled. "Oh, no. They're always jockeying. The Sicilians are looking strong right now, but I see power shifting like the tides. Each group will forever move up and down the ladder depending on how they adapt to the ever-changing landscape of rackets and politics. It's my belief that these three will probably be the leading players for at least the next hundred years, though."

"Dom, you know my mind is moving a thousand miles an hour with what you're putting together down here."

"I know, but you have a lot on your plate as it is. And Jon will be handing the reins over to you in under five years, so you'll have even more stress in your life. It's not that you wouldn't be an asset in helping to coordinate this thing, but your skills are needed in Chicago Heights. You're already the most important person in keeping The Heights's stature in The Outfit where it belongs, always near the top."

"I guess," I said.

"It's very important to Jon and me that you know you aren't being left out of anything. This thing we're organizing between Italy, Rome, Chicago, parts of the Middle East, and South America is bigger than any one guy. We're building the most profitable corporation in the entire world."

"I understand. And I appreciate your words. But I'm not thrilled that this was being organized without me knowing."

Dominic put his hand on my shoulder. "And Jon and I appreciate that. But we're planning something that is so massive, it's crucial that the circle of people who know about it be kept very small. It's for everyone's protection. You should feel respected that you know what's going on at this point in the project."

I thought for a second and realized Dom was right. "Thanks for talking to me like this, Dominic. I miss you. Guy says he'll try to come visit you and the family in the next year or so."

"You're keeping him busy, I hope."

I smiled. "He's one of my most trusted men. So, yes, I have him busy,"

The conversation helped me put things in perspective. Jon had obviously been talking about retirement again. I couldn't deny that I thought I deserved to be in the loop and that, in the back of my head, I felt like I was ready to run The Heights.

I was more ambitious than I'd realized.

TEN DAYS LATER, I was back in The Heights and Cal City. One of my favorite things to do when I came home was visit my sisters, nieces, and nephews. Kids didn't appear to be in my future. Even though I was still more than young enough to have them, I doubted I would find the right gal to settle down with.

I didn't like to dwell on it, but it depressed me.

I spent most of my time around showgirls. Not that they couldn't make good moms, but the odds were stacked against it. And I had a reputation, so the parents of any nice girl in The Heights wouldn't be too thrilled if she brought me home. Anyway, I spent a lot of time at my sisters' playing with my nieces and nephews. I never had favorites, but I was always drawn to Concetta and Tony's boy, Joey, like a flower to the sun. He was a ray of light, with a zest for life I wished I could bottle up and hold close. I sometimes wondered if I'd ever found that much joy in everyday experiences. If I had, where had it gone?

Not long after, I had an interesting meeting with Accardo, Ricca, and Giancana in River Forest. After ten minutes of catching up and talking about my trip to Italy, the subject switched to California—and the tone turned more serious.

"Sal, we understand you'll be heading West when heat from the G-men gets to be too much. You've bought a cabin near Tahoe and are looking for farmland near your sister?"

My hackles started rising. "Am I being spied on or something here?"

Accardo looked me straight in the eyes. "On the contrary. We want you to do the spying."

"You're a star in The Outfit," Ricca explained. "We try to know what all our guys are doing, let alone someone in leadership."

"Okay." I wasn't sure where this was going. "I do plan on going to Cali every now and again for multiple reasons. Who do you want me to keep tabs on?"

"Handsome Johnny Roselli," Accardo said. "He's outta college from that Hollywood union charge and has amassed a decent amount of wealth."

"Not to question the order," I said, "but he still belongs to Los Angeles, correct? He's still under their jurisdiction?"

Ricca answered. "We here in Chicago believe his ego might cloud his judgment. We need to make sure he doesn't get weak in the knees if they start putting heat on him. Simple as that."

"I understand. I can make contact with him whenever you boys want. I can also have my boy Bomps in San Diego keep his eyes and ears open for me."

"That'll work, Salvatore. We can't think of a better man to make sure Dragna's boy isn't talking to the G," said Accardo, referring to Los Angeles boss Jack Dragna. "I don't want to rely on info about Roselli from other families." Accardo fidgeted in his chair like he was ready to end the meeting.

"I have it covered. I understand your concerns, and I'll make sure Roselli and I get better acquainted while I'm out there."

Ricca's eyes were cold. "Just because this sonofabitch has a lot of money, it doesn't make him untouchable. It may get him clout out there in LA, but that doesn't mean shit to us. Capice?"

"Agreed."

Just like that, I had another thing on my plate.

I didn't blame them for wanting to keep tabs on Handsome Johnny. He did maybe half of his ten-year sentence, and the higher ups get a little suspicious when guys get out of jail early. I didn't think Roselli was talking to the feds about us, but he knew a lot of people on the street and in the government. He was an accomplished sniper during the war, and the CIA was rumored to be talking to him. Even Bomps talked about him during my last trip to California. I'm sure the fellas in Chicago knew that, too, so it was surely one of the reasons they wanted me to keep tabs on a major influencer like Johnny Roselli.

The very next day, I had Francis, Ricky the Bomber, and Marco all trying to get a hold of me. Based on who was calling, I assumed it was related to Joliet.

I was right.

"Marco, you're my first call. I want to hear what you have to say before I call back the other two fellas."

"Hey, Sal. A bar owner in Joliet is refusing to put Automated's vending machines into his place."

"Did he give a reason, or he just doesn't want to?"

"Our guys have visited him two times already, and both times he's cursing out our boys. Get out of here you, dirty degos. I'm not working with you fucking guys from Chicago Heights. You can all go fuck yourselves. That kind of talk. In front of the whole place, while guys are drinking at the bar."

"Have our guys done anything to him or his place?"

"No," Marco said. "We were waiting to see how you wanted to handle this strunz."

"Good. I'd like for this asshole to fall in line without bringing any attention, if you know what I mean."

"Absolutely."

"This guy gets two more visits before it gets ugly. Capice? I want you there to personally observe how it goes down"

"Got it."

"Not that anyone did anything wrong," I assured Marco, "but maybe they need to be more original in order to get the point across."

"I follow, Sal."

"I'll tell Francis and Ricky the same thing, but I want someone at this guy's place before tomorrow."

"I'm on it."

I hung up with Marco, then spoke to the other two about how I wanted this thing handled before it had to get ugly for the owner.

Early that same evening, Marco was at Ricky's house with Francis discussing the matter before they showed up at the bar. Ricky had a son named Michael who wanted to be just like his old man. He had moxie and was a pretty smart kid with a reputation for thinking on his feet. Or so his father said.

Michael convinced his father to let him go in there with me. I promised to keep Michael safe, as it was clear he was going to keep pushing until Ricky the Bomber agreed to let him come along.

Michael and Marco showed up at the Joliet bar around seven thirty that night. As soon as they walked up to an empty space at the crowded bar, Marco was recognized by the bartender.

"What the fuck do you assholes want?" the bartender growled.

"Now, now" Marco said, "there's no need to talk like an imbecile. We're here to discuss business, and hopefully we can all make some money."

"We already said we aren't doing business with you filthy wops from Chicago Heights." The bartender was so loud the entire bar could hear him. "Can't you take a hint when it hits you upside the head?"

Marco stayed calm. "Lower your voice. We think you and your boss haven't really thought this through, and we want to make sure you do. This is a good opportunity for all parties."

"We're not putting your dago Chicago Heights machines in this bar. Now get the fuck out of here."

"Are you sure this is how you want it?" Marco asked one last time.

"Get the fuck out!"

Michael chimed in. "No problem. We get the point. Do you think we can get a couple whiskeys and have a cigarette before the drive home?" He pulled a pack of smokes from his inside jacket pocket.

"Suit yourselves. I will take your dago money."

The bartender returned with two whiskeys.

"Can I bother you for matches?" Michael asked. "I don't have any in my pack."

The bartender tossed a pack of matches onto the bar.

"Thanks, pal." He gave me a look that said there's a reason for all of this.

The bartender stood and stared as Michael fumbled to light the match, knocking over both glasses of whiskey and spilling booze all over the bar. Michael then struck another match and made it look like he'd accidentally dropped it on the floor.

"Holy shit," Michael said, "that was close. With all that booze on the bar, that match could have sent this place up in minutes. What a tragedy that would be, huh?"

Michael smirked and Marco threw some change on the bar. "Thanks for your time. We need to go deliver your message."

Michael's theatrics were taken seriously. Before they got back to Cal City, the bar owner had already gotten a hold of me with one question: "When can I expect your guys to come deliver the vending machines?"

I couldn't have been more pleased. This was a much better outcome for all parties. I really don't like to use violence if it can be avoided.

But if required, it has to be swift.

And brutal.

THE REST OF the late forties were fairly quiet. Things were running pretty smoothly throughout the territory and for The Outfit as a whole, and between Automated, Co-Op, and Royal Vending, we were on a hiring spree. As we continued to increase the number of establishments our machines were in, I was in constant need of more installers, mechanics, and collectors. The collectors were my guys, but the mechanics and installers were employed by legit businesses. Well, mostly legit, with the exception of the skimming and cleaning of Outfit cash.

We all got hit pretty hard in early 1947 when we learned that Al had died. He'd remained ill on Palm Island since his release from prison and died there of a stroke and pneumonia.

I was arrested later that year on a reckless driving charge in central Illinois. I was going well over a hundred and tried to evade the officer when he turned his squad car around to pursue me. What can I say, I like to drive fast. I had no trouble getting the charges dropped.

But it was the first time I got a mugshot that I couldn't have destroyed.

CHAPTER 22

Boss of The Heights

In the early fifties, the Cal City Strip was a well-oiled machine and our political capital was secure. We still had the mayor under our thumb because Jon bailed him out with the IRS, and we had kept the entire police department on our payroll. Cal City was bringing in high-quality entertainment, too. Sure, there were a lot of strip joints around, but we wanted to offer high-class shows as well. Hell, we had Martha Raye, Sophie Tucker, and Louis Armstrong performing in Cal City.

During one night that I'll never forget, Ricca, Campagna, and Accardo brought Jimmy Durante to Cal City. He'd been performing in Chicago and told his hosts that he wanted to check out Cal City because he'd heard great things. The next night, we hosted Jimmy D and showed him a great time. He loved all of it. The gambling, the girls, and some high-quality female singers were all organized for his visit. He especially loved Tara Solara, an exotic knock-out built like a goddess with a striptease act called The Statue That Comes to Life. She eventually left Cal City and headed to Hollywood, where she starred in a few successful B movies.

I suppose the early '50s did present a couple headaches that needed addressing, though.

That pain-in-the-ass Senator Estes Kefauver launched his high and mighty special committee to investigate organized crime in 1951. Eventually, after enough interviews, Calumet City showed up on their radar. This put a bit of pressure on the Cook County sheriff's department, and they broke my balls with a couple small busts in Cal City to save face. One night, they raided the Owl Club. Of the five hundred men in the club, less than forty were arrested. That same month, authorities raided another one of our joints on the Strip called the Four Aces.

I'd had enough of the bullshit. While I knew the sheriff's department was trying to save face, guys were getting nervous about coming out to the clubs for fear of being raided. I called the deputies on my payroll and figured out how much it would cost me to make this go away. What a friggin' pain. But all it took was a few grand, and we were back to business as usual.

Our influence throughout the Midwest intensified in the early fifties, too. The Outfit actually spoke for Milwaukee and Madison in Wisconsin. Because of my cousins and their connections, we'd had clout in the state since Prohibition, but now I was actually friends with Milwaukee's boss, Franky B. I was even his son's Reconciliation sponsor. It was a beautiful occasion. My cousin, Guy, attended as well.

We also spoke for Springfield and Rockford in Illinois, and Kansas City in Missouri on the National Commission for La Cosa Nostra. And because I'd been spending more time and investing money around the West Coast over the last eight years, our quiet presence in Los Angeles and California was also undeniable. Not that we had influence over the California families' businesses dealings, but we were there and had interests to protect.

Our influence had also reached outside the U.S. to Havana and Mexico as early as the 1940s. During that time and into the early fifties, I made trips to Tijuana. Pizzoli traveled with me in those days. He was becoming my main point man when I was gone. We'd head to San Diego first, spend a few days there, then get down to business in Mexico. It was usually me, Bomps, Pizzoli, and Four-Fingered Frank. Yes, we were trying to expand our gambling interests in Cuba and Mexico. But at the same time, these locations—along with New Orleans and Montreal—were key with regard to what Dominic, Jon, Luciano, and Lansky were building with our partners in Italy.

Must've been about 1952 when the FBI was informed by the National Bureau of Narcotics that Jon and Four-Fingered Frank were being indicted by the Italian government for conspiracy. The charges stated that they were part of a narcotics smuggling ring led by Luciano. People often think that New York casts the widest net, but The Heights's crew grew The Commission's interests considerably through its connections. I mean, the facts are the facts. But because we kept such a low profile, our influence was always underappreciated, which goes back to my philosophy of insulating yourself from exposure.

Take the fortune. Fuck the fame.

Nothing ever came of the charges, but it was around this time that Jon permanently retired and left or transferred many of his Outfit interests to his son, Steve. The conversation between Jon and I was something I'd thought about for a while, as I felt like I'd already been in charge of day-to-day operations for years.

Jon told me about his retirement when I visited him in Miami. He opened the door of his modest ranch-style home just a block or so west of the beach with a grin. "Thanks for coming down. I hope you're also getting some much-deserved R&R. Let's have a drink or an iced tea. What'll it be?"

"I'll start with the tea, please, and I'm certainly trying to relax while I'm down here. I also took a loaner car from our friends at the dealership. I wanted to leave my car parked so anyone watching thinks I'm still in The Heights."

"Smart move. I like it."

"Well, they may not like it when I return the car with twenty-three hundred miles on it," I laughed.

"So," Jon said, switching to business, "you may have an idea of why I asked you to come down here. I'm getting out of the rackets. I've had a good run, but I've attracted too much attention lately, and I'm too old for this shit. I want you and Steve to take over my holdings. You're Boss of The Heights, Sal."

I nodded. "You know I'll take care of our interests and do my best to keep a protective eye on Steve for you."

"I know you will. You're a natural born leader. Been telling you that for decades now. I mean, you've been working towards this for … Jesus, thirty years. In fact, I'm sure you've felt like the boss for the last ten. It's your time, and you're ready."

"I'm honored."

"That's it, then. Let's have a real drink now, and get ready for dinner. I'm taking you out with some friends for a low-key celebration."

I stood up and gave him a hug and kiss on both cheeks.

In the eyes of The Outfit, I was now Boss of The Heights. This Thing of Ours was something I had dedicated my life to since before 1920. And honestly, with Jon spending so much time away from The Heights since the mid-forties, in my own mind, I'd already felt like I was in charge. It wasn't the title that gave me satisfaction. It was the respect that my partners showed me that meant the most.

But by the end of that night much of my happiness had been replaced by the stress of knowing that there'd be people looking to push me out or knock me off. It's the nature of being a racketeer.

That day, which I had pondered for years, was disappointingly anticlimactic.

I liked knowing I was getting what I deserved but that was about it. I had to change my focus because I kept having one recurring thought.

If this doesn't bring me happiness—if this doesn't fulfill me—maybe nothing will.

WHEN I GOT home from Miami, I had six angry music producers questioning why their artists' records were not in Co-Op's or Automated's jukeboxes.

Steve Allen, Jon's son, was handling the Co-Op meetings and Francis took the Automated meetings. Most of the meetings went exactly the same. They all started out with these hotshot producers coming in all cocky, trying to throw their self-perceived weight around.

"Welcome. How can I help you today?" Steve or Francis would start, knowing damn well why the hell they were there.

"Well, I would like to know why my Top 40 artist isn't in your jukeboxes?"

Now, a Top 40 artist deserved attention for sure. It also meant the producers and record labels had a marketing budget for them.

Steve and Francis would provide the standard answer. "Company policy. If you want your record played in our five-hundred jukeboxes, it costs two-hundred and fifty dollars."

In fact, it was more like a thousand jukeboxes between Co-Op and Automated.

"Two-hundred and fifty dollars to get our record in your machines? That's insane!" they'd cry.

"Well, it's not insane. It's company policy. That is the fee to get your record placed into the machine."

"This is preposterous," the producers would say. "The clientele where your machines are located want to hear the latest and the greatest. You owe it to them."

"You see, we actually owe them nothing. They will find something to play to satisfy their moment, whether your record is in there or not. Company policy."

"Can I assume the two-fifty gets my artist in the first five of the rolodex?"

"No. It gets you in the machine. If you want your Top 40 Artist to be one of the first five records, it is another two-hundred fifty dollars and that needs to be renewed every eight weeks."

Predictably, their jaws would hit the floor.

But they all ended up abiding by our "company policy."

To help put our influence in perspective, The Outfit had roughly seven thousand jukeboxes in Chicago alone, which cleared somewhere between $30 and $40 million a year. Sounds impressive, right? However, we controlled more than half a million jukes across the country that brought in about $300 million.

With control of that many machines, one can also understand how we could make a star.

It was easy to go above and beyond when we were pushing talent who actually possessed it. Carol Lawrence comes to mind. Heard of her? Was married to Robert Goulet. Did West Side Story on Broadway. She's a Chicago girl. Her real name is Carolina Laraia. Her father, Mike, was appointed comptroller in Melrose Park by Joe Bulger, who was a trustee and president of Melrose Park.

Joe Bulger was also the president of the Unione Siciliana.

Back when Accardo was building his estate in River Forest, Mike Laraia—being a comptroller who was aware of the best craftsmen and artisans in the area—made sure only the best worked on the Accardo home. So years later, when Laraia's daughter was launching her singing career, Bulger reached out to Accardo.

I remember the conversation I had with Accardo, which came

up during one of our regularly scheduled sit-downs.

"So our last piece of business to discuss is Carol Lawrence," he said.

"Okay ..." I said, a bit bewildered.

"We're going to help one of our own. This young lady will have no idea who is behind her."

"One of our own, with the last name of Lawrence?" I asked with skepticism.

"Lawrence is Laraia, Sal," Accardo said in a tone ordering me to be more patient and trusting of the subject matter.

"Laraia ... the comptroller's daughter?"

"Yes. Her father encouraged her to make her name more American before releasing the single."

"Okay. No problem. So you want her record in all the jukes?"

"Yes but not just in the jukes. In the Top Ten of the machines, Sal. Once you hear her, Sal ... Fuhgeddaboudit. We're gonna make this girl a star."

Accardo said this as we stood up to leave, the decision having been made.

And that is exactly what we did.

Accardo was right about something else, too. Carol had no idea how much of a push her career got because The Outfit gave her record Top Ten placement in a half a million jukeboxes. Now, she's a seriously talented kid and absolutely deserved it. We just gave her the initial push.

Speaking of Top Ten and Top Forty hits, Giancana and Jules Stein over at MCA records dreamt up some metric system to measure popularity and came up with Top Ten Hits, which morphed into the Top Forty. Yes sir, The Outfit's national influence was far more reaching than the public's perception of organized crime.

***

PART OF MY weekly routine in the 1950s was checking in with all my managers and bouncers on the Cal City Strip. It was important that I make myself available to my top men. I did this for a couple of reasons. First, to let them know I heard their concerns and took them seriously. Second, and most important in my eyes, if I am absent too long a few fellas might get the idea that while the cat's away, the mice should play. And that just invites problems for all, especially me.

For instance, not long after returning from Miami and putting the record producers in line, I was catching up with my brother-in-law Tony. I still had him running the Owl Club nightly with Joe Baker, and I knew if Tony was there I would get an accurate and detailed update of what I missed.

"What did I miss?" I asked as I closed the office door behind us. "Not a lot I hope?"

I sat at my desk and Tony relaxed in a chair across from me. The club was packed and the noise from the main floor invaded the office.

"Nothing major," he said. "I just have a slightly comical tidbit for you, but tell me about your trip first."

"Well, Tone, Jon officially announced his retirement. I got the nod and Accardo, Ricca and Auippa gave their approval and blessing. I'm running the show," I said matter of factly. "I'm Boss of The Heights."

"Holy shit, Sal!" Tony jumped up and headed for the dry bar across the office. "There isn't a more qualified person to take this thing over. I mean that, even though I am biased."

He finished pouring the drinks and handed one to me. "Thanks. I am going to tell the family at the picnic tomorrow."

"Saluti," he toasted as we hit glasses.

"Thanks, Tone. But enough about me. What's been going on here?"

"Well, Sal, this one might actually make you laugh," he chuckled in his signature way.

I leaned back in the chair. "Okay. I like a bit of humor instead of bad news when I get back from being away."

"So last week Joe Baker pulled me aside to make me aware of a very, very drunk regular who has a reputation as a horrible gambler. He gets up small and starts pushing, then always loses it all and a lot more. The lovable loser type, Sal. You know what I am talking about."

"I do."

"So, Baker pulls me aside to tell me that he has this regular flush out of cash who has been raising hell over getting a marker. Baker knows we don't do that for guys like him, but because he comes in all the time Joe wanted to get my opinion on the matter. By the time Joe and I came out of the back office, this fella was being rude and loud to every employee in the joint."

"Okay," I said. "I have a feeling where this one is going."

"You only think you do. So, Joe taps the guy on the shoulder, merely to divert his attention from the tellers he was berating, and this strunz turns around and cocks Joe right in the face."

Here's where I should give you a little background on Joe Baker.

Baker lived in a motel just on the Indiana side of the border. He had no wife and no family. He was loyal, didn't steal, and had tight lips. If and when we'd get raided, he wouldn't say boo. Baker was an ideal employee, and he and Tony were good pals and worked terrifically together.

Baker was also pound-for-pound one of the most powerful men anyone had ever seen. He was a five-foot-seven inch barrel of a Jewish man, and I can't emphasize enough how physically strong he was. Baker had hands like a bear and a reputation for being able to knock guys out with an open hand slap across the jaw.

"He sucker punched, Joe?" I smiled and got up to refill our drinks. "Uh-oh!"

"It didn't faze Joe in the least," Tony said. "But before we could believe what this guy just did, he cracked me across the face."

"Oh shit!" I said as I poured fresh drinks for Tony and myself.

"So Joe and I literally carry this strunz out by his neck and legs. We took him around the back and beat him unconscious. I was pretty pissed off at this point and Joe was apologizing to me for even considering getting this guy a marker.

"He says Tony, I am so sorry. This shouldn't have happened. I should have bounced him just based on how drunk he was. So I says Joe, don't worry about it. Let's get this piece of shit away from the club so he won't be associated with being here. We can't leave him out cold behind the club. That's when Joe had a great idea. Tony, he says, let's leave him on the tracks. If this piece of drunken shit gets hit, he gets hit. They'll just figure he was drunk and passed out too close to the tracks. A horrible accident.

"So we left him on the tracks, and finished up our evening like nothing ever happened."

A funny story, but I had a feeling. "The story doesn't end there. Does it, Tony?" I asked.

Tony shook his head. "So, the very next night, this guy walks into here, all beat to shit, and is acting like nothing ever happened. He saw us both and had no reaction at all. And, of course, he's back to his losing ways, except sober tonight.

"Joe was in shock. Tony, can you believe the nerve of this guy? Showing up the very next night after we almost killed him. How does he have the balls to show up like this? Joe asks me in total bewilderment."

"So," I said "what did you guys do, Tone?"

"I told Baker that this fucking guy was so drunk he may really not remember what the hell happened. So I told Joe that we should go over to him and ask him about his face to see what he says. Joe walked over to the guy, who was shooting craps at the time. Hey, Joe says, we noticed that your face is all fucked up. I saw you here last night and your face was in one piece. Do you remember what happened?"

I'm enthralled. "What did the guy say?"

"He told Baker that he blacked out and that he must've gotten rolled outside when he left the club. He said he woke up to the horn of a freight train and was able to get himself off the tracks when it was about fifty yards away." Tony finished the story in his signature giggle.

"Too funny," I said. "Unreal."

"Right! We let him be. Since he wasn't drinking, maybe he learned a lesson. Although he was right back to giving us his paycheck, so I guess he has a few more lessons to learn."

I finished my drink and was starting to feel exhaustion. "Wow. Thanks for the crazy story, Tone. But I am going to head out. See you at the family picnic?"

"Of course."

"Great," I said, heading for the office door. "I am looking forward to playing with little Joey. Tell my sister hello for me and that I'll see her at the picnic."

"Absolutely, Sal. Drive safe," Tony said. "And watch your speed!"

"Nah, don't worry. I am not in central Illinois."

I laughed as I shut the door behind me.

CHAPTER 23

Ducking Heat

It was 1957 before the well-oiled machine needed some maintenance. The IRS went after Accardo and myself for underestimating income from the Owl Club. I eventually settled out of court on an amount but he went to trial.

The trial put a spotlight on Cal City that it hadn't had to deal with for quite some time. I wanted my name off the Owl Club's title after that, and after a talk with Tony I transferred the club's title to him and my sister Concetta. As I explained to him, they were not putting out any cash, but they were my new front and he would get a bigger cut every week. Tony didn't have a problem with it because he trusts me, but I could see him going over the odds of getting indicted in his head. I promised we'd keep the heat off him. The last thing I wanted was to get my sisters pissed off at me and get my nieces' and nephews' dads thrown in jail.

At the same time, I needed to be more insulated moving forward.

I also had to talk with Joe Cosenza immediately.

"Coz, come in, come in. Can I pour you a drink?" I asked as he passed Tony on his way into the Owl Club's back office. "I'm going to have a short cigar, too. Want one?"

"Sure, thanks." Coz took the cigar and lit it while I poured the drinks. "What's up, Sal?"

"I want you to take over the day-to-day for me in Cal City, effective immediately."

Before Coz could respond, there was a hard knock and the door swung open. It was Steve Allen, who shut the door and looked at me.

His eyes were filled with shock.

"My dad's dead," he managed. "Heart attack. Mom just called from Florida."

I pulled up a chair for Steve as we hugged and cried.

Jon, my mentor—my big brother and surrogate father after mine passed—was dead.

When I would seek out Jon's knowledge, he could tell whether I was looking for fatherly advice or if he needed to be my boss. If he needed to act like my boss, he'd tell me to meet him at his office. But when it was paternal guidance I needed, Jon would tell me to come over for dinner and we would talk over a drink. I couldn't even begin to count how many times Jon and his wife had me at their house when Jon knew I needed that kind of attention. And even though Jon had his own son, there had been room enough in his heart for one more. He would always tell me how much he has enjoyed watching me grow up into the strong, intelligent man I'd become.

As quick as my talk with Joe Coz started, it was over. But there wasn't much more to discuss. After setting his almost full cocktail on the desk, Coz kissed Steve on the side of his head, placing his right hand on Steve's cheek while holding his lit cigar away with his left, then closed the office door behind him.

AFTER THE TRIAL, Accardo unsurprisingly decided to step down from his day-to-day role in The Outfit and let the more publicity-hungry Momo Giancana take over. Accardo, along with Auippa and Ricca, were always there to advise and maybe even pull Momo's strings once and while. Their leadership was deep and strong. And even below those guys, I could rattle off six or so names capable of running Chicago.

It's those types of events that made me crave California. Once Coz had taken over Cal City, I could focus more time on my interests out West, particularly the new tungsten operation in Nevada and our hotel that was under construction—the Stardust.

I would usually stay at the Cal-Neva, but on one trip I left the state-bordering resort for my cabin. I needed to be in the quiet, alone. A lot had happened in a short period of time and I wanted to focus on the hurricane raging around me. I then headed for Stockton, not far from my sister's place in Linden, where I toured some property with a beautiful agent. She took me to a lot that looked as stunning as she did.

I got out and looked out at the vast fields. "This is where I want to build a home."

"So can I assume you'd like to purchase the property?"

I grinned. "Let's talk about it over dinner."

I was happy at that moment. I had my cabin in the mountains. I just bought a great piece of property and was about to go on a date with a gorgeous woman.

I was the Boss of Chicago Heights.

Then I thought of Dominic over in Italy. I was sure word of Jon's passing had reached him by then. I was also sure that he was proud of me. He told me thirty years prior that someday I would be in this position. He was right. But I had unfortunately come to the realization that my business was less fulfilling than anticipated.

Property and houses are wonderful but not as special

without a wife and kids to fill them.

I picked up the property agent at her place a couple hours later, and we remained in contact while the house was being built and I got my tomato ranch set up. But that was as far as we went.

AS SOON AS I returned to The Heights, Momo Giancana got word to me that he wanted to have a meeting about something about to happen in New York. I got to the meeting—which was a restaurant Giancana liked that was closed to the public until 4:30 p.m. but open to us—to find him and Accardo in deep discussion. There were no drinks or food on the table so I knew this was serious and to be quick.

I looked at my watch. "Did I miss something already? I'm not late."

"No," Giancana said. "Please sit."

"What's up? What's with the frustration?" I asked.

"The Commission wants to hold a conference at Joe Barbara's estate in Apalachin, New York," Accardo said.

"Huh. Who is supposed to attend?"

"Fellas from around the entire country are supposed to attend," Giancana said.

"Why? What good comes out of having a hundred fellas at one location? Glad I'm not going," I added in case anyone had any ideas about nominating me to make the trip.

Giancana looked at me, annoyed, but I didn't give a shit. There was no way I was going.

"Don't worry, Sal," he said. "I wasn't going to ask you. I am going, mainly because I'm the new acting boss for The Outfit and I want those New York pricks to know we don't give a shit about their posturing and backstabbing bullshit. You probably heard that Anastasia was hit. Well, it's causing a lot of friction in our thing over there. Stefano Magaddino is using the meeting as a way to assert himself on the national stage. He wants to show his cousin, Bonanno, that he's more important. Bottom line is, they just need to get this shit sorted out so it doesn't affect us all. I want them to hear that from me."

I turned my focus to Accardo. "Are you sure the location is secure?"

"We've expressed our concerns regarding a conference of this magnitude but New York said they want to do this. We offered to have it in Illinois, but our offer was graciously declined."

"Be careful up there. I heard Barbara's been sick and may not have his guard up about security like he normally would. I appreciate the fact you had no intention of asking me to go."

"No worries," Giancana said. "I wish I could just send a couple of jamokes but, like I said, they need to hear it from me."

THE FOLLOWING WEEK it was all over the news. Major Mob Bust in Apalachin, NY, the headlines read from coast to coast. Momo Giancana escaped without being caught after he sprinted out the back of the house and ran until he reached a service station about ten miles away.

A couple of days after he got back to Chicago, Giancana, Accardo, and I met at his HQ, The Armory Lounge on Roosevelt Road in Forest Park.

"I'm glad you got out of there unscathed," I said as I hugged him hello.

"What a shit-show, Sal! I swear, I wouldn't be surprised if someone set us up."

"I'm in the process of trying to get some answers," Accardo

said, in part to appease Giancana, I think.

"I told you to tell the guys in New York that something of this magnitude should be held in Chicago!" Giancana was yelling out of frustration. "Before it started, I told the guys there the same thing!"

"I know. Total shit-show," I said with a little relief knowing I wasn't there and Giancana didn't get picked up.

"You're right," Accardo said. "And for the record, I did offer Chicago to New York, multiple times."

"We have four towns that we could've held that conference in. Four! I told them we could've had it in Chicago Heights, Cal City, Elmwood Park or in Melrose Park. Four towns we have locked down. They have five fucking families, plus Buffalo, and not a one could provide security for such an event. I am done!"

He made more than valid points in my opinion. I could've easily arranged for a meeting of a hundred men in The Heights or in Calumet City without it getting busted. It would have been easy. In fact, I agree that Accardo and Giancana could have arranged it just as easily in Elmwood or Melrose.

"Gentlemen," I said, "I have a larger concern about what lies ahead for all of us after this bust."

"G-Men?" Giancana guessed.

"Exactly. The FBI. J Edgar had denied the existence of a national organized crime syndicate. Well, we just proved him wrong. It's now undeniable and we're going to have to adjust and insulate."

Giancana turned to Accardo. "Looks like your timing was pretty good. I get to inherit these headaches now."

"Whatchya gonna do," Accardo said with passive aggressive inflection.

***

AFTER G-MEN interviewed the twenty guys who got pinched at Apalachin, the FBI set up what it called the Top Hoodlum Program in cities where they felt organized crime had a strong hold. It would be another couple years, but eventually the G-Men opened their file on me. And with J Edgar unable to deny our global syndication, I knew it would be a whole new ball game.

Not only would they start to surveil me, the G-Men would start following guys linked to the poker games set up by Tony Fazio.

My brother-in-law would have to leave The Heights for weeks at a time, so he'd head to Mexico to lay low and schmooze our friends down there. Giancana, Accardo, myself and other higher-ups had no problem with Tony Fazio representing our interests if asked. We would also make sure our friends down there ensured that the G would lose sight once Tony or any other friends needed to cross the border, regardless of the reason behind the stay. Tony also shared a love for the West. He loved touring the ancient trails in the western and southwestern states. The Fazios were also cousins with my sister's husband's side of the family, so he, too, would visit my sister's farm in Linden. We also shared some investment interests—namely mining.

I remember when the heat was bad on Tony after those bullshit raids in Cal City, so he and Concetta were headed to visit our sister Val out west for a month. Tony was literally packing up the car, but it was during the school year, so my sister was a little worried about leaving the two kids home alone. Joey was probably fourteen or fifteen and Nina was about eighteen, so I didn't see the problem.

"Concetta," I said, "they're good kids. Nina will keep an eye on Joey and I'll check in on them regularly."

"I know, Sal. I know. But Joseph won't do his own laundry. I told Nina to do it, but she'll be out gallivanting around while I'm away. I'm no dummy."

"Come on, sis. Tony is about done. Go kiss the kids. Tony said he gave each kid the same amount of money so they can take care of themselves and one another. They're going to be fine."

She finally listened to me. Tony kept a low profile until he was able to come home and my sister got a nice long visit with our sister in Linden.

I remember stopping in one night to pick up Joey and Nina to take them for dinner. They had probably been home alone for ten days. Well, I say alone, but with all my sisters living in The Heights, they had dinner—or it was delivered—with someone every night, and this was my turn.

"Take your time, kids," I said when I walked into the kitchen.

"Make yourself a drink, Uncle Sal," Joey yelled from across the house. "I'll be down in a minute."

"Way ahead of you, kiddo," I said, laughing.

I jogged up the stairs, drink in hand, to bust my nephew's chops and make sure his sister wasn't going to make us late.

"Hey, Junior," I blurted when I pushed open his door, which was already slightly ajar.

"Oh, hey," he said, laughingly glancing at the pile of dirty shirts on the floor to his left and the giant stack of brand new, still folded shirts piled on his desk.

"Did some shopping, Joey?" I asked in shock.

"Well, Nina sure as heck isn't doing my laundry. All I do is underwear and towels. So I had to get a few shirts, Uncle Sal."

I grinned. "Joey, you have a new shirt here for everyday that your parents are gonna be gone. Madone! Your mom was right."

Oh, did Joey know how to make me laugh and smile. My nephew—and all my nieces and nephews, for that matter—was always able to get me into that good place that's so hard to find in my line of work. I mean, the kid had thirty to forty shirts stacked up to get him out of washing delicates. He may have only been fourteen, but the kid had a plan.

"Hey, she wants me to wear clean shirts every day, right?" Joey said as he hiked up his dress pants.

I left him to finish getting ready and yelled into the bathroom. "Ten minutes, Nina my darling."

"Okay, Uncle Sal," she acknowledged with frustration.

A COUPLE OF years later, Tony and Concetta were in Cali visiting our sister and I was again helping keep an eye on my nephew. Joey had just gotten his license and a new, special-order rocket Pontiac, and word had gotten to me that he had been racing.

"Joey, does your dad know what you are doing at Route 30?" I asked my sweet but confident nephew when I walked into my sister's kitchen.

"Look, Uncle Sal," Joey held up his trophy to show me. "I won my division. I'm getting pretty good at this drag racing thing."

"Nice. Just don't let your mom find that trophy," I advised him. "I'd keep it at your girlfriend's house. Capice?"

Joey smiled. "Good idea."

"How's school been going?"

"Hate it."

"Well, you don't need to like it but you do need to go. And if I find out that you haven't while your parents are out of town, we're gonna have a problem."

"Don't worry. I am going and doing my schoolwork."

"That's what I want to hear. How about Francis and I swing by the high school tomorrow and take you out for lunch? We have some things to discuss but we can do it after we drop you off."

"Sounds great. I get out for lunch at eleven twenty-five."

The next day, Francis and I were parked out front of Bloom Township High School talking about the shit going on in Joliet when out trotted Joey.

"Good afternoon, Mr. Curry," Joey said as he jumped into the back seat of my Buick.

"Afternoon. I heard you just celebrated your sixteenth birthday. That's exciting."

"Yes, sir. I am pretty excited to be driving, that's for sure."

It was almost noon, but we ate at one of Tony's and my favorite breakfast places. The aroma of fresh-brewed coffee and bacon there always brought me back to the Sunday-morning meals my mom would make for the family after church.

"I recognize this handsome young man," our waitress said as we slid into my regular booth at the end of the restaurant. "You come in here with your dad, right?"

"Yes, ma'am," Joey answered.

"This is my nephew, Joey Fazio. How are you this morning, darling?"

"What can I get for you gentlemen?"

"Steak and egg special for me," I started.

"Turkey club with fries and a coke, please," Joey said.

"I'll have the same," Francis followed.

Francis knew how to talk to kids. He had his own. In fact, he had a son just a bit older than Joey.

"Hope you are staying out of trouble with that new driver's license of yours," Francis said to Joey.

"Actually, he's not," I interjected, busting Joey's balls. "The kid is winning trophies at Route 30."

"Drag racing? Does Big Tone know?"

"I think my dad knows," Joey said, looking guilty. "Definitely not my mom, though."

We were just about done eating when Francis decided to really spoil my nephew.

"Listen, Joey. I don't want to get your parents mad at me, but my son just got a new motorcycle last week." Francis continued talking to Joey but looked at me. "You think you want his old Indian?"

"Are you serious, Mr. Curry? An Indian motorcycle? Are you sure your son will be okay with this?"

"Absolutely. Just promise you'll drive it in good health. Your uncle is going to get word out to your parents as soon as possible, and if there is a problem, I'll be at your house the next day to pick it back up. Okay?" Francis smiled. "Happy birthday, Joey."

We dropped Joey back off at the school, and I thanked Francis for being so generous.

"No problem," Francis said. "He's a good kid. You think he wants in on the business in a couple years?"

"I don't want him to. It's not in him, and I don't want it to be in him, either."

"He definitely looks up to you, Sal. We'll see."

I have to be honest, at that moment in time, I thought it would be nice if my nephew got involved with us. He was well-liked, and I could easily groom him for it. But there were already too many guys for Joey to leapfrog without someone getting their panties into a bunch.

Anyway, Francis and his son delivered the Indian to Joey the next day, and I saw Joey riding that thing around The Heights all summer long until my sister made him get rid of it later that year.

Too dangerous for her liking, I guess.

CHAPTER 24

Car Lot Casino

By the late fifties, we had to get more creative with our gambling operations to stay a step ahead of the G. I had come up with a plan for a new casino, so I called a picnic at my house because I wanted the opinions of Tony, Guy, and Pizzoli.

I was looking forward to this new barbeque my brother-in-law Joe DeCarlo had built for me out of a fifty-five-gallon metal drum. He'd cut it in half and installed a hinge, creating a clam shell that made it one hell of a smoker.

"Thanks for coming, fellas," I said when it was time to get their attention.

"What do you have for us, Sal?" Pizzoli asked.

"We need a new casino because Cal City is getting heat and the Corral Club will probably be compromised within twenty-four months. And I've been thinking about where we could hide the cars so it wouldn't draw attention. Then I thought about our boy, Ralph, at the Pontiac dealership." I gave them a second to follow my train of thought, then explained as I spread out the hot coals around the sides of the barbecue. "I want to build a second floor on the dealership to act as a casino. Think about it. We can hide cars in plain sight if they are spread around the dealership."

"It's genius," Guy said as he raised his beer. "You've done it again, Sal."

"Obviously there are a lot of details to figure out, but I would like to start construction of the second-floor next month."

"A casino inside a car dealership, that is some next-level stuff," Toots added. "I got to say, it really is a great idea."

"In the meantime, I am thinking about having my nephew, Joe, and a few of his friends use their cars as guide cars, leading fellas to our moving location. We'll only select places we know we have protection, and only for a short period."

Seven months later, we had our new casino. I honestly couldn't believe we pulled it off, but it worked just as planned. Guys would pull their cars to the back of the building, then the valet would direct them to the stairwell and park the cars around the dealership so they blended naturally with the rest of the lot. When on the second floor, the men would walk through a few offices, one of which had a huge double-doored closet. A false wall in the back of the closet opened up to a room that was nearly two-thirds of the second floor.

It was a thing of beauty, a well-lit, windowless casino with slots along two walls and poker tables, blackjack tables, and roulette tables spread evenly throughout the floor. You truly had to see it to believe it.

Accardo, Giancana, Auippa, and Ricca couldn't seem to believe it even after they did see it.

"You keep outdoing yourself, Sal," Giancana told me when he came out the first time. I told him that there are a lot of opportunities out West with a lot less interference from the G. He was intrigued and encouraged me to keep him posted. Giancana was always interested in new opportunities to make money—and for ways to clean the cash we already had.

We were expecting an influx.

A couple months after we finished above the Pontiac dealership, the Stardust hotel in Las Vegas opened its doors. On Tony's recommendation, I sent my two best dealers from the Owl Club to get the new hires up to speed. It was my loss, but my brother-in-law assured me we wouldn't miss a beat because he had some capable guys who were eager to step up.

Like the Pontiac joint, I loved the Stardust when it opened. It had a 105-foot-long pool shaped like the Big Dipper that was really something to see when it was lit up at night. They ended up erecting a tower in the early sixties, but at first it was just two floors of rooms.

The Outfit's grip on Vegas started growing, and within a few years we also had big-time interests in the Desert Inn, the Riviera, and the Freemont. We financed through our partners at the Teamsters' Central States Pension Fund. We took our cut before most winnings were counted. You know, just a little skimming off the top. No biggie.

I didn't stay at the Stardust very often. My place was still the Cal-Neva. The backdrop of Tahoe and the mountains, I mean, Vegas just can't compete with that. Fuhgeddaboudit. Giancana and I loved it there, along with our friends, Dean Martin and Frank Sinatra.

Ol' Blue Eyes and I got to know each other pretty well over many years of professional dealings in Vegas, Palm Springs, and of course at the Cal-Neva. Sinatra also brought his parents to Tahoe and Palm Springs off and on for years during the 1950s and sixties. They loved coming to the Cal-Neva and all the other beautiful resorts, too, but they just liked being with their boy. They would often ask about my favorite places in the West or in Chicago. I told them about a ranch owned by some family and that I'd take them there sometime for a nice weekend. Complete privacy. Total relaxation.

One time when we were at the Cal-Neva, Frank wasn't there yet. My valet tells me that there may be "eyes" there. He'd seen three black sedans moping around the property and the parking lots just a few minutes ago. Sure enough, the men returned, but this time they started asking questions at the front desk. I wasn't going to stick around, and I called Sinatra to let him know that there were guys sniffing around the resort.

"Sal, listen," Frank said, "I don't want my parents around any of that either. When do you think they'll leave?"

"Probably three days or so. I called my family and am going to stay at their ranch last minute."

"Is that the ranch you'd always tell me about?"

"Yup. That's the one."

"Well, maybe you can help me get my parents away from these guys for a few days? Maybe they could stay at the ranch with you?"

I only had to think about it for a second. "I think it's a great idea, Frank. I've told them I want them to see it. This is as good a time as any for sure."

"Sal, you're beautiful. Listen, this is what I'm gonna do. I got this new plane, see. My pilot will pick you and my parents up at the Neva. He'll fly you to the airport nearest the ranch. How does that sound? Does that make it worth the hassle of having to entertain my parents? I mean, you know they'll be doing their own thing. Going on walks. Staying out of your hair. Or what you got left of it." Sinatra asked with a hint of a chuckle.

"Absolutely. They'll be welcomed like family."

"So, Cuz, my pilot will pick you three up whenever you are ready. He can be to you in under six hours once I tell him."

"I don't want to fly at night. No offense to your pilot. It's just the way it is. How about he gets us in six hours? I'd like to vanish as quickly as possible."

As scheduled, Sinatra's secretary knocked at my suite's door to escort me and his parents to the car that would take us to Frank's latest wings. This was in the single-prop days, years before he had the Learjet. We landed at a small regional airport about a forty-five-minute drive from the ranch.

When we arrived, Tony Fazio's aunt was there to greet us and show us to our accommodations. Per my request, my quarters were in a quieter area of the main house. It worked out great. Frank's parents had a lovely stay for four or five days, then Sinatra made arrangements for them to meet him in Palm Springs. I made my way to Arizona for a little fun and to check in on some mining interests.

Throughout this time, I was throwing money into various mining operations out West. I remembered what Giancana had said about opportunities and all of that Vegas cash that needed cleaning. Mining is a cost-intensive business with a very slim profit margin. But that's the beauty of it when you need to clean millions from the Vegas skim.

For example, I had a gold mine that I partly owned with some family out there. It takes a lot of capital to fund that kind of operation, so we did so at a loss through the use of phony loans funded with the skim. At the end of the year we'd file our taxes, tally all of the breaks and refunds from the losses, and collect a nice clean sum. We didn't take out exactly what we put in—it was like getting like forty cents on the dollar—but we were still ahead, and the money was clean.

A Jewish guy we partnered with once told me that we Italians would "make all of this cash, but then what? You stick it in a crawl space 'cause you can't spend it 'cause you don't know how to clean it. You have to think smart, look for opportunities. And sometimes you have to lose a little to make more, know what I mean? Don't be so greedy all the time." He was totally right and I have never forgotten that. I ended up having mining interests in Nevada, California, Colorado, and Arizona. I even brought a couple of my equals into some of these mining interests with me.

Guys were always looking for ways to clean their money or put it to work.

If I wasn't busy enough juggling all my interests and responsibilities, the end of the fifties threw more curves at me.

In late spring of '59, there were some serious raids in Cal City thanks to a new chief of police. They hit some of my most notorious joints, raiding the Derby Club, Folies Bergere, Four Aces, and Riptide, which was owned by the Mancini brothers. The cops arrested more than one hundred people and confiscated a trove of club records. But most of those arrested were strippers, and they didn't know boo about who really ran the clubs. It's why I begged Jon to insulate ourselves decades ago. And even if some of the strippers, patrons, or servers heard names associated with the clubs, they were too smart to say anything. The risk-reward just wasn't there for them to rat anyone out.

Neither me, Peter Banino, nor the Mancini brothers were charged following the raids, but I had to make quick plans for my high-roller games at the Owl Club and Club Corral. The heat was getting to be too much for Cal City and some of the other towns where we had set up shop. At least the casino on the second floor of the Pontiac dealership was chugging away untouched. That helped a lot. If I didn't have that casino, I'd be scrambling frantically instead of just scrambling.

Then there was that scathing Chicago Daily News story that came out in early June of that year. The article outlined how I avoided notoriety over the years by installing brothers-in-law as owners of my businesses, and how law enforcement didn't have photos of me. That newspaper article really put a spotlight on me and it drove me bananas.

And finally there was Accardo's tax trial, which was just getting underway. Three state's witnesses in his case were Boys in The Heights—including Vince Friggin' Pizzoli, my right-hand man!

This is the shit that keeps me awake at night. It's nonstop, I tell ya. The life of a racketeer is a lot like a boxer. We just bob and weave and try not to get hit too hard. We have to stay on our toes because if we get caught on our heels we'll get knocked the fuck out.

All witnesses testified that Accardo was selling his Foxhead beer illegally out of his car. When Pizzoli was being questioned, it came out that he was a partner in Automated Music Company. To make matters worse, he told them who his partners were. So just like that, me, three of my five brothers-in-law, Toots Potenza, and several others were officially part of Accardo's tax trial record. And once this info becomes public, it's there for the authorities to reference and helps them fit the puzzle pieces together. I understood why Pizzoli said what he said, but madone, that was a tough pill to swallow!

In the end, Accardo got off on appeal, but then Ricca was doing a few years for tax evasion around 1959-60, too. My monthly sit-downs with The Outfit guys were getting more and more important. We all seemed to have tails on us and feds digging through any record of our business dealings they could find. We all needed to be more vigilant than ever.

It was at one of these monthly meetings in late '59 when we decided to consolidate our poker games, mostly due to my encouragement. Cal City wasn't the only place The Outfit was coping with the headaches of raids. Cicero had been getting pinched as of late, too.

"So how bad did they get you guys in Cicero this week?" I asked Giancana once we started talking business.

"The Big Game is badly compromised," he said. "We need to move it as soon as possible."

"We're thinking about Will County," said Rocco Fischetti, who ran the Cicero gambling with Giancana. "It's quieter out there and we have great protection, no?"

"Will County would work for sure," I said. "You know my guy out there, Francis, would need to get a cut."

"Absolutely, Sal," Fischetti said.

An idea was forming, and Giancana was great at reading body language. "What are you thinking, Sal?"

"Well, I am on the verge of needing to move my game from Club Corral. I am thinking if you want to come out to Will County, we should combine them. This way, our two games wouldn't run too close to one another and cause any gripes between us. We would be working together to run the smoothest and biggest Big Game ever." I pitched. "Of course, for that to happen, I would need—with approval—to become a member of The Bank."

They looked at each other.

"Accardo thought you may suggest that," Giancana said. "And we told Accardo that, if you wished it, we would make it happen."

"Let's do it."

"Okay," he said. "Each member of The Bank will now put in twenty thousand nightly."

And just like that, the two Big Games in the Chicago area were consolidated into one that attracted the biggest players from the entire metro area. I think they wanted Will County because they knew the Boys in The Heights had our political capital there under pretty solid control. It would just be fewer headaches—and well worth cutting in Francis and allowing me to become a member of The Bank.

And boy, did Francis and I deliver. That game could have two hundred guys at it, nobody ever raised an eyebrow. Shit, I think that game ran untouched for two years.

CHAPTER 25

Cal-Neva

A bright spot appeared at the dawn of 1960. Something I had longed for had become available, and I finally bought a stake in the Cal-Neva Lodge with Giancana, Deano, and Sinatra.

For a while, I was spending more time at the Cal-Neva than my cabin, which was only an hour away. The Cal-Neva, as one could guess, straddled the California and Nevada border. The property was gorgeous, on the sparkling shores of Lake Tahoe, which is truly one of my favorite places on Earth. And after visiting the Cal-Neva resort for nearly a decade, I finally owned part of it. I couldn't have been happier.

In addition to the Rat Pack, I became fairly well acquainted with Johnny Kennedy at the Cal-Neva, too. We'd seen each other there since the mid-fifties and had exchanged greetings when mingling with Hollywood stars or when Giancana was there. He and Momo would hang out all night with the ladies. They even shared girlfriends, but everyone knows about that already.

What was more odd to me was how the Kennedy brothers passed their girlfriends down the line. Take Marilyn, for example. I met her a few times and saw her at the Cal-Neva with Giancana and Jack, separately. Jack was done with her crazy ass and his douche of a brother, Bobby, was sitting there panting with his tongue hanging out the corner of his mouth, waiting for Jack's table scraps to hit the floor.

That boy quickly forgot what his daddy did for a living. Bobby's lavish life was funded from illegal money, but somehow he was now above it? Bullshit. He was motivated by headlines, which fueled his career. I saw Bobby's demise coming for a long time.

I think Giancana just wanted to sleep with Marilyn to drive the Kennedys nuts. A week before Marilyn's death, he, Sinatra, and Marilyn had a weekend-long tryst. I had people at the Cal-Neva who filled me in on any major goings-on. I also received a call from a buddy out there from New York, Jimmy Alo. They called him "Jimmy Blue Eyes," and he just happened to be at the Cal-Neva the same weekend the Lawfords showed up with Marilyn.

Sinatra and Giancana were having a ball, Alo said, but when they knew Marilyn arrived they took it up a notch. Giancana was overheard saying, "Wait until the Lawfords tell the Kennedy brothers about Marilyn's weekend with us, Frank. It's going to eat Bobby alive from the inside out." Alo told me that she was "out of it" all weekend long and what Frank and Giancana were doing to her, keeping her all drugged up and passing her back and forth, was "disgusting."

I provided my workers at Cal-Neva with great tips and thanked Alo for keeping me abreast of the situation. The next week when I received the phone call about Marilyn's death, I happened to be staying at the family ranch where I had taken Sinatra's folks.

I was in my monthly sit-down days after I got back to The Heights after Giancana's incident with Frank and Marilyn at Cal-Neva.

"Well you two are pretty brown," Fischetti said to Giancana and myself.

"You sound like a jealous schoolgirl."

"Because I am!"

"Okay, boys, enough," Accardo said, trying to get things on point.

"Okay," Giancana said. "The Outfit is ready to expand its

interests in Mexico and we have made plans for a representative of ours to meet with officials and our partners in Mexico City in two weeks. We're hoping to add interests there and in Acapulco, and create some in Cancun and Ixtapa."

"Who's going?" I asked. "Tony Fazio?"

"We were hoping so, Sal," Giancana said. "Can you let him know?"

"The Mexicans like him," Accardo added, "and Fazio knows how much he can negotiate without us there. And when it's time to come back to report."

"He'll have no issue going at all," I said. "He's probably looking to get some heat off of him anyway. I'll let him know first thing tomorrow, and we should all meet before he leaves so everyone is on the same page."

"Okay, that's it," Giancana said. "Our business is done for today. Now, Sal and I need to get back to Cal-Neva."

"Ah, fuck you two sons of bitches," Fischetti laughed as we made our way for the door.

"Hey Salvatore, hang back," Accardo said. "Owl Club talk."

Giancana glanced back at Accardo, and I sat back down knowing damn well it wasn't Owl Club business that he wanted to discuss.

"What's up, old friend?" I asked.

"It's about all this business with Giancana, Sinatra, and Monroe mixed in with the brothers." By brothers, he meant the Kennedys.

"I know, it's a mess. Be thankful she didn't off herself at Cal-Neva when that was happening. We'd have a massive catastrophe on our hands."

"I'm acutely aware of that which is why I want to talk to you, Sal."

"Okay," I said pointedly.

"When Giancana is out your way, make sure I hear anything

unbecoming for a man of his stature. I know you can't step on his toes. I understand the hierarchy here. I just want you to make sure you are aware of his activities when he is out West. The powers of The Outfit deserve to know how he is representing everyone while he is out of Chicago. New York called me about his Cal-Neva shenanigans." Accardo was visibly frustrated. "Speaking of out West, I also want you to keep even closer tabs on Handsome Johnny Roselli out in L.A. Capice?"

"Sure. And hey, can I say something real quick?" I asked. "Old-timer to old-timer?"

"One hundred percent, Sal. Shoot."

"Roselli makes me nervous. He feels like he'd be a talker if squeezed just hard enough. He has avoided me in the past, and I think I make him nervous. Like I can see through him."

Accardo nodded, absorbing what I'd said.

"Anyway," I continued, "I think we should have Roselli make himself useful and get a copy of Monroe's autopsy report. We need to make sure there isn't anything in there that is damaging to The Outfit. This can be done by us in good faith in case you believe New York has the perception we aren't on top of things."

"Do it," Accardo said, monotone.

ONLY A FEW weeks after Tony Fazio's return from Mexico, we had to bury Guy, who died of a heart attack at his home. Dominic was torn apart because he couldn't attend his brother's wake or funeral. I kept Guy on the payroll for as long as I could to keep cash coming in for his family.

Guy's death should have been a wake-up call for me. I was starting to experience shortness of breath and other symptoms that made me think my heart wasn't as strong as it ought to be. I already knew my lungs were getting weaker because I had to spend the entire December of '61 in the hospital being treated for pneumonia. And once authorities got word I was stuck in St. James, they had people watching and asking about every move I made and everyone who visited me inside that place. They'd even ask about what I ate. I realized that, once healthy, I'd need to keep moving every week or two to avoid surveillance.

At the same time, guys in our line of work don't spend much time thinking about growing old. It doesn't happen for a lot of us. It's not like I had taken great care of myself over the last twenty years. Big meals with the boys, lots of top-shelf booze, being up half the night with work shit. Eventually, the good life catches up to you.

My more metaphorical headaches had already been ramping up. I was dodging U.S. Senate committee subpoenas by moving around the West Coast every four or five days. And while I was avoiding being served, a Chicago Tribune reporter busted our balls and published an article about vice being run in the wide-open.

The story mentioned the Mancinis were once again running the Folies Bergere when it was supposedly shut down. It also mentioned a few other joints I had the Mancinis running for me. The story also mentioned my guy in Blue Island, who we called Tuff. The article talked about my horse parlor in Steger and called out Marco's, which sat in unincorporated Will County. They called Co-Op Music's sale of sheet music and records a front. They mentioned a few brothers-in-law by name.

A total fucking debacle.

The Senate wanted to question me regarding Cal City and which interests had moved from Cal City to other areas like Lansing and Thorton. I wouldn't have testified even if they found me in time for the hearings. I mostly didn't want to be seen on national television or be quoted in national newspapers. We've been over how I need to stay below the radar, right? And here's what I found ironic: once I was able to take a breath after those hearings ended, my pneumonia set it in. Surely they wouldn't have had a problem finding me in December 1961, right?

BUT NONE OF those problems were as bad as what happened a year after the FBI officially opened their file and assigned the G to me. That was 1963, the year of that wicked raid on The Heights. Oh, Madonna Mia!

It was the largest one I'd seen in The Heights since the twenties. Not a bad run, huh? In April of that year, about three hundred G-Men raided about as many of my handbook operations throughout southern Cook and Will counties. The G pinched Pizzoli, Steve Allen, Toots Potenza, a Zingaro brother, and more. They questioned Joe Coz and one of his brothers.

The FBI also found records of some Co-Op Music guys who shouldn't have been on the payroll—like Guy, who was earning $20K a year. Records also showed Co-Op still paying Dominic $20,000 annually—I was giving him Jon's salary as tribute—even though my cousin had been in Italy for twenty-eight years.

In the end, me and my top guys escaped indictment. But the raids forced us to increase our gambling revenue outside of the dens we were accustomed to operating. We pushed our bookies to ramp up their sports booking operations. Gamblers didn't need to be present, and sports viewership only increases every year. Sports books also had no operating costs when compared to running a nightclub and casino. It is also easier for our friends in law enforcement to turn a blind eye because it isn't visible to the communities. Sports bookies became, and still are, big revenue sources for The Outfit and all organizations across the country.

We continue to prove that we, as an organization, will evolve when it appears our backs are up against the wall.

CHAPTER 26

Villa Venice

There were some good times mixed in between '61 and '63. It wasn't all bad press, dodging subpoenas, and cleaning up after raids. For example, late in '62, Giancana had just finished fixing up the Villa Venice a little northwest of the city on the Des Plaines river.

He had nearly a month of high-end entertainment booked to celebrate its opening. Momo secured Dean Martin, Sammy Davis, Eddie Fisher, our buddy Jimmy Durante, and, of course, Sinatra. Giancana didn't have a hard time getting everyone on board. Sinatra knew he owed Giancana for a lot of this Kennedy shit. See, Sinatra asked his friend Momo to help get the vote out for JFK. The Outfit didn't rig or stuff the ballot boxes, but they threw their influence behind Jack via the unions.

And don't forget, Joe Kennedy was a bootlegger and racketeer. Chicago thought if they helped his son get elected, perhaps the government would back off. Well, shortly after JFK's election, he made his brother Bobby the United States Attorney General. And what did Bobby do? He declared war on organized crime. Let's just say there were some pissed off gangsters from coast to coast. Bobby definitely forgot where he came from … friggin' strunz!

Anyway, in addition to the top-notch entertainment, in one of our meetings at the Armory Lounge, Giancana expressed a thought. "Wouldn't it be great if we had gondolas ferrying our guests during the reopening celebrations?"

I rocked back in my chair. "I actually may be able to help you with that."

"Really? Do tell." Giancana's eyes widened. "You got a gondola guy?"

"My good friend over at the Morici's Chicago Macaroni Company may be able to help out. He has import-export connections in Italy and may be able to bring some over for you. Do you want me to look into it for you?"

"Absolutely, Salvatore. If he can do it, see how many he thinks he can ship over and let me know. I think I'd take up to six. This would be huge if it works."

"I'll see what I can do and get back to ya."

After that meeting, I stopped into Fagman's, my favorite clothing shop in Chicago. I wanted to pick up some new digs for the season. I also used their phone to make calls once in a while, like having an office in the city.

"I gotta make a call," I told Fagman, so he took me back to his office.

"Tone," I said when my brother-in-law answered the phone. "It's Sal."

"Hey Sal, what's up?"

Concetta was best friends with Paolo Montecelli's wife, and I knew I could get a message to Paolo via my sister. "My sister around? I need to ask her something."

"She's out with Gladys. Can I have her call you?"

"Funny she's with Gladys. I need to talk to Paolo and see if he can have some large items shipped over from Italy."

"I'll make sure he gets the message," Tony said. "If I don't see him tonight, I'll tell Concetta to let Gladys know you'd like to talk to him."

I said goodbye to Tony and walked back to the front of the store to see all my stuff boxed and wrapped.

"I threw an extra shirt in with the slacks that I thought would look nice, Mr. Sal," Fagman said as he passed the two bags to me. "On the house."

The next day, I got a call at Co-Op Music from Paolo Montecelli. He worked almost all day, and I don't like bothering people who are working, so I was fine with him calling me at his convenience. Unless of course a week went by. Then I might have other thoughts, but Paolo wouldn't do that to me.

"Thanks for calling me back in such a timely fashion," I said. "How's Gladys?"

"She's great, thanks. If I could just get her to stop going out and spending money with your sister every day, I'd be a lot happier."

"Not sure if I can help you with that one, Paolo," I joked back. "That's a conversation you can have with Tony."

Pleasantries out of the way, Paolo got to the point. "So, what can I help you with?"

"Gondolas, Paolo. A friend wants gondolas from Italy and I thought you may know the best way to get them here."

"I need to make some calls, but I can do that for you without a problem. How many does your friend want?"

"He said he'd take up to six if it was possible."

"Can I call you back as soon as I get word it can be done?" Paolo asked cautiously.

"Absolutely."

Four hours later, my phone rang at Co-Op.

"Sal, it's Paolo. I bought six gondolas. They'll be here in about eight weeks. I hope that works for your friend. If not, I now own six gondolas."

"Eight weeks works for everyone," I assured him, knowing Giancana would be ecstatic. "And Momo won't forget you did this for him."

Here's what I loved about Paolo. He never asked who the friend was that I was asking for and when I did tell him, he acted like Giancana was no big deal. The guy was a total pro. "I did it for you, my friend," Paolo said coolly. "Not him."

"I appreciate you saying that, but this was big. I'll even pay you back today and then have him pay me back. Can I swing over tonight and drop off what you're owed?"

"Whatever works for you works for me. In fact, won't you stay for dinner? I bought some new wine I want you to try."

"You know what? I'll take you up on that," I said. "I haven't seen Gladys in a while and she always makes me laugh. I'll bring some flowers for her."

"She'll love that, Sal. Come over any time after five. We'll eat at seven or seven-thirty. Sound good?"

"See you at six."

The Montecellis were an honest and hardworking family. It's one of the main reasons I wanted to pay him back on the same day. I didn't want to cause Paolo one headache over this thing.

Of course, when I told Giancana at lunch a few days later, he was gushing about the gondolas.

"Sal, this is huge. As many tickets as you need for any night, Sal, just let me know."

"That's generous, but whatever tickets I ask for I'll pay for."

"Sure, Sal. When the time comes, just give me dates and how many tickets you need."

"I'll give you plenty of notice. All I know now is that I need nights when Sinatra is singing."

"No problem at all." Giancana pulled out an envelope stuffed with cash. "For the gondolas. And when the Montecelli's come to the show, let me know so I can stop over and thank him personally."

"Will do, and I'll get the dates and the number of tickets I need to you as soon as possible."

A few weeks later, Joey Fazio tracked me down.

"Uncle Sal, how many tickets do you think we can buy for a Villa Venice show?" he asked. "I heard my parents talking to the Montecellis about what days would work."

"I could probably get as many as your parents need. Why?"

"Well, I was wondering if the same night my parents are going, if I could invite my girlfriend, Donna, and her family," Joey said. "Her two brothers are also great friends of mine, and her parents are great people. You know how my dad loves them too."

I smiled at his strong lobbying. "I'll get five more tickets for the same night you are going. Is that good?"

Joey beamed. "Is that good? Uncle Sal, that is awesome. Thank you so much!"

"You know I got you covered whenever I can."

"I know Uncle Sal. You know I am going to marry this girl, right?"

"Whoa, easy now. You're only eighteen. How old is she?"

"She's sixteen. I mean, we're not getting married now. I want to get married when I am twenty."

"Sounds like a solid plan. And when you're ready, I will be there."

Joey came in for a hug, and I squeezed him and covered his face with kisses. He tried squirming away when he knew I was playing around with him but I covered him solidly before I let him go.

THE VILLA VENICE was tucked away far enough that if you were on River Road, you'd have no idea what lies back there. Security there was fairly lax, and Giancana made sure there'd be no trouble with authorities. You either belonged there or you didn't. Every car was greeted by a few guys as they drove off of River Road towards the joint. They would direct drivers where to park, and the nicest rides were instructed to pull all the way up to the valets.

"Uncle Sal!" I heard echoing from the Des Plaines river one

evening there before the shows started. Joey and family were in a gondola with Montecelli and his wife. It looked like Paolo was giving them a tour of all the gondolas brought over from Italy.

Damn, those shows were something else. All that talent on one stage for almost a month. I'd look through the smoke at the faces in the crowd and it would just be eyes wide open and smiles abound. The straight-up, extra-dry martinis, sweet Manhattans, Rob Roys, and Sloe Gin Fizzes were being served up fast and accepted even faster. It was shoulder-to-shoulder, but no one cared while they were having the time of their lives. The gals were in their finest beaded dresses and tops and full-length leather gloves, their hair and nails impeccable. The gents were adorned in new silk suits, expensive ties and Italian leather shoes. The ladies' perfume mixed with the sweet scent of the cocktails, the thick smoke, and sweat.

Sammy Davis Jr. was simply fantastic that night. When he'd goof around with Frank and Dino, the crowd would just lose it in laughter. One time when they were clowning around, Sammy put his arm on Dean's shoulder. Dean slowly removed Sammy's arm off his shoulder, looked at him and said, "Sammy, I'll share my money with you … share my booze and women with you … and if you need anything please let me know … but don't ever touch me!" They then hugged it out and laughed hysterically and the crowd went nuts. Dino and Sammy stole the show in my opinion. Nothing against Sinatra, but those two were just stellar.

There was a point in the show that night, however, when Sinatra called out a heckler and the place went up for grabs.

Sometime after Sinatra's third song, some guy in the crowd yelled, "Play Nice 'n' Easy!" Frank ignored him like he didn't hear a word. But after this strunz shouted "Nice 'n' Easy" after the fifth and sixth songs, Frank had heard enough from this guy. "Hey buddy, I don't tell you how to deliver milk!" Sinatra yelled and the crowd exploded in laughter and applause. That was Frank. For an entertainer, he certainly didn't take shit from anybody. Everything had to be on his terms.

What a night. What a month. Giancana probably brought in three million bucks between the ticket sales, booze and casino gambling made available nearby. However, the handful of shows with the Rat Pack at the Villa Venice will go down in history. My nephew couldn't stop talking about how much everyone loved their evening, and thanking me for making sure his girlfriend and her family could be part of something so special. Joey kept to his timeline with Donna. He was engaged sometime in 1963 and got married in mid-'64.

The wedding was spectacular and the reception was massive. There were eleven hundred people in attendance at the Legion Hall in Chicago Heights. If I have seen a bigger cake than that, I sure as hell can't remember where. Accardo came in and out of the back door of the Hall, and we both came and went through the kitchen. There were G-Men in the parking lot taking license plate numbers, so we had rides to avoid them. I had gotten word that the G had been trying to locate me, but word was that they believed I was in Italy. This brought me some pleasure. If I was careful—as usual—I could relax a little bit as long as they thought I was back in Sambiase or Rome.

And as the night was winding down, I needed to talk to my nephew and his lovely new bride. "What a beautiful day this was. I couldn't be happier for you two. And Donna, what a stunning bride you are. Joey is a lucky man."

"Oh, I think we're both lucky," Donna said sweetly.

"Here's my envelope," I told Joey. "Put it in your jacket."

"Thanks, Uncle Sal," Joey said as he stuffed the cash inside his tuxedo jacket. "I appreciate it."

"Listen, make sure you find Tony Accardo's envelope before

you leave. He probably gave you kids five hundred bucks." And he had.

"Oh geez!" Donna gasped as she looked bright-eyed at Joey.

I smiled at her enthusiasm. "So, Vegas for you two love birds, huh? That should be fun. I am excited for you guys to go. I kind of wish I could be there at the same time but I can't swing it. When are you planning on leaving? When is your flight?"

"Oh no, we aren't flying," Joey said. "Tickets were too much money, and because we aren't in a hurry, we were just going to drive."

"Well, if you're driving, you're driving my new car. I just picked up that green Buick a few weeks ago and it needs to take a road trip."

"Uncle Salvatore," Donna said nervously, "we can't take your car cross-country."

"Sweetheart, it's just a car and I insist. It's a convertible with A.C. When are you planning on making the drive?"

"We were thinking about leaving tomorrow afternoon or the day after," Joey said.

"Leave the day after tomorrow if you can," I told him. "I want to make some calls beforehand. I'll swing over to your parents' house tomorrow morning to drop off my car and your dad can give me a lift to the dealership so I can get a loaner."

I walked into my sister's house the next day for some coffee and breakfast if it wasn't too late.

"I can't believe you're giving the kids your new car to drive out to Vegas," Tony said.

"Me either," my sister added. "Are you sure?"

"Enough, both of you. It's just a car. Let the kids drive first-class."

Before they could continue protesting, Joey and Donna walked into the house.

"Hey, lovebirds. Still planning on driving to Vegas?"

Joey nodded. "We're planning on leaving the first thing tomorrow morning."

"Perfect," I said as I pulled out a piece of folded up paper from my pocket. "I made those phone calls."

"What's this?" Joey asked me as I handed him the paper.

"That list is the date of the best shows, where they're located, and who I want you to ask for as soon as you walk into the venues. Capice?"

"Thanks, Uncle Sal," Joey said. "Anything else we should know?"

"You're staying at the Stardust, right?" I asked.

"Yup," both the kids replied in sync.

"Good. I got you all set up. Go have fun, and call me when you get home. I'll want to hear all about your honeymoon."

A couple weeks later my sister and Tony had me over for dinner with Joey and Donna upon their return from Vegas.

"So tell me kids, how'd you like Vegas?" I asked as we began filling our plates and taking our first sips of wine.

"Well," Joey said, "before we even got to Vegas, a crazy thing happened to us. We got pulled over in Wyoming for speeding, but that was a bunch of crap. I was only going a few miles over the speed limit. The cops brought us to the station and said we needed to pay a hundred bucks in cash. I had it so it wasn't a problem, but it was quite a headache and I think Donna was a little scared."

"Why do you think you got pulled over?" I asked.

"I think they saw two young kids in a super fancy car and decided to mess with us. That's what I think," my nephew said, trying to not raise his voice.

"I think you're absolutely correct," Tony told Joey.

"Anyway," Joey continued. "We got on our way and made it to the Stardust with no more drama."

"What did you think when you pulled up to it for the first time?" I asked, a grin on my face.

Donna laughed. "Our eyes popped out of our heads!"

"I also recognized a few dealers from the Owl Club," Joey added. "Speaking of dealers, one night Donna was playing a little blackjack before we headed out for a show. The dealer looked young, like my age or just a little older, and he helped Donna win."

I grinned as I continued eating. "Oh yeah? How'd that happen?"

"He'd deal the cards and then just hit or stay for me," Donna said, "without me ever saying a word or making a motion."

"Sounds good to me," my sister said as she kept putting more food on all our plates without anyone asking.

"And one day I was playing keno next to Jerry Vale for about an hour," Joey added. "That was pretty fun."

"Did you two get to all the shows?" I asked.

"Oh yeah," Joey said. "We saw the Lido show you told us to see. We saw Connie Francis, and Don Rickles, who was friggin' hilarious."

"Oh, Don cracks me up," I said.

"He asked the guy in the front row, Hey, you sleeping with her? The guy seemed embarrassed and said no. Rickles doesn't hesitate to ask him, Then why the hell are you buying her dinner?" Joey burst out laughing and had to gather himself before continuing. "The room lost it. People were wiping tears of laughter out of their eyes. We also saw Louis Prima and Pat Henry. We hit your entire list."

"So everything went smooth?" I probed.

"Like silk, Uncle Sal. We'd walk into the venue and I would ask whoever was at the door for whoever's name was on your list for that show. Without hesitation, the person would know what to do or get that person. We always had the booth in the middle of every room, set back just far enough not to garner any attention but still be the best seat in the house. And they'd never give us a bill, nor were we allowed to tip our server. They'd just say, Sir, we can't accept your tips but thank you. We are being taken care of for taking care of you."

"We felt like movie stars, Donna said. "It was all so very special."

"The icing on the cake came when we checked out of the Stardust," Joey said, "and we didn't have a bill!"

"What?" my sister said in total shock.

"I know, Donna said. "We charged a sports coat, a dress, and some accessories to our room. When we checked out, they just said, It's all been taken care of, Mr. and Mrs. Fazio. We hope you had a wonderful stay at the Stardust and we hope you come back soon to see us."

"Utter shock," Joey said.

"Honestly, we don't know what to say," Donna added.

Joey got excited. "Oh, there's one last story that happened on our way home. The total opposite of getting shaken down by the Wyoming cops."

"Do tell," I said.

"So Donna and I were just wiped out from the trip and driving home, so we decided to pull over in Tulsa for the night. Well, completely randomly, there was a PGA event being held in town and all the golfers were staying at the resort that we checked into."

"Oh, no way," my sister said as she began clearing the table. "How fun."

"What made it funny was that these guys, like Palmer and Trevino, were all gassed up and laughing their asses off, flying around in golf carts with girls. They were like kids, totally goofing around at Olympia Fields like nobody was watching."

"Well," I said, "it sounds like the honeymoon was a ten out of ten."

"Donna and I don't really know how to thank you except to keep telling you how wonderfully we were treated and how much fun we had." He leaned back in his chair and raised his wine glass to me.

I smiled and raised my glass to Joey's. "You are thanking me by telling me what you did and that you had the time of your life."

What Joey didn't know was that the Stardust contacted me, ready to offer Joey a job as a pit boss. But his father and I decided it was not an option. Neither one of us wanted Joey to be part of that life, so we had the offer pulled before Joey ever knew about it.

The joy I saw on those kids' faces made my year. I cared immensely about what my family—especially my nieces and nephews—thought of me. I was always fearful they would learn more and think differently of me, that my family wouldn't respect me or love me anymore.

At that point, my nieces and nephews were my kids.

They were all I had.

CHAPTER 27

Kiss A Good Thing Goodbye

A week or so later, I headed back to San Diego because Bomps wanted to introduce me to his "good friend" Jimmy Fratianno, who did a stretch in Ohio before the boys in Cleveland sent him out West with their blessings. Handsome Johnny Roselli sponsored him, and Jack Dragna made him.

Bomps called me down so Fratianno could sell me on coming in on his new trucking business. We met at one of Bomps's favorite joints for dinner. I arrived twenty minutes early to make sure Bomps got us a good table, and to relax with a drink before we started talking business. I was in my sixties by then, and I'd already had a long day of traveling before meandering into the dark but rich looking steakhouse. A truly classy joint. Black suede panels covered the windows. Huge crystal chandeliers hung over the red carpet and large booths adorned in black leather with white tablecloths. And everyone was dressed to the nines.

I opted for a Dewar's on the rocks and lit up a robusto while I waited. I was a little wary of the upcoming sales pitch, but Bomps was an old buddy and I am always willing to hear about new ways to invest my cash. Fratianno was selling his new plan for a legit trucking business with some fringe benefits.

"It's like the kickbacks I got in the Occidental Oil deal," Fratianno pitched, "but this will be on the books, see."

He told me about some of the other trucking deals and jobs he had done in the Sacramento area. He sounded like a cheap car salesman, and at times I felt like he was insulting my intelligence.

"Well how much fucking equipment do you got?" I interrupted as we all puffed our cigars.

"Sal, I'm getting bigger all the time but I need to be careful because of my parole and all. They fucking watch me like a fucking hawk. I did just buy five transfer units, called Slam-Bangs. I'm the first guy in Sacramento to have them. You can do so much more for cheaper because these things can haul twenty-five tons at a time versus the standard dump truck."

"How much did that set you back?"

"Well, they are thirty-three grand each. But Sal, I got a guy in Stockton who falsified the down payments. He takes the price up to thirty-eight grand so the bank thinks I put five grand down, see."

"Sal, this fucking guy has more junk on a ball than Sandy Koufax," Bomps said, laughing at his own joke. "He may be one of the best bullshitters I have ever met."

"Maybe that's what fucking scares me, Bomps," I said while staring down Fratianno.

"This is all good," Fratianno continued in his annoyingly cocky way. "All my drivers are union guys, Teamsters, but I have a way around paying the union."

"How the hell do you manage that?"

"Say one of my drivers gets hurt. I date back a check for the month prior in their name. When the agents in Sacramento or Redding question me, I just tell them I'm paying straight to HQ in San Fran. See? I never pay welfare, vacation, pension, or health. I do pay workman's comp, but there's just no way around that."

"Sounds decent," I admitted.

"Because I'm in the Teamsters, whenever contracts come in from other parts of the country, my union guys hand them my card, see. Because I get all the jobs, all the truckers want to work for me. I got fifty trucks working on fifty percent commission on top of the twelve trucks and heavy equipment. I'm sitting pretty but I am obviously looking to expand, which is why I wanted to talk to you."

This all sounded good, but I wanted to know how Jimmy Fratianno made his bones and cut his teeth. I've heard some things. Some people's version of an earner or tough guy is different than mine, to say the least.

"Say, Jimmy, how'd you earn? Booking? Shylocking? Gambling? What do you have going on in Sacramento?"

Fratianno had been booking since he was a kid but wasn't as into it by that point. He told a few other stories meant to impress, and after some deliberation I secured a quarter-million-dollar loan and brought in a couple of brothers-in-law. Tony and Joe DeCarlo each put in for fifty-five grand. This was supposed to be like an annuity that would fund their retirement.

The trucking business went smoothly for a few years until Bomps called me to come to San Diego to discuss an "issue" that had come up. Two days later I showed up for the dinner meeting with Bomps and Fratianno.

Bomps didn't have his normal face on, and Fratianno looked like he was guilty of something. As the maître d' escorted me to the back corner booth, I remember wondering what I'd gotten myself into. "Scotch with three ice cubes, please," I told the waitress as she approached the table.

"Sal, good to see ya!" Bomps said, sounding a bit fake.

"You two get here fifteen minutes early to get your stories straight?"

"Calm down," Fratianno said. "We haven't even had a chance to even tell you what's up."

"Listen, Little Jimmy, don't ever fucking tell me to calm down." Based on his reaction, I don't think anyone had ever called Fratianno Little Jimmy before, which only helped drive home my point. "This is calm. When I am not calm, you'll feel it throughout your entire body. Capice? I got shit going on in Lake County, Indiana, that needs addressing and a new headache out here is the last fucking thing I need. Don't try to schmooze me. I'm smarter than you and I see through you like newly cleaned glass, okay? Now what the fuck is going on?"

I think I made my point.

"Well, see, one of my guys roughed up a driver who was out of line and the guy went to the authorities," Fratianno confessed.

"What the mother fuck, Jimmy? How'd you let this happen? What specifically do you mean by out of line?" I was spitting through my teeth, fighting my urge to yell. And the urge to lean across the table and choke him out.

"He refused to sign the Owner-Operator driver's contract."

"And you thought beating a signature out of him would be worth it, versus letting the strunz go and finding another driver? You know goddamn well how I feel about attracting attention, you stupid fuck." I was fuming. "What do you have to say about this, Bomps?"

"Obviously, this is very disappointing news. I'm pretty fuckin' pissed."

He'd said the right words, but Bomps sounded defeated. So, I turned my attention back to Fratianno. "How the fuck are you gonna fix this?"

"Honestly, I don't know. The damage has been done."

"Great. Fucking call me when there's nothing I can do to help. So now what?"

"Waiting for subpoenas from what I hear," Fratianno said without much fear.

"Well, I've dodged them before. I guess I'll do it again." I stood. "You really fucked me on this, Little Jimmy. Unfuckingbelievable."

"Where you going already?" Fratianno asked.

"I'm sure as hell not sitting here any longer. I'm disappearing. Good luck to ya."

SURE ENOUGH, THE government launched an investigation. I did like I needed and ducked the subpoena, but Jimmy Fratianno's strunz cost me just over $400K and I had to stay out of California. The charges against Bomps somehow got dropped, which seemed a bit fishy but I dismissed it. Fratianno received a fine and a few years' probation. I was just happy I dodged another bullet, but my brothers-in-law lost a lot of their savings. Sure, I lost almost eight times what they did, but they had families. I was sick to my stomach, but they were ready to pick up and move on. True pros.

That thing in Lake County, Indiana, was Chicago asking me to take the territory. My buddy was retiring and the fellas in line to replace him had tax and legal problems. Chicago didn't want to go farther down pecking order there and they knew I was the best, regardless of the time I spent out West.

But Ricky the Bomber wasn't so sure.

"Sal, I'm hearing that Ricky's not too pleased with the Lake County thing going to you," Pizzoli told me soon after I got back.

"I've heard the rumors made it up to Auippa," I said. "Ricky's making a stink and his stench is wafting far from home. I've got his number."

"Anything I need to know or do?"

"No. For now, we just keep on our toes and keep doin' what we're doin." Which, around that time, was expanding our vending footprint deeper into Will and Kane counties.

Pizzoli nodded and leaned in. "Who you thinkin' 'bout putting in charge of Lake County's day to day?"

"I think Toots is the guy who deserves it and will run it in my style."

"I agree. You know I trust him. He goes way back with us, and he's waited his turn. I like working with him a shit ton more than Ricky and his new buddy, The Greek, that's for sure. Though that one's a motivated earner, I'll give him that."

"Yeah, I know The Greek. He's eager to move up with Ricky and he's not afraid of anything. None of those guys working the chop-shops are. We definitely take him seriously within the organization. Anyway, Tell Potenza tomorrow to come see me."

Next thing I know, I'm catching word all over The Heights that Ricky the Bomber is talking. Not only is he talking. He's talking shit.

The subject came up during a big family cookout at Concetta and Tony's house. As usual, I held the business talk until my sisters were busy doing the dishes and getting coffee and desserts ready.

"I want all cool heads here," I told my brothers-in-law. "We're not young kids anymore. Hell, you all have your own kids, and most of them are grown. Ricky's an earner and he wants more. Potenza getting Indiana was just a hot iron poker in his ass."

"We could have our guy do his thing," Joe Rosetta suggested.

"We are a long way from that. He isn't being replaced by anyone here, so let's all take a deep breath and relax."

"He fucking threatened us, Sal," Tony said. "Did he not?"

"One of my guys said that he did. But it was in a roundabout way."

"Roundabout?" Joe DeCarlo said in disbelief.

"He was talking about after I was retired or dead," I clarified.

"Do you know what the fuck he said exactly?" Rosetta asked, visibly angry.

"He said ninety percent of my brothers-in-laws could be dead if they weren't retired when I was gone," I told them.

"Motherfucker," more than half the guys said at the same time.

"I will arrange a sit-down if I need to," I said. "This is nothing. Everyone just relax. However, if I did die, you all should seriously consider retiring. This thing is changing fast and it's time to realize that no amount of money is enough to go to war or die over. These chop-shop guys are determined. Not only are they determined, they're ruthless. The bodies will start piling up and that draws serious attention. I want all you guys away from their operations."

"Sal, what are you talking about?" Fazio asked. "That's not even gonna happen. We don't need to discuss such ridiculous things."

"If I do this another ten years, I'll be in my mid-seventies. It really wasn't my plan to do this at such an old age. I think I'll be ready to sit back and look at the fields in less than that."

"When you're out, Sal, we're out," DeCarlo said.

At that, all the guys held their glasses over the fire pit.

"I'm not going anywhere right now," I joked, "so none of you jag-offs go to your rooms tonight and start dreaming about buying a boat in Miami. You all still got jobs to be at tomorrow!"

Half the guys started busting my balls when I tried leaving, which caused my sisters to come down and insist I sit down until after pie and coffee.

CHAPTER 28

The Sit-Down

A few months later, my expansion west caught the attention of the mayor of Aurora, Nevada. This character decided to contact the Illinois Investigation Commission. Because of this, authorities managed to serve me a subpoena—after forty years of dodging them. You got to admit, that's a hell of a run.

Those legal troubles slowed us down a bit. They named and pinched Aldo Fazio, Steve Allen, Francis, and myself. The charges were eventually dropped on Don, and Steve and I refused to answer any questions. But it was a major fucking headache for all involved, to say the least. There was a damning newspaper article in September of 1966 about it, too. The Trib really pissed me off because they called out my brother-in-law and snapped off some photos of me and the fellas. But what really took my anger to another level was the fact they put photos and addresses of our homes in the article! Total fucking harassment as far as I'm concerned.

Then, just when I thought that things couldn't get any hotter in '66, they did.

And in a big way.

That's when this thing with The Bomber really escalated. This fucking guy kept pushing me and pushing me. If it had been thirty years earlier, I would've just taken care of him. But he was too big an earner now, though he had really pushed deep into my territory with full intent of taking over my interests.

"Sal, we gotta talk," Pizzoli said with an earnest face.

"What do you have for me?"

"Ricky's got The Greek angling with him out here. Ricky must be cutting him in on whatever he takes. Something for sure."

"Do you have any specifics?"

"They infiltrated the Eagles in Cal Park from what I hear. One of our bartenders there."

"Do we know which one?"

"I'm actively working on getting that info."

"Once you know, send a message. That piece of shit, whoever he is, thinks he's going to spy on us for a puny fuck who is my subordinate. Make sure this guy has served his last hi-ball."

"I'm on it, Sal."

"You know who I want to handle this. When it's done, tell him I'll send Rosetta to his place with an envelope."

"It'll be taken care of, Sal."

A few days later, I heard my Number One hitter was waiting outside the Eagles A-Go-Go for our rat bartender to leave work. Roger P, an ex-cop in The Heights, was my manager there at the time, so we knew when this strunz's shift was up.

As our bartender friend went to unlock his car, Rosetta turned on his headlights to catch the rat's attention. When the bartender looked up, my guy put a gun to his head and ordered the bartender into his own car

"No quick moves or you're a goner."

"What's this all about?" the bartender asked, visibly shaking.

"Who have you been reporting to?" my guy asked while pointing the gun as they headed out of Cal Park. "Take a right."

"What do you mean? I work in Sal's place."

"I hear that you are actually reporting to someone else. Take a left."

"I don't know what you're talking about. Really!"

"We're done talking. Take a soft left."

After thirty minutes, with Rosetta following, my guy instructed the bartender to park in an abandoned industrial site in Northwest Indiana. After seeing his bleak location, the rat started to talk.

"Okay. Okay. I'm working with The Greek and Ricky. I report to Ricky on what I see and hear. Please—"

My guy put two in the back of his head and stuffed him inside the truck, then wiped down the car best he could. Rosetta was right there and ready to take everyone home. The cops found a freaking diary on this guy detailing the happenings at the Eagles A-Go-Go, and my plants in the department confirmed the bartender was with Ricky and The Greek. I was ready to kill them both myself, but I knew better.

A couple days later, word got back to me that The Bomber thought Roger P had pulled the trigger. Roger was a friend for a long time, so I put word out that he was under my protection and shouldn't be touched.

He was found a few months later in a ditch along West Avenue in Chicago Heights, beaten and shot in the head.

I was at my breaking point with Ricky and could feel things escalating out of control. Sure enough, a couple months later, an associate of mine who worked at a collection agency in Blue Island—which was under Ricky's control—was found shot and left for dead in his trunk not far from the agency's office. The Bomber had thought the guy was spying for me, and he was right.

But this was the final straw.

It was time for me to insist on a sit-down with Accardo and Ricca. If they couldn't get Ricky to respect the boundaries, I was going to kill The Bomber before he got me or someone in my family.

RICKY DIDN'T STAND a chance. Especially after I had Milwaukee Phil and Teets Battaglia in my corner. These guys were seriously respected by Accardo and Ricca. Milwaukee Phil went way back as a friend of The Heights crew. Teets and I were also close, mostly through his relations with the Battaglia brothers south of us in Kankakee. They both assured me that they had my back and would put the word in for me. With that, I called for a meeting in neutral territory. We met at a restaurant that's friendly with the Boys in The Heights and set the time for late morning, before they were open to the public.

Ricky the Bomber wasn't so cocky. He knew he broke the rules, and was probably happy he was sitting there instead of at the bottom of the Cal-Sag river.

"Ricky," Accardo said, "why are you pushing back on Sal?"

"Push back?" I said. "This fuck killed two of my guys and Roger P wasn't to be touched."

"Sal, please," Ricca said with sympathetic eyes.

"He's in California or somewhere all the time and he's got family on cushy payroll jobs," Ricky said.

"I'm gonna kill this fucker right now." I wasn't yelling, just stating it quite matter-of-factly.

"No, you're not," Accardo and Ricca said simultaneously

"He's an earner," Ricca said. "And isn't scared of trouble."

"I can replace him before this meeting ends," I countered.

"With who?" Ricky asked with disdain. "Another brother-in-law?"

I shot Ricca and Accardo a look that said Resolve this now, or I will.

"Enough," Accardo said, trying to diffuse the agitation in the room.

"Ricky," Ricca said, "you wouldn't even be here if Sal and Guy Scalea—may he rest in peace—hadn't let you into The Heights. So, here's what we're gonna do. You get all of Blue Island, and you stop your assault on Sal's people and turf."

"That's it?" The Bomber complained. "Just Blue Island?"

"Listen," Accardo said, his frustration showing through, "we all go back to the early twenties. Sal is largely responsible for most or all the interests you are looking to hijack from him. You're off-base. Either accept this or be on your own. Understood?"

"Understood," Ricky conceded, though I knew immediately he wouldn't stick to it. Some of these younger guys like Ricky had started to feel entitled when they should've just been grateful to be getting a piece.

The Bomber may have had new boundaries, but he never let his beef with me die. He was just more discreet about it because if he didn't at least appear to stand down, Chicago wasn't going to protect him from me.

Us Capone guys looked out for one another.

IN LATE 1967 or early '68, I started getting calls from Jimmy Fratianno again. He'd been trying places I liked to eat and hang out with no luck until finally reaching me at home on a random night.

"Sal, you're a tough guy to get a hold of," Fratianno said when I picked up.

As soon as I heard his voice, I poured myself a big-ass scotch.

"That's because you cost me a fucking fortune," I said. " What's up now?"

"I want you to invest in a casino with me. I have a couple in mind."

"Which ones?"

"My first choice is Crystal Bay in Lake Tahoe. My fallback is the Tallyho. I'm sure you're familiar with both."

"You know, Little Jimmy, I can't believe you got the balls to ask if I want to get involved in another one of your business ventures. Do you just take me for one of your marks? What the fuck?"

"The last thing I am trying to do is insult you. I come to you with ideas because, yes, you got the cash most don't have. But you also have vision, Sal. Guys from New York don't think outside their Family, let alone outside the state. But nobody carries more clout than you right now west of Chicago. You know what's going on out here better than anyone. Fuckin' fuhgeddaboudit."

He wasn't wrong, so I decided to mull it over. "If I call you back, I expect to know who your front is going to be."

"I'm working with Nick Palermo. You know, the mayor with ties to the San Fran and San Jose Families. He's supposed to help me find the face of this thing."

"You think the mayor of San Francisco and his people want to get back into bed with you again?"

"If they think it's a winner, then yes."

I had to think about this one long and hard. Fratianno was a weasel and I didn't trust him as far as I could throw him. "I'll get back to you."

I was interested in the Tallyho. And as much as I didn't trust the guy, I figured if Fratianno brought in the right guys, who knows? I could use a home run to make up for the trucking company debacle.

Anyway, I packed up and headed to California. We decided to meet at the Nut Tree, a familiar place where we had meetings during the Fratianno Trucking days. Bomps showed up, too, but Palermo couldn't attend in person. He was in the middle of exploring a possible gubernatorial run, so he sent his brother-in-law.

"Thanks for coming, everyone," Fratianno said. "Especially you, Sal. I really appreciate the trouble."

"What do you got?" I asked, getting to the point.

"It's been my lifelong desire to own a casino," he said, "and I'm thinking this could be my last chance."

"It does sound attractive … if it can be accomplished," I said.

"As I told you guys earlier, I'm looking into the Crystal Bay and the Tallyho."

Before he could continue, I wanted to steer him toward my preferred choice. "I did a little research into the Tallyho, and Hughes is divesting his Vegas interests."

Palermo's guy decided to jump in, too. "Why do you want my brother-in-law involved? Considering what you've already put him through."

"Because he is such a well-heeled attorney along with everything else," Fratianno said. "He can be a conduit to form new relationships and help us navigate the regulatory waters."

Palermo's in-law sat back into his chair. "Okay, I'll listen."

"I like the location of the Tallyho and the price," I said. "I think it may be an easier deal to get done."

"I'm good with either one," Fratianno said. "I feel it's better for us to have a couple options when looking for money and a face for the casino. This leads us to our next point—who?"

"My cousins out here in Cali know a lot of builders and ranchers who have cash and a clean face to front," I said. I can start asking around."

"I'll put some feelers out too," Bomps finally chimed in. He was sitting quietly, which wasn't like him at all.

We ended the meeting and arranged a follow up two weeks later, again at the Nut Tree. We planned to compare notes.

This time, I started the meeting. "I got good news. My cousins have a couple ranchers and a prominent industrial builder willing to invest and or be the face for the casino."

"Nick is willing to help you throughout the legal and regulatory processes," Palermo's brother-in-law added.

"And I reached out to the families in San Fran and San Jose," Bomps said. "They'd be interested if the money and front were solid."

Fratianno raised his glass of beer, which was loaded with ice. "This is great news! Looks like it's time to apply for our license with the gaming commission."

"The only thing is," I said, trying to sound casual "for whatever reasons, my people are overwhelmingly set on the Tallyho and aren't interested in the Crystal Bay."

I should have known it was too good to be true.

The Nevada Gaming Commission rejected our license application because they figured out Fratianno was involved. I wasn't necessarily surprised, but I was extremely disappointed. It was going to be impossible to make up for the trucking losses unless I stayed active back home.

Ricky the Bomber was going to love hearing that I wasn't retiring just yet.

When I returned to The Heights, I found out that authorities were still keeping a close eye on Co-Op Music, and state revenue agents had taken away some of our Royal Vending machines for not displaying the required tax stamps.

The headaches were going to continue in 1969, so after I took care of the pressing issues, I went back to my tomato ranch in California to contemplate my next move and escape the prying eyes.

CHAPTER 29

The Exposé

And now, I'm still sitting in my wraparound porch on this picture perfect California day. I love sipping an iced tea—or something stronger—when the trucks are loading up tomatoes. Today I opted for a glass of scotch on the rocks.

Hey, it's almost one in the afternoon, I joke to myself. I'm a bachelor. What difference does it make?

"Mr. Sal, the mail arrived," one of my field workers says." Here you go sir."

"Thank you. How's the crop looking?"

"Looks great, Mr. Sal. The guys loading the truck even commented on how beautiful this crop looks."

"Outstanding. Thanks, Edwardo. You guys need anything, let me know."

"Thank you, Mr. Sal. We are okay."

The mail is mostly coupon books and junk mail. But in between all the crap is my favorite magazine, LOOK. I'll read it and then bring it over to my sister's, like I do with all my magazines. I'm absentmindedly glancing over the cover when …

Holy shit! There's an article in here about Nick Palermo—our friend, current Mayor of San Francisco and possible gubernatorial candidate—and his mafia ties. I frantically open the magazine and jump to page seventeen. It is all about Palermo's ties to Fratianno and the families in San Fran and San Jose.

Then Bomps is mentioned. "Oh shit," I say as my heart sinks

into my gut.

Then I keep reading.

I am all over this article. They even have a candid photo of me, from out here in California. How the hell did they get this? Unfuckingbelievable! My mugshot was taken back in the forties when I got pulled over for that bullshit reckless driving ticket, but that's the only pic the government's ever had on me. At least, that's what I thought. But if some magazine photographer found me and snapped this picture, then the G surely has photos of me. Sonofafuckingbitch!

People all over the country, if not the world, are reading about me at this very moment.

This is bad.

Really bad.

Fifty years of racketeering and now I get noticed. How could I let this happen? Am I getting too old? I'm sixty-eight and I've never missed an angle. Never. Accardo will be stunned and The Bomber will be friggin' lovin' it. Fuck! I have to do some damage control back home, and quickly.

I jerk myself upright and hustle inside to make some calls. I need to book a flight for tomorrow morning, go back to Chicago and show Accardo and Ricca the situation is just some temporary bad publicity for me, that it won't affect The Outfit as a whole. And I desperately want to see my family. Eating and drinking with my sisters and brothers-in-law will help me relax. I only feel like myself when I'm at a family picnic or dinner in my sister's basement. I miss laughing with their kids, who are my kids, too. Yes, in times like these, you need family. They have your back. But more importantly, their love is unconditional. I've always consulted with my sisters and brothers-in-law, and one thing I've never lacked is confidence.

But now, for the first time in my fifty-plus year career in the rackets, I lack confidence in what the future holds. And as I pick up the phone receiver with my left hand, I throw back the nearly-full drink with my right.

CHAPTER 30

A Position Unfamiliar

I damn well know that I can't think effectively in a state of panic and rage, so I have to calm myself. As I zip my suitcase shut, I sit down on my bed and take a deep breath. I have to rethink my departure. I can't go into an airport, where all people do is pick up magazines to pass the time. There will be copies of LOOK everywhere. I'll drive back to Chicago. But I can't drive a car registered in my name.

I have my foreman locate my favorite farmhand. This kid is a hard worker, comes from good parents, and never complains about nothing. I instruct him to head into town to find a paper with classified ads. I'm going to buy a used car to drive home.

"Here you go, sir," the kid says as we stand out on the porch. "The cars are in the back."

"Thanks. Have a seat while I look through. This won't take long."

After just a few minutes of perusing, I see a slightly used Chrysler that will do the trick. I point to the listing. "Meet me at the front of the house in ten minutes, then I'll drive us to this address," I tell the kid. "I'm buying you a car today, son."

"Yes, sir," the kid replies, looking utterly dumbfounded.

I go inside and into my bathroom, stand on the toilet, then push up and slide over a ceiling panel. I pull out my stash box and take out some cash to purchase the car.

A bit later, the kid is fidgety as I drive us to the address in the ad.

"Listen kid, you aren't doing anything wrong today. I can assure you that."

"Okay, sir."

"I am buying you a car, but this is how it's gonna work. I need a car to borrow that's not in my name or in a relative's name, Capice?"

The kid nods, so I continue. "Just go up to the house and tell the owner you are interested in the car and would like to take it for a test drive. I am going to sit here with a newspaper covering my face the whole time. If the owner looks suspicious of a young kid like you buying his car, just flash him this." I pull the cash from the inside pocket of my sport coat and hand it to him.

"I understand, Mr. Sal."

"Now, don't take a long test drive. Just a few blocks in either direction to make sure it shifts smooth, okay? Hit the gas hard once or twice from a stop, and hit the brakes hard to make sure they are good enough, capice?"

"Got it, sir."

"Lastly, don't haggle too much. Offer him forty bucks under his asking price. I don't want to pay full right away because everyone negotiates a little. If he insists on full, give it to him."

"Will do, Mr. Sal."

"I'll follow you back to the farm in my car when it's all done. Then I'm going to drive your car to Chicago. You'll get the car for good when I drive it back to California in, like, four to six weeks. Sound like a fair deal?"

"Of course, sir. I'm not sure what to say, but thank you. A lot."

"You're a good kid from a good family. You guys deserve it." I pull up to the curb and park the car. "Now go buy yourself a car."

SEVEN HOURS LATER, I am on the road headed east. I've been doing this for almost fifty years and I feel like a dumbass kid with his head too far up his culo to see daylight. This is most definitely a position unfamiliar to me, but it is what it is, and I needed to go talk this over with Chicago, man-to-man.

I have nothing but my thoughts as I drive mile after mile. Hours pass and I feel like I am thinking about the same thing I was just ten minutes ago. I figure the only way for me to get through this journey is to turn on the radio, find some good music, and keep it turned up to keep my mood stable and my mind from turning negative.

But there are a few things that I can't stop thinking about no matter how hard I try.

It's time to retire, but will The Bomber or The Greek try to take me out before I get the chance? I also can't stop going over what I am going to say to Accardo when I see him. Regardless of his level of discontent, I need to make sure he's confident that I won't attract any more attention or associate with Bomps or Fratianno—who I'll call Jimmy the Weasel from now on.

I'M AT A service station just outside Springfield, Illinois, when I see a phone booth next to the building. I close the door behind me and call Accardo to see if he's up for a visit before I see my family.

His wife answers, so I try and sweet talk her into giving the phone to Accardo. "Hi, it's Sal from The Heights. I hope I am not interrupting family time, but if Tony is free I would love to talk to him for a second."

"Of course. Wait just a minute while I grab him. He's just out back."

I keep throwing change into the phone to keep the call going. It starts to aggravate me but I keep my cool. I have no choice. Then I finally hear Tony coming.

"Sal? This you?"

"Yeah, it's me. Sorry to bother you on a Sunday."

"No worries. Where you at? Cali?"

"I am actually in Springfield. Driving home. But I feel like I need to come talk to you, first. I assume you saw the LOOK article?" I wipe my brow of the sweat beads forming as I stand inside the booth.

"I sure as shit did, Sal. It's LOOK. Who hasn't seen or heard about it? Not so good, partner. Not so good. I know this is the last thing you want … or any of us want, for that matter, so I am not going to treat you like a schmuck over this one." Accardo sounds calm, even though I know he's pissed. This is one of those things that set him off.

"I thank you," I say, trying to infuse my voice with as much gratitude as possible. "But I'd still like to swing by tonight. I need your opinion on some things."

"When will you be coming through?"

I glance down at my watch. "I can be at your place around seven-forty-five. Will the family be done with dinner by then?"

"Yeah. Head on over. We can warm up the leftovers for you, then talk after you eat and have a glass of wine."

"Appreciate it, Tony. And sorry again."

I hang the phone up feeling a little better than I had the last couple days.

I PULL INTO Accardo's driveway four hours later—within minutes of my estimate—and his guards recognize me as soon as I step out of the car.

"Evening, Sal. Mr. A said you can just walk inside."

"Thanks, fellas."

Tony's sweet wife greets me as I enter.

"Sorry for the Sunday-evening intrusion," I say. "I promise I will be outta here shortly and you can put him back to work around the house."

"Stop, Sal. He's in the kitchen. Go on back."

"Thank you, again. And I will be quick. I promise."

I make my way to the kitchen, where Accardo is cutting up peaches and grapes and putting the fruit in his glass of wine. He stands to greet me and we embrace, genuinely.

"You have to be wiped out, partner." Accardo unwraps a bowl of pasta that he'd covered for me. "Sit down and I'll grab you some dinner."

"Thank you. And yeah, I think I made it in record time. I wasn't speeding like normal, I just couldn't grab more than three to four hours of shut eye a night, ya know."

"Well, you're here and you have my attention. Let's talk."

"I think I am going to step aside when you and I feel like the time is right," I say without dancing around the point.

"Really, Sal? Just like that?" He sounds a bit shocked.

"Well, not today. I think you and I need to pick my successor. I understand that a smooth transition is essential, and that we don't want to create a power vacuum."

"You considering any of your brothers-in-law?"

"No, no, no," I say. "They're all pretty much retired or out of the thing. Ricky warned them against seeking leadership after I'm done. And they don't want anything to do with the guys left down there quite honestly. They see how things will be when I am out."

"There are some hungry earners down there … and they are ruthless. Well, at least Ricky and The Greek, from what I know."

"That is why timing and Chicago approving new leadership has to happen before I fade away."

"You think they let you fade away, or do they try to grab it forcibly?"

"Well," I say, "I'm hoping you will get word out that if any moves are made in the interim, guys will be eliminated. Permanently. I think that would keep them in line. Ya know?"

Accardo nodded. "Who you thinking about replacing you?"

I don't hesitate for a second. "Pizzoli. He's been loyal and at my side since the forties. You and Chicago know him inside and out. He'd make for the smoothest transition and things should go on like I never left. Toots is great too, for sure. I know you could trust him. The others are great earners, but I don't know about their leadership, and I honestly don't trust 'em."

"Agree on all fronts, Sal. Vince Pizzoli is the guy unless we discuss differently."

I nod. "I'll obviously keep you informed as things move forward with the guys. I know nothing is set in stone, so we'll keep Vince's name between us for now."

"Sounds good. Now go home and get some rest. I'm going to get word out that if anything happens to you ..." Accardo makes a slashing motion across his neck.

"Thanks. And I appreciate you seeing me on short notice like this. Especially on a Sunday night."

"The way you dropped everything after that magazine article to come see me, fuhgeddaboudit. You've always been a pro and kept the lowest profile of any of us. I got your back."

"Means a lot, Tony. Really. I might get some real sleep tonight."

I feel great as I drive home. A lot of stress has been put aside for now. I don't need to worry about Chicago coming after me because of the LOOK thing, and I know Accardo's gonna protect me until I can step down under my and Chicago's terms.

I fly up my driveway. Open the door. Toss my keys into the key dish on the ledge next to the door. Take a quick shower. Slide into bed.

Then, sleep.

CHAPTER 31

The Jockeys Start Jockeying

It's only been two days since I spoke with Accardo, and I have already received three calls from guys asking for sit-downs. I scheduled them all back-to-back to back at Savoia's during lunch hours today. The Greek is first, then Ricky the Bomber, and finally Vince Pizzoli.

I naturally arrive about fifteen minutes early. Per my request, the restaurant put us in a far corner booth where I can see the entire place. The owner is here and assures me no customers will be allowed anywhere near us. I thank him kindly for his discretion and sit, waiting for The Greek.

I'm starting to get hungry, the scent of garlic and red sauce permeating through the establishment, when in walks The Greek, right on time.

"Sit down," I instruct politely, holding up my palm, inviting him to get comfortable.

"Thanks for seeing me, Sal. I really appreciate it."

"It's nothing. You are a good earner and hard worker. Not afraid to get dirty, so there's no reason for me not to. Want something to eat? Drink?"

"No thanks, I'm all good."

The Greek sounds ready to talk business. I wave off the attentive waiter, who is twenty or so feet away.

"So," I begin. "I suppose you hear I am thinking about stepping aside?"

"Yeah. I'm wondering about the timing, and I would like the higher-ups to consider me for promotion."

"Regarding the timing, that is still very much up in the air. Could be months or a couple years. Chicago has some say in that, ya know? Once I'm gone, I think you would move up in the organization no matter what. I assume you wanna be boss around here." I lean forward a few inches. So, why you and not Ricky or Vince Pizzoli?"

"No disrespect to those guys. You know I have no beefs with either one, but I am a lot younger. I am hungrier, and think I'd have more staying power as a leader."

"Really?" I'm shocked he would say that. He's the last guy I'd say that about, but I'll never let him get the feeling I think that.

"Yes, I am young and think I can keep the other guys in line. I also have some ideas about new ways to earn. I'm keeping those close for now, though."

"You say you can keep the boys in line, but you think you can make them happy? Also, you have ideas and haven't shared them with us yet. That makes me wonder. Sorry, got to say that right now." There's no way I can hide my growing aggravation and skepticism of this guy.

"I know. Sorry about that. I'll share with you when I get more organized thoughts about the whole thing, but it involves cars. Anyway, I just wanted to throw my hat into the ring for consideration, ya know?"

"This takes more than street smarts," I say. "If you want to be a leader to your crew and have Chicago think you are capable, you need to give an impression of intelligence that is above the average soldier or enforcer, capice? Not looking to insult you here, but these are the details that go noticed by those above you and below you. But I appreciate your drive and you making it clear to me that you want to lead. That doesn't go unnoticed."

"Appreciate it, Sal."

The Greek stands, as he and I both know there's nothing more to discuss. We shake hands. I want to show him some respect, even though I don't trust him at all. Just before he turns to leave, The Greek has a look in his eyes. He is one hundred percent capable of anything.

Guys like that are valuable but you always have to watch them closely.

After The Greek exits the restaurant, my waiter returns and I ask him for water.

"Anything to eat, sir?"

I shake my head. "I'll wait on ordering for now. Grazie."

I'm glad I avoided temptation, because just like clockwork, here comes Ricky the Bomber.

I stand to greet the man who wants to take me down. "Lunch Wine, cocktail or beer?"

"Nothing for me, thanks."

I motion the waiter again to leave us in peace. What is it with these guys not even taking something to eat or drink? They can't wait to make their pitch and get out. Cut from a different cloth, I suppose.

"Sal," Ricky begins before he's even sitting in his friggin' chair, "I obviously heard from some friends in Chicago that you are thinking about taking a smaller role. I also heard Accardo is making sure no moves are made against you."

"This is true. I need protection from some of my own guys." My tone grows dark. "Guys like you. Have you not already made threats against certain people in my family if they sought future leadership?"

"That's in the past, I hope. I am fully aware that your brothers-in-law are out, or will be out with your retirement. No one needs to feel threatened. I want to move forward and discuss your future, and hopefully mine."

"The timing is unknown, but, yes, new leadership is on the horizon. You should know that your name is on that list. You have been doing good work for over twenty years and that hasn't gone unnoticed. It's just a matter who Chicago wants to deal with day-to-day, and who they think The Heights crew will respond to with the most respect and confidence."

"What are the factors in timing, Sal?" Ricky asks.

"Mostly, when my internal clock tells me it is time. There are some external factors, though."

"What are we talking about, Sal?"

"That LOOK article, for one. If the G puts heat on these guys that they can't handle … fuhgeddaboudit. Chicago will need me to step aside. That's the honest truth."

"I appreciate your frankness. I just have one more question. Who else has thrown their hat into the ring for promotion when the time comes?"

"You, Vince, and The Greek."

"No Toots?!"

"Not yet. He hasn't reached out, so I assume he doesn't want the spotlight."

"Huh, okay."

Ricky is obviously surprised, but also done with the meeting. He pushes back his chair and stands to shake my hand. "Thanks for your time, Sal. We'll talk soon. Back to business."

After he's gone, the waiter again makes his way over to the table. "Can I get you another water, sir?"

The Bomber was so anxious to leave that I have five minutes before my trusted right-hand man comes. "Dewars on the rocks, kid. Make it a double."

"Yes, sir. Right away, sir."

I take this extra time to reflect on the previous meetings, and my own timing for stepping down. Jimmy the Weasel and Bomps … I have to find out quickly what they are up to and the level of heat on them.

Before I realize, Pizzoli is being directed towards our table by the owner.

"Thanks for seeing me, Sal," he says as we hug and kiss each other on the cheek.

"Of course, Vincenzo. Goes without saying."

The waiter walks up, cautiously.

"Hungry or thirsty?" I ask.

"I am if you are."

Now we're talking! I turn to face the waiter. "An order of calamari and a couple orders of angel hair, please. Bring a bottle of chianti too."

"Pleasure, sir. I'll be right back with the wine and a couple glasses, gentlemen."

"Vince, I'm glad you wanted to eat. I'm starving."

"The way the garlic punched me in my nose when I walked through the door, how could I not get hungry?"

"I've been feeling the same way, partner. I assume you want to talk about news that came down from Chicago?"

"Of course," he says, genuinely worried. "Do you think you are in danger? And are you really retiring?"

"I think I am safe, but I'll keep my head on the swivel it's been attached to for the last fifty years. I am also probably going to pull back from day-to-day soon."

"Okay, so it's true. Well, Sal, in that case, I just want to officially say I am interested in taking over for you, whenever that is. I think my qualifications are beyond question, and—"

"Let me cut you off right there. You don't need to sell yourself to me. You have been by my side in The Heights, Cali, and our many trips to Tijuana. Chicago knows you inside and out. They trust you, and are fine with whatever a transition of power to you would look like."

"Thanks, Sal. We have been running around together for a long time now, haven't we?"

I smile. "Listen, Vince, for your own safety, what I am about to tell you has to stay between just the two of us."

"That always goes without saying, but okay. What's up?"

"You are our top pick. Mine and Chicago's. It would just be too dangerous right now to let guys know of your impending promotion. You'd be a target for those who will surely become jealous, capice?"

"Capisco, Sal. I totally agree. The Bomber, The Greek, or someone else may try to eliminate me before it's official."

"Now I have a question for you, Vince."

The waiter walks up with all the food, refills our wine, and leaves as quickly as he can while still doing an attentive job.

"Oh my God," Pizzoli says. "Doesn't this smell amazing? I'll be sweating out the garlic rest of the day. Anyway, what question is that, Sal?"

"Vince, I am honestly surprised that I haven't heard from Toots regarding the top spot."

He starts spooling some angel hair around his fork. "I have, Sal. He reached out and said he doesn't want the attention it will bring. He hopes that I get the job and wants to be my right-hand guy. Of course, I told him there isn't any other choice than him if I were to get the nod."

"I figured. And of course he's the best choice for your confidant. Honestly, is there really any other guy you can trust as wholly as him?"

Pizzoli nods while swallowing his pasta. "It gave me more confidence to see the top spot."

I start preparing my first bite. "Okay, no more business.

Nothing more to say for now, anyway."

He holds up a glass of chianti.

"Saluti."

CHAPTER 32

Friends No More

Things have been settled here for a few weeks and my crew is aware of the coming changes—with exception to who will take over for me. It's Christmas Eve, and I am ecstatic at seeing my sisters, their kids, and their kids' kids in The Heights. I enjoy our traditional Christmas Eve dinner, which seems extra special this year.

Part of me wonders how many of these I have left. My health has been suspect, and I'm still afraid Bomps or Fratianno are talking to the G. I'll look into this more thoroughly as soon as I get back to California.

For now, the smells of Christmas Eve dinner seem better than I remember. The strong aroma of oil from the fried shrimp and calamari fills my sister's home. There is also angel hair in a red snail gravy, lasagna, and fettuccine alfredo. It is magical to forget about all my external stressors and take in the magic of a holiday spent with family. But near the end of the night, while I am having my coffee and cookies, I decide to head back west on Christmas morning. I have no kids to watch open Santa's gifts, and my nieces and nephews will be busy at their own homes creating Christmas memories. No need for me to intrude on those.

I want to ring in 1970 from the solace of my farm or cabin near Tahoe, so I hit the road as soon as I wake up. I take my time driving, and make it back to my California farm in three and a half days.

I'm back a couple days before I realize how many times Bomps or Jimmy The Weasel tried making contact with me. It just doesn't sit well with me. They both went through every avenue known to them. I may be wrong, but I decide to break all future communication with them. If they have turned informants, then they already have more than enough info to pass along to the G, especially Bomps. I've known him since the early forties and have taken many trips to Mexico with him. My dealings with Fratianno were supposed to be legit, but he knows me too well for my liking at this point. I feel no remorse cutting off ties with The Weasel but I do miss Bomps. We are friends. I think.

Accardo continues to keep The Bomber from undermining me, and he gave me a pass after the LOOK exposé. I don't want, nor can I afford, to let him down by keeping poor company. I quickly make contact with a friend of mine within the L.A. family to see what he knows about my former pals.

Here's what he tells me.

Fratianno no longer has friends in California because all the families here know he's been questioned by the G. Bomps is under suspicion of cooperating, though that hasn't been proven by anyone yet. He's trying to keep a low profile but is no longer being brought into the loop regarding any current or future dealings. It's my guy's opinion that Bomps will be hit sooner rather than later.

This information sends a hollow pit into my stomach that isn't going away. I will almost surely develop an ulcer. I travel between the farm and my cabin to try and relax, but my thoughts are constantly filled with my past acquaintances becoming government witnesses. Thoughts of jail are impossible to keep out of my head, too. I go from feeling sorry for myself to wanting to personally hunt these two down and remove them from the face of the Earth.

I continue to make inquiries across the West, and they all echo the same. No one is a hundred percent sure, but it's assumed

Fratianno and Bomps are rats. I go back and forth, debating where I am safer from the G's watchful eye. These doubts are beyond aggravating. Uncertainty has been nearly nonexistent throughout my life. But now, my freedom isn't in my own hands. I am hoping past acquaintances don't sell me out. Never before have I left things to chance, yet here I am, hoping.

Hoping isn't planning. Hoping isn't being in control. Hoping is for those who are unprepared.

And if word gets back to Chicago that these guys are rats, I am going to have to retire immediately to keep the heat off The Outfit. Chicago knows I would never talk, but if the heat comes down on me I will appear weak and unfocused.

This is when a different kind of trouble can rear its ugly head.

A hit won't come from Chicago. It would be an unsanctioned move by those within my territory. And Chicago, perhaps, would have less to say, and asking forgiveness rather than permission is easier to get when a leader is painted into a corner. Fungul.

I fidget in my bed all night trying to get comfortable. I eventually fall asleep rubbing my feet and legs against one another. Four scotches helped knock me out too, I suppose.

Early the next day, I get a call from Chicago. They just received credible info that Bomps and Fratianno are cooperating and they say I should head back home. And so, after just a few weeks back in Cali, I'm making the long drive back again.

CHAPTER 33

Dealer's Choice

It's early spring in 1971, things have been quiet for some months now, and I think maybe The Weasel and Bomps aren't cooperating.

Then I have my regular visit with the top brass in Chicago.

The meeting is with Accardo, who is all but retired and present to make sure grievances are resolved fairly, and Auippa, currently in charge of the day-to-day.

"It's inevitable that those guys are gonna talk," Auippa says. "We keep hearing the same thing from our sources, who work independently from each other. It sounds like a move is gonna be made against Bomps sooner rather than later. We hope that's the case for your sake."

Though we'd been planning for this day, I'm sullen as I start to speak. "Sounds like I need to step aside."

"It's time, partner," Accardo says gently.

"We'll move ahead with Pizzoli as we discussed before?" I ask, glancing at both but lastly at Auippa as a sign of his position. We go back a long way, too. And make no mistake, Joey Doves Auippa deserves everyone's utmost respect. He's had mine for decades. And if certain alliances were to be made, and Auippa okayed them, then that could be that for me. I am grateful for his friendship and absolutely respect him as my boss.

"That's the man we feel most comfortable with," Auippa says, confident in the choice.

"His right-hand man is gonna be Toots," I say. "I assume you like him, too. He goes way back and can be completely trusted. Is Chicago comfortable dealing with Toots in that new role?" I already know the answer, but the question has to be addressed formally at this point.

"A hundred percent," Accardo says. "We love him."

I stand to embrace them both. "Well, if that's it, I don't want to waste anymore of your time. I have an announcement to make to my crew."

Accardo kisses me on both cheeks as we hug. "Sal, it saddens us both to have this conversation. But we still feel like you are going out on your own terms. We all know how much you love California. Retire and relax out there, partner."

AS I AM DRIVING home, I decide to tell the gang during a picnic at my house. It's going to be almost 70 degrees in a couple days. I'll plan it for then. That will give me enough time to get word out to those who should be there.

I get word to Pizzoli, Toots, Ricky, The Greek, the Cosenzas, a couple Stefanos, my brothers-in-law, and about fifteen others to be at my house at four in the afternoon. The day arrives, and I am full of anxiety. Pizzoli is more than capable, but when you envision something and it's finally upon you, sometimes it's hard to believe.

I cook sweet peppers and onions down earlier in the day, and I grill some sausage and burgers, too. We have beer, wine, and I have some bottles of booze sitting out on an outdoor bar. Everyone has a sense what is to be said, so I rip off the bandage.

"It's no secret that I would be making this announcement someday," I start. "I don't want to bullshit anyone. I am going to step aside because there is a chance some of the fellas I ran around with in Cali are gonna talk to the G. It's in my best interest if I fade away to protect myself and The Outfit. I am aware that it's been hard for some of you"—I glance over to The Bomber—"to believe I have been connected and hands-on when I have been spending more and more time out West. Well, it looks like I will be spending even more time out there trying to avoid any connection."

"No way, Sal!" I hear Coz yell from the back.

"Yes, way. It's time. My decision. And there are a handful of guys here capable of replacing me. Those who want to lead came to me months ago. I heard you. I appreciate you. I respect you." I take a few steps toward Pizzoli. "I know you're all dying to know who's going to be the boss, So without wasting any more time, I want to introduce my replacement, the new Boss of The Heights, Vince Pizzoli."

Applause and whistles fill the air. It's quite a raucous scene for a minute. Louder than I expected.

"Let the party continue. You guys can stay as late as you want. If anyone wants to talk about what was just announced, I'll make myself available inside. This is your chance. After tonight, I don't want to hear anything more about it."

I make my way inside and tell Toots to bring to the kitchen anyone who wants to talk. Those who want to wait can sit in the family room.

After sitting in the kitchen for twenty minutes or so, Toots pops his head in.

"Just one guy feels the need to talk," he says, slightly sarcastically because we both know who it is.

"Come sit, Ricky," I say politely, fully expecting him to be pissed off.

"Why did I get looked over?" The Bomber asks, hate filling his eyes.

"You definitely were not looked over. A lot of thought was put into this. Myself and Chicago are fully aware of the decades you have devoted to The Heights. You were in the top two of those who threw their cap into the ring," I say, trying to show him some respect and appreciation of how bad he wanted this promotion.

"No disrespect to Vince, because he is deserving, but I kinda want to know what the deciding factor was."

At this point I begin to lose patience but do my best to not raise my voice. "Here's the last thing I am going to say about it, and you best listen—for your own health." I poke a finger into my chest. "I picked Pizzoli. He was my number one choice. He was also the unanimous number one choice in Chicago. Unanimous, Ricky. We are The House. We hold the cards. We decide how many decks are in the shoe. It's dealer's choice, Ricky, and that's that."

Ricky stands and reaches out his hand. "I understand, and I will respect the decision."

I accept the handshake, hoping The Bomber and I are finally done. "I know this is a tough pill for you to swallow, Ricky, but this is what Chicago wants, so you best make peace with it as soon as possible."

"I will, Sal. I'm going to go outside and congratulate Vince."

I sit back and pour myself another Dewars on the rocks. That's it. I'm out.

Then I think about the two rats running around California who may still bring me down.

So much for relaxing.

CHAPTER 34

Time To Rest

It doesn't take long for my greatest fears come true. My old pal, Bomps, and Jimmy the Weasel are definitely talking to the G. Word is that Bomps will get hit but The Weasel is supposedly taking witness protection. Even if the Cali Families get to them, I have to assume the damage to me will be catastrophic. The thought of me spending my last few years behind bars is too much for me to handle. Whenever I think about my inevitable incarceration, not just a passing thought but really envision what prison will be like, my chest tightens.

But I'll get a break from that tonight. Concetta, Tony, and I are dinner guests of Joey, Donna, and their two daughters. Can you believe they have kids now? I haven't seen my nephew for months and I can't wait to hear how things are going.

Donna greets me as she's bending over chasing her two little girls around the family room. "Uncle Sal!"

"Oh my! Look at those facce bellas," I gush, glancing down at my grandnieces.

Donna waves her flat hand across her crinkled nose. "I'll meet you in the kitchen as soon as I change this diaper."

"Nephew, how's Sears? Running the place yet?"

"Working on it, Uncle Sal. Working on it."

"I am so proud of you for busting your ass the right way. Donna's father is another great example. Follow his lead. No offense to your dad"—I look at Tony, who gives me a that's fair look—"but your father-in-law is a true role model. Nothing comes easy, but look at what waits for you every night when you get home. That's what it's all about. You're doing it right."

"No. No offense. I tell him the same thing all the time," Tony nods agreeingly.

"Thanks, Uncle Sal."

We destroy an antipasto tray and enjoy a couple drinks as my sister and Donna prepare dinner. It doesn't take long for the entire house to smell of simmering gravy and the chicken cutlets that are baking in the oven.

But after dinner, my mind starts wandering back to the darkness. I look around and think about what I am going to miss. How my sisters will inevitably deal with sneers and whispers that aren't so discrete.

"Sal, you okay?" Tony asks as he moves toward my chair. "You don't look so good."

"Fine, fine. Don't you worry."

Concetta comes up behind her husband, but she's not about to sugar-coat it. "Brother, you don't look fine! You need a doctor."

"Nonsense."

But she's not wrong. Something is up, but I don't want to worry my sister and the kids, so I stand to go into the bathroom.

Maybe I can splash some water on my face, snap myself out of ...

I MUST'VE COLLAPSED, because the next thing I know I am laying in a damn hospital bed at St. James.

"You gave us quite a scare, sir," a young, strawberry blonde nurse says.

"I must not be in Hell because you are way too cute," I say, but it comes out a whisper. My body is in such pain. It feels like weights are just laying on top of me. "What do you mean by a scare?"

"You had a heart attack," she says. "It was touch-and-go for a while there, but you pulled out of it. You're quite a fighter, it appears."

Unbelievable. I'd probably be better off dead. That way, at least I wouldn't see a jail cell. Okay, maybe not. I am grateful I didn't drop dead in front of my family. That would've been traumatic for them.

"You've had a lot of calls inquiring about your condition," the nurse says. "Also a lot of people are requesting to come see you when visitors are allowed."

I'm in no mood to talk or see anyone. I lay here for a couple hours, thinking about how I avoided subpoena after subpoena for decades, but my life of racketeering is finally going to catch up to me.

I'm picturing the inside of a federal pen when a doctor walks into my room. "Mr. Liparello, you're a lucky man. You survived a serious heart attack. We need to keep a close eye on you. Your vitals still aren't as stable as we'd like to see."

"Wonderful, doc. I feel like I just got hit by a friggin' truck."

"I would expect nothing less. You just need to try and relax and rest."

"I can't relax. There's tons of stuff running around in my head that doesn't go away." I'm aggravated at him, even though none of this is his fault.

"Stresses of life. I am sorry, but you still have to try to rest a little. I'll be back in a few hours to check in to see how you're doing. Okay?" The doctor puts my chart at the foot of the bed.

"Sure, doc. Do whatcha gotta do."

A couple minutes later, a different nurse sticks her head into my room. "Sir, there is someone here to see you and he's refusing to leave. I am sorry to interrupt your rest, but he is being quite relentless."

"It's fine. Send him in."

She opens the door all the way, and I see my trusted, right-hand guy, Vince Pizzoli.

"Sal, you okay? 'Cause you look like shit," he says, smiling.

"Don't make me laugh," I say, grabbing my upper chest. "It hurts like a sonofabitch. Fungul."

"I don't want to keep you from rest, but I had to see you with my own eyes. I had to see how bad a shape you're really in."

"And?"

"Like I said, you look like fuckin' shit."

"I said don't make me laugh," I grimace in pain as I chuckle.

"Rest up, and you'll be outta here before you know it. You'll beat this, no problem." Pizzoli is trying to stay upbeat even though I am pretty messed up this time.

"Even if I get out of here, what's waiting for me down the road?"

He knows what I'm alluding to. "It could be years or never. Try to stay positive. You know?"

"Yeah, yeah. But the last two guys I spent time with in Cali are gonna rat me out to the G. My gut is telling me I am not going to dodge this one. I would've been better off dying."

"Stop it, Sal. You mean too much to your family. Look how much you have helped them, especially after your dad died."

"I've tried. They're all I got."

"Sal, you've managed to keep such a low profile to protect them from our thing. It's so-"

"Let's be frank for a minute, okay. Why did I always want insulation and try to keep a low profile? What's the real reason, Vincenzo?"

"To avoid heat."

"Right. To avoid going to jail. My own selfish reasons. If I really wanted to protect my family from this life, I wouldn't have been in this life. I have been a racketeer for fifty years. Fifty fucking years, and you have been there with me for nearly the entire way."

Vince gently places his hands on mine. "It's been a fun ride and an honor to be with you, Sal. I wouldn't have wanted to serve under anyone else."

"I've also lived a solitary life. I don't think I ever gave love a chance. Was I punishing myself unconsciously, Vince? I don't know. Maybe I could've pulled it off, but I was too scared to try. It was easier to keep telling myself that I didn't want to worry any more people than I already was. Sure, keeping a low profile has been beneficial for my extended family, but I did it for myself. Period. I'm petrified of jail. I've avoided it for fifty years and now you think I'm gonna go?"

That fucking elephant sitting on my chest is getting heavier by the second.

"Sal, you're getting worked up," Pizzoli says. "Last thing I want is for you to have another heart attack."

"It's fine," I say through labored breaths. "The best thing for me and my family would be God just taking me while he has the chance." I suck in more air. "If I go to jail, it's going to destroy my nieces and nephews. It'll kill me, but it'll really kill them. Ya know?"

Pizzoli puts his right hand on my shoulder as my body screams for oxygen. "You're not going to jail, Sal. Just stop thinking like that. You need to rest."

Can't.

Breathe.

"Not feeling … good." I'm gasping now. "Chest … killing me. Bring … water."

"Sure, thing, Sal."

Pizzoli stands and leaves, always the good soldier for me. He knows what's coming.

But now he won't have to see it.

***

ONE MINUTE LATER, Vince Pizzoli returns to the room, giggling with the nurse, holding a cup of ice water. When she sees Sal, she rushes to the bed and frantically calls for help.

"Sweetheart, stop. He wants it this way." Vince pulls up a chair and sits next to his lifeless friend. "It's over, Sal. No stress. No jail. You did it. You dodged your last bullet."

Then he leans down and kisses Sal's cheek.

"Rest easy, Boss."

ACKNOWLEDGMENTS & NOTES

The thought of writing a historical crime fiction novel lingered in my head for years. During a phone conversation with my relative, Matt Luzi—author of The Boys in Chicago Heights: The Forgotten Crew Of The Chicago Outfit—I felt the final nudge to tackle the project. His book provided much of the historical information I used to create my stories. Louis Corsino's book entitled The Neighborhood Outfit: Organized Crime in Chicago Heights was another historical reference for my novel.

This being my first book, I came to many realizations during the writing process. I discovered how much I enjoyed creating scenes and dialogue, and getting lost in the story after stressful days at work. However, there were times I wasn't left with a sense of accomplishment. Many times after a writing session, I felt apprehension about writing such a book, even if it was fiction. First, I was raised thinking the mob was never to be glorified. Second, even with names changed, anecdotes created or embellished, and facts already made public by previous works of nonfiction going back to the late 1960s, I was getting ready to divulge many personal stories shared with me. Stories I only told a few of my closest friends. However, facts discovered by Chicago Outfit historians and authors—specifically Matt's book on The Heights crew—married to the stories I knew were something out of a television series or movie. That kept me excited and motivated to tell an entertaining story that no one else could.

This book wouldn't be possible without my team at Blue Handle Publishing. I can't say enough about them. They believed in my rough manuscript and saw its potential. I truly believe I found a partner in this project, and for that I am sincerely grateful.

I'd like to thank my first copy editor, Christine Tilles, for giving my manuscript the rhythm and flow I intended but could not achieve without her expertise. I wouldn't have had the confidence to submit for publication without her help.

A huge thank you to Leslie Liautaud, who I emailed countless times. She mentored this first-time writer during the entire process; outlining my story, writing it, and keeping me positive during the submission process.

I want to thank all my family and friends for their endless support and encouragement throughout this journey. A special thanks to my work friends who cheered me on daily for the last couple years.

Thank you to my loving wife, Nicole, and three beautiful daughters—Ellie, Lia and Kira—for encouraging me and giving me the time and space to finish this project after work, which is supposed to be family time. You are my world.

I want to thank my sisters for always looking out for their little brother. Lastly, I thank my parents for making sure their kids learned what is truly important in life. An education, honesty, hard work, and sincere kindness are key ingredients to finding happiness and fulfillment. They led by example, which made their lessons more meaningful.

This is who we are. This is our true legacy.

ABOUT THE AUTHOR

Ray Franze has spent nearly thirty years trading options at the Chicago Mercantile Exchange and the Chicago Board of Trade after graduating with a BBA from the University of Iowa. He grew up with his two older sisters in the Northwest suburbs of Chicago, where his loving parents and grandparents helped instill a strong work ethic.

Franze lives with his wife of twenty years, Nicole, in the Chicago suburbs, where they raised three daughters.

The Heights is his debut novel.

For more great titles from Blue Handle Publishing authors, visit BHPubs.com or follow us on Twitter and Instagram **@BlueHandleBooks**

Our Founder, Charles D'Amico, is **@Charles3Hats** on all platforms

Our authors on Instagram

Leslie Liautaud
@author.leslie.liautaud

Jordan Reed
@author.jordan.reed

AJ Whitney
@aj.thewriter

Ray Franze
@TheHeightsNovel